OKANAGAN COLLEGE LIBRARY

P9-DUG-893

GOVERNOR OF THE
NORTHERN PROVINCE

GOVERNOR OF THE NORTHERN PROVINCE

a novel

RANDY BOYAGODA

VIKING
CANADA

Thank you to Ellen Schlosser, Ken Alexander, Bruce Westwood,
David Davidar and Nicole Winstanley. —RB

VIKING CANADA

Published by the Penguin Group

Penguin Group (Canada), 90 Eglinton Avenue East, Suite 700, Toronto, Ontario, Canada M4P 2Y3
(a division of Pearson Canada Inc.)

Penguin Group (USA) Inc., 375 Hudson Street, New York, New York 10014, U.S.A.
Penguin Books Ltd, 80 Strand, London WC2R 0RL, England
Penguin Ireland, 25 St Stephen's Green, Dublin 2, Ireland (a division of Penguin Books Ltd)
Penguin Group (Australia), 250 Camberwell Road, Camberwell, Victoria 3124, Australia (a division
of Pearson Australia Group Pty Ltd)
Penguin Books India Pvt Ltd, 11 Community Centre, Panchsheel Park, New Delhi – 110 017, India
Penguin Group (NZ), cnr Airborne and Rosedale Roads, Albany, Auckland 1310, New Zealand
(a division of Pearson New Zealand Ltd)
Penguin Books (South Africa) (Pty) Ltd, 24 Sturdee Avenue, Rosebank, Johannesburg 2196, South Africa

Penguin Books Ltd, Registered Offices: 80 Strand, London WC2R 0RL, England

First published 2006

1 2 3 4 5 6 7 8 9 10   (RRD)

Copyright © Randy Boyagoda, 2006

Author representation: Westwood Creative Artists
94 Harbord Street, Toronto, Ontario M5S 1G6

"Water Spider," the first chapter of this novel, originally appeared in *The Walrus* magazine.

All rights reserved. Without limiting the rights under copyright reserved above, no part of this
publication may be reproduced, stored in or introduced into a retrieval system, or transmitted in any
form or by any means (electronic, mechanical, photocopying, recording or otherwise), without the
prior written permission of both the copyright owner and the above publisher of this book.

*Publisher's note: This book is a work of fiction. All names, characters, places and incidents
either are the product of the author's imagination or are used fictitiously, and any resemblance
to actual persons living or dead, events, or locales is entirely coincidental. The character
of Sam Bokarie is based on a real life West African warlord who was killed in 2003.*

Manufactured in the U.S.A.

LIBRARY AND ARCHIVES CANADA CATALOGUING IN PUBLICATION

Boyagoda, Randy, 1976–
Governor of the Northern Province / Randy Boyagoda.

ISBN-13: 978-0-670-06564-6
ISBN-10: 0-670-06564-1

I. Title.

PS8603.O978G69   2006   C813'.6   C2006-902454-5

Visit the Penguin Group (Canada) website at **www.penguin.ca**

Special and corporate bulk purchase rates available; please see
www.penguin.ca/corporatesales or call 1-800-399-6858, ext. 477 or 474

For Anna and Mira,
the grace and wonder of my life

Anything—anything can be done in this country. That's what I say; nobody, here, you understand, *here*, can endanger your position. And why?

—Joseph Conrad, *Heart of Darkness*

The measure you give will be the measure you get back.

—Luke 6:38

WATER SPIDER

I.

He laughed at what passed for tragedy in his new country. Last week, the body of a little girl was found pressed against a sewer grate. She had been catching water spiders on a creek swollen by the spring thaw. A floating barrette alerted a man walking his dog.

Little Caitlin. In the newspapers at the convenience store where he currently worked, and on the televisions at the laundromat where he attempted to wash his new clothes, and during the elevator chatter at the apartment where he now lived, so high above the earth. Little Caitlin. She was everywhere, as was talk of public safety committees and the need for a protective barrier around the creek when it rose too high. Bokarie would attend the memorial service planned for that Sunday, intent upon fitting in but also a little curious. His manager told him that hundreds were expected, perhaps even a thousand. Each had been asked to wear something pink. That was Little Caitlin's colour. If the petition circulating was successful, the town crest would gain a sash, in loving memory.

His old country occupied a corner of the Friday newspaper's front page. Sopping with sweat, Bokarie carried in the stack at the start of his morning shift. It was April northwest of Ottawa, but he remained suspicious of Canadian sunlight. Because his back and shoulder muscles were still in scar tissue atrophy (an unexpected help during his asylum hearing) he stooped over and twined his arms around the bundle to pick it up. Hunched, he shimmied through the door. His wet cheek pressed against the topmost paper, smearing across a thumbnail picture of his old leader, the General. Peeling away the damp smudge, he saw the dark sunglasses and the counterfeit medals and the smart beret that, he had been taught, displayed the elegant monstrosity of blood-and-coin patriotism. The General was smiling. He might have been on his way to prison for crimes against the People, or to the People's Palace for finally disposing of the President. Bokarie did not turn to page A-20 to find out, just as he switched the radio dial to music whenever he heard "According to UN monitors, the situation in west central Africa today became ..."

This was the gift of immigration. The past, even if it never became past, remained over there. He was happier this way, safer, over here. He understood that the General, whether as convict or President, had to blame him for what were now known as the Upriver Massacres, even if they happened under his orders, because Bokarie escaped. INTERPOL, RCMP, FBI—they might be searching for him already, depending on what deals had been struck. He dragged cinder blocks against his apartment door each night.

He was not angry with the General for his betrayal, or for trying to have him killed, or even for the men he bribed to do it. This was the way in their country.

The scorpion got across the river on a turtle's back and stung it just before the shore. A fish swallowed the scorpion. If the fish didn't choke on the stinger, if the fish wasn't speared, if the fish swam hard enough, some-times it reached clearer waters. Then a bird swooped down.

A woman walked into his store just as he finished stacking the papers. Her eyes, he thought, were like this country. Big and empty. She had a kerchief tied around a sweep of straw-coloured hair. Buttons sprayed with slogans and symbols fanned out across her wide skirt. She wore the indignantly pink T-shirt that he often saw these days on the bus and at the supermarket. She was holding a pink box shaped like a dollhouse. Her lips pursed. She was about to make a speech. He knew this. He had made speeches in his old country. Oh, such speeches.

There will always be growing pains when a great nation is reborn! If a few sandals fall into the fire, or a little woman blood mixes into the ashes, what great loss is this? My brothers, it is no loss. My own mother, my own woman, my own child—they have fled, have starved, have been killed in the first wars of the new history, after the British and the French and the Germans left us to fight amongst ourselves for the right to tend our own fires. Meanwhile, the tribes Upriver have guns and electric and water and maize. They have as many goats in their fields as we have vultures above our huts. Do you wonder why? They worship the swine that squeals in the capital city, our self-appointed President-for-life, who sells our wives and daughters to Nike Red Cross U.S. of A. Who protects the Upriver villagers and fills their troughs because they are all of that snub-nosed, mongrel tribe.

There is one man who can put an end to this. The General. And he has told me that only the eldest and purest people of our beloved home-land can help him cleanse what has been soiled. This is why he has asked us to reclaim our ancient lands as part of his National Restitution Campaign. This is why we must crush the chirping locusts that sing of the President's greatness and slaughter the dancing baboons that step to his orders. This is why we will at last greet rosy pink morning from the moist

earth that your fathers' fathers left to you. Brothers! When they desire
mercy, you shall make of them a sacrifice! For our sons, for our General,
for our nation!

Bokarie remembered his speeches while adding cherry syrup to the
Slushie machine. In his new country, he picked out scratch cards for
old ladies. They treated him with pity and fear and kindness and
curiosity. They gave him zoological stares. He answered their question
each time with a different country. This was for practical reasons,
though it was also a satisfying entertainment. Yes, I am from Haiti.
Indeed, I was in Rwanda. Madam, you can tell that I lived in Sierra
Leone. In truth, I did flee the Congo. He confirmed their vaguely
Christian, blandly Canadian sympathies. The civil war was even
worse than what is shown on television here. The earthquakes swallowed my home and family. When the Americans came in their tanks
looking for more oil, we had to flee from their boasts of freedom.

II.

Her lips opened.

"Good morning. Will you put this on your counter? It's a donation
box for the Little Caitlin Fund. This is my charity certification card.
It says my name is Jennifer. If you agree, this establishment will be
added to a growing list of local business sponsors. I will give you one
of these official ribbons. Little Caitlin's family and friends will be very
appreciative. We need all the help we can get to raise awareness. I'm
honoured to be in charge of the community's response to this tragedy.
I recently quit my job in the field of human resources management
to devote myself fully to making sure Little Caitlin is never forgotten
and her tragedy never repeated. The government has recognized my
efforts with monthly support. Will you join me, join us?"
He responded to her slow loud words with the pidgin English he had
practised with a friend in the oil tanker's hold while heaving across

the Atlantic. Towards this little pageant of Canada, convenience stores, and Caitlin.

"Thank you. It is much worthy cause. You show courage in giving yourself to it, and your government is very kind to you. I know this truth. In my old country, the heavy rains and the heavy boots bring much death to our children."

The woman tilted her head, thoughtful like a dog hearing a new sound.

"Oh, you poor man. So you must know what's it like to lose a loved one. And to come to your new country to escape such things and find them here too. Little Caitlin isn't the only one, but with your support, we can help make sure she's the last."

"Yes. But I must ask manager if allowed to put box here. I like much the pink ribbon. Is it okay, you give? Where I come from, pink means the colour of the dawn."

Her fingers pressed against the walls of the dollhouse, her mouth turning with impatience, forethought.

"Such eloquence! You're probably one of those brilliant foreign intellectual types who can't get a job when you come over, so you get stuck doing this kind of stuff. Last week I was in Ottawa, visiting the Parliament Buildings. I do that now and then. I was late to catch the bus back to town and needed a ride—"

"Ottawa?" he interrupted, eyes mooning extravagantly.

"Yes, that's the capital."

He nodded and smiled for her to say more.

"Anyway, my taxi driver was from Bangladesh. He said he was a doctor. You should do ESL at night school. It's funded. You just need to believe in yourself. Like Little Caitlin did. How about the box?"

"Ottawa is the capital."

"Yes, it is. You should probably visit it at some point. Next time I'm going, I could let you know. But I don't plan to go there until enough awareness has been raised around here of what Little Caitlin means to all of us. So, the box?"

"I ask boss man. My ribbon?"

"Sign this petition. And come to Centennial Park this Sunday for the memorial rally. I'll look for you there. How come you're still wearing your parka?"

III.

Bokarie would send his young and hungry men off to each raid with a speech given from the flatbed of a derelict aid truck and later arrive to crunch an elder's jaw plate against a gutter or to shoot a lingering dog. To proclaim victory. He would inspect remnants of the burnt-out villages reinvented as cities of the new nation, dividing the charred land into lots for squadron leaders baptized as local constables. On the General's behalf and in the name of peace, he attended muggy prayer vigils for the souls of the dead travelling to the cool gardens of the afterlife. The Promised Land. He would spindle his copper-wire arms around the shuddering survivors in sympathy, those who had had enough time to flee into the brush when they heard the rebel anthems sounding up the road. Husbands and mothers and wives and fathers, they had no choice but to accept his comfort though they knew who and what Bokarie was. The terror of possibilities blunted their knowledge of his crimes.

After each visit, he would report to the General. They spoke by satellite phone to make plans for the next incursion. He would receive instructions and then a reminder of how he had been raised up, how his help was needed to bring order to their nation. Mention would be made as well of future rewards. Bokarie would then return to the corrugated shed where he lived with two brothers and a cousin. He had promised each of them a village, a television with DVD, and local virgins, once the General named him governor of the northern province.

But men's plans are in agreement for the space between a butterfly's wings, or, as in his old country, the span of a razor blade. His militia was only awaiting a final order, poised southeast for its triumphant entry into the capital city. He imagined that the General would greet him personally, that he might even be asked to address the National Assembly, but by the time Bokarie took the last village, bones and rumours of the first raid had reached the demilitarized zone and the foreign press pool. Soon, donor nations were murmuring. In the light-bulb cafés and at the dust-whorled checkpoints, strange words began squawking out of the transistors. *Power-sharing* and *reconciliation* and *sanctions* and *multilateral intervention.* Suddenly the General was on CNN embracing the President. A smiling American peacebroker was standing behind them, his hands pink meaty grips on their shoulders. When the General stepped forward and addressed the nation, his tongue was hot and sharp with the language of the new world politics.

"A security coalition will rid our stricken nation of the terrorists and evildoers butchering the river people to the north. With the support of the international community, firm and fearless leadership will bring an end to this tyranny. Freedom will march where it is needed."

Three days later, Bokarie's younger brother carved a wide arc across his back while he was reading a map. He had just found a shallow creek crossing into the unmonitored brush of a neighbouring country. His cousin shot the assassin in the ribs and neck. Searching the body, they extracted a pair of dark blue passports, payment in advance from the now impossible-to-reach General. Quickly tracked down, Bokarie's older brother pleaded his innocence. It was unconvincing. Fortified by cane liquor, his back bleeding through a poultice of banana leaves, Bokarie then set out for the river with his cousin. His turtle.

The passports were good enough to barter in Africa but too crude for travel beyond. He traded the first to get through the sandpaper-and-scrub interior. The second dropped him into a tanker headed to the deliciously named Newfoundland. Wedged between the barrels, he befriended a nervous Liberian and helped him prepare for his asylum hearing. He learned his story. Later, when he crushed the man's windpipe, the others in the hold shifted positions to absolve themselves of witness. The altruism of survival. In a St. John's impound yard two weeks after they reached the shore, a German shepherd sniffed out the body. By then, Bokarie was in a warehouse dormitory studying refugee relocation pamphlets.

IV.

He stepped off the bus and entered Centennial Park. Everything was thick and wet with spring. Damp in his heavy coat, he dripped and squelched his way into a solemn pink sea. The family was on a stage flanked by monstrous posters. Baby Caitlin, toboggan Caitlin, school Caitlin, birthday Caitlin, soccer Caitlin. A flotsam of cameramen and civic leaders was crushing them.

As he drew close, Bokarie saw the big and empty-eyed woman from his store, Jennifer, teetering at the edge of the stage, trying to control the roseate flood of frothing sympathizers. An old longing returned. His talents were needed.

Tilting her sunglasses, Jennifer glimpsed a pink ribbon flailing in a black hand; it was raised up and floating forward. She remembered him, the pitiful and eloquent African engineer stuck behind a lottery-and-cigarettes counter. He was starting to figure this place out, she sensed, noticing the clump of a winter jacket he had just dropped on a chair as he plotted towards her. He had lost a child to flooding as well, she recalled, deciding that there was currency in skimming a sympathetic new Canadian onto the stage. She was planning to run in the next election, her campaign centred on a private member's bill for drainage security. Think Pink would be the motto. A global dimension could help. She beckoned and he scuttled up. They nodded at each other. She was, for a moment, surprised by what happened next.

Bokarie broke past her, his thin frame cutting towards the family. He embraced them with an ancient comfort. Though startled to be wrapped up in this unexpected black man's soaking clinch, they were too polite to writhe. The audience was quietly, curiously watching.

After a measure, Jennifer intervened, now in control of the stage. She swivelled Bokarie around and guided him forward, her hand pressing against the crest-shaped scar on his back as she whispered instructions. He did not recall the pain. He was smiling. New words started crawling across old sentences. There were photographs. There was applause. There were only possibilities in his new, temperate country. Such a shiny microphone!

NONE OF THE ABOVE

I.

When she was nine years old, Jennifer sank ankle deep into the thicket mush behind her family's cornfield and had a mystical experience. She had been off on her own, as was her habit, her station. The other children endured the vibrating July heat by ranging across town. They searched through floridly named subdivisions and behind barren strip malls for ants and the odd frog to burn with bifocals liberated from their grandparents' bureaus. They dropped vengeant fistfuls of pennies in the mailboxes of retired teachers, dental hygienists, and other local warlords known to be at their afternoon naps. But Jennifer was bulling through the swollen cornstalks of her family's few acres. Their green tongues were slapping at her with rain catch dropped down by a sun shower. Which had just stopped.

Coming out on the other side of the drooping green poles, she wiped the water and sweat from her forehead. Everything was dripping warm. She parted the reeds and came upon something that looked like an upside-down fancy candle, or maybe, she thought with a vault in the chest, an iced cruller. She walked forward. She didn't mind the ooze sucking around her shoes when she neared the indifferent elm tree, or the sensation of her bag-of-potatoes body sinking into the wet bottom. She craned her neck and squinted against the sunlight that shot through the higher branches. Because something was happening.

Hanging from a bent twig was a twirling braid of wet mottled fatness. Two yellowy, whitish slugs, pocked with red dots, wrapped around each other. Twisting and turning, taffy-slick and slow-mating in the tumid thick of Ottawa Valley summer. Jennifer watched them for a long while. Then a bird came at them and they dropped onto the leafy, squashy ground with a SMACK! But only for a moment before another swoop down and a scoop up. Following the bird back to its perch, Jennifer wondered if the slugs were still swinging because they hadn't quit doing to each other, or if they were now just dangling from the beak. But then the bird threw back its head and its throat bulged and they were gone.

Slogging home, something pulling at her ankle, she couldn't decide what it was about the slugs and that bird in the woods. But she would look for them again.

II.

At the start of her final year of high school, Jennifer Ursula Thickson declared for Graduating Class President. She ran unopposed. She lost.

"And for Graduating Class President, well, it seems that Jennifer Ursula Thickson has been defeated, has lost to—I'm not sure of how to put this—well, she's lost to 'None of the Above.'"

Mrs. Bureaux, the civics teacher, had been unsure of what to do. This was without precedent at the high school Jennifer attended, in a conscientiously unremarkable town where not unhappy lives shuffled to hushed ends. Whose Latin motto, invented in a Civic Pride contest during the once and once only, federally funded exuberance of 1967, was provided by a clever favourite son who had gone on (escaped, as he later put it to colleagues) to lecture in Classics at a university in Ottawa. *Status quo.*

A simple majority of an otherwise genetically indifferent graduating class had crossed Jennifer's name off the ballot and written "None of the Above." They did this with a bland insolence inherited from the blended loins of generations in the Ottawa Valley, those Scots and Irish and French farmers whose tribal hatreds and seeding secrets and uglier ethnic features got all mixed up in cars and fields after a century of harvest dances and Canadian Legion wedding receptions and Knights of Columbus bingo nights and all-church Christmas parties. Who, thus combined, gave to each successive crop dispositions formed to resist someone like Jennifer because she was trying to raise herself higher than her family, her history, her teeth allowed for. This being the mortal sin of every small town. So it was decided by tacit referendum that she should be prevented, the decision passing among her classmates like the silent, purposeful spread of fog on a warmed-up autumn morning in their postage stamp of a township northwest of the capital. There was no other discernible source for the decision, no evidence of a vengeful campaign, no traces of animosity, and no alternatives offered.

Everyone just understood. Jennifer. She wasn't supposed to be Class President. She had heavy ankles. She would have made sense as Correspondence Secretary. She would have been acceptable as Treasurer of the Prom. But anything more than that would have been off, unbalanced, mutually embarrassing—like using the good dishes for dinner with lesser relations, or a wife referring to the front porch as the veranda in front of her in-laws. Jennifer would have to push against this sullen, grain-fed logic in her every effort to be something more than was preordained as her lot by virtue of being born into a large-boned, small-farm family.

In place of a president, the faculty decided on something fancifully known as a Provisional Collective Authority, comprising the smarter students and better athletes and prettier girls. Jennifer was still invited to join. With the embarrassment of receiving unexpected and unwelcome company, they had to acknowledge her shunted desire to participate in school life. To their relief, she declined the offer. She would show them.

She required neither the pity nor the charity. She was not upset by the loss. She had gained a view of the life that she decided had to be hers. She knew this much from the sucking thrill, the ache of expectation, the cold steel taste in her mouth the unsleeping hot night before election day; and from her ragged heartbeat in the moments before and then after the historic results were announced. All of which gave her a stabbing excitement that her prior pursuits—crossing guard's assistant, recess monitor, Friday night handler for the backward child Benjy one farm over—had only pricked at. Waiting for the election outcome, she had been wrapping and then unwrapping her blond plaits around her thick fingers, as was her habit when excited. When she heard, she let go and went limp for a moment. But then something else.

She was supposed to agree, graciously, with the unassailable logic of the late teen electorate, for whom such elaborate and meaningless high school elections were devised and regularly held as natural preparation for their full immersion in the political life of the nation. Jennifer was supposed to recede back into the Canadian Shield whence she seemed to have come. Instead, she got hungry.

She went in search of knowledge to prepare for the next election. It didn't matter what it was for, when it would happen. She sensed already that there is always, *always* another chance to get people to put their finer senses aside and be willingly duped into seeking their betterment in billowy slogans and cold buffet promises. Having watched enough chatty sewing machine salesmen from Cornwall and haughty farm subsidy officers from Ottawa come by the house and have at her parents, Jennifer only had to discover how to master what she sensed was this universally accepted, even necessary trickery. But she needed more to work with. Her family wasn't ever going to make enough money, which was clear enough from their recent crop yield and long-standing policy of reheating leftovers until the plates and pots were finger- and thumb-licked clean. She also knew there was little in the way of ambition in the bloodline; her father was hopeful of someday saving enough to put down a little on a cabin up north, not even thinking about a cottage, mind you, and with river frontage at best. Plus, Jennifer had come to terms with her own slabbish frame and had never been interested in the dress patterns from the *McCall's* books that her mother occasionally showed her and gamely described as slimming options for the coming Christmas dance. She didn't bother with any of that. She was never going to trim down and tit up enough to get pregnant enough to marry well enough, like other ambitious poor girls in town did.

Instead, Jennifer approached the civics teacher, Mrs. Bureaux, for assistance. This was reasonable: she had been the elections monitor, and once the other students had slouched out of the portable after the results were announced, she had pulled Jennifer aside and offered a mess of therapeutic pottage. *If there was anything more she could do*; *When you need to talk*; *It's not you, it's society*; etc.

Mrs. Bureaux was sorting through overheads for a unit on the Red River Rebellion when Jennifer came up beside her. After checking her shock that the girl seemed interested in actually taking up the offers to talk and such, she went worried that Jennifer was going to make a scene. She calibrated her distance from the intercom and tried to remember the code for the school's on-call guidance and emotive care counsellor. A scene being a venal, not mortal, sin in a small town, but still to be avoided along with any near occasion to commit it. The teacher listened, blinking rapidly, to Jennifer's request, followed her jabbing finger as it pointed at the prime minister's portrait hanging beside the smudgy clock. She was immediately relieved by the option that presented itself. A good book or two on politics is better than a boring lecture any day! The bait worked. The girl left.

But like a door-rapping Jehovah or a tent-smacking deer fly, something kept coming at her. That ponytailed bloodsucker, the teacher thought, would have clung on until she had taken enough and then more of whatever it was she wanted.

III.

Hortense Spillway was demonstratively unmarried. Which is to say that at fifty-two, she was gradually blending into the static landscape around her, noticed by others with less and less frequency, like wallpaper patterns in gently rundown homes. She walked as if on padded feet. Her body, only a few pounds heavier and plusher than when she was in her twenties and first took the job in the school library, was, in her early fifties, a slender, barren willow branch. Her wrists and neck were always garlanded with colourful, clinking jewellery, the cut glass resembling bits of bruised fruit. The acceptable flourishes of a respectably aging, single woman. She was companioned by two cats, Charlotte and Emily. She lived for her monthly reading group—the Hoarfrost Romantics, a name she had helped devise. It was composed of a half-dozen town ladies and one single but artistic man. He was a night school drawing instructor and occasional director at the Community Playhouse. Save Christmas visits to a very married sister in Renfrew, the Hoarfrost Romantics was Hortense's only let-up from the litter box of her daily life. Otherwise, it was along the gravel of the town's streets that she went, passing from her first-floor rental to the school library's front door to the greengrocer's to the family pew in the gingerly upright and echoing Anglican church, then back to the first-floor rental, repeated every week since she first took rooms a few months after her parents had passed on. There had been a man, once, but having failed to secure her father's blessing, she was alone, measuring her days in the steeping of teapots and the collecting of Victorian figurines from a mail-away collectibles society based in Brixton.

She was arranging date slips at the front counter when the osprey diorama that hung in the middle of the library was suddenly blotted out. There was a largish girl standing in front of her, staring with massing insistence. A girl at a hulking right angle to Hortense. She sensed that the girl was lonely, being heavy-set and plain, and there arose the dim prospect of fellowship, which was welcome. The reading group adjourned in May, under the collective ruse of crowded summer months. But Hortense was too quick. Before the girl could explain what she had come for, she was directed to paperback copies of *The Stone Angel* and *The Edible Woman*, their mustardy pages stacked together providentially on the nearby returns cart. The overture did not have its intended effect.

The girl wanted to know about politics, about how great men were made, how they came to become what they were.

"Politics, please. That's what I want to know about. Mrs. Bureaux said you'd have books on politics in here. You keep your fairy tales, Miss Spillway. Books on politics. Please."

This was an aggressiveness that Hortense knew didn't run in Jennifer's diffident clan. She wondered if maybe the girl was trying to impress a boy by reading up on his interests but then remembered hearing about the unfortunate election results some months earlier. Sympathy came, momentarily. The stupid hurtful pointlessness of rejection.

But then she went angry, wasp-stung by this thick-lipped, this thick girl calling her proffer of literary titles, of friendship, fairy tales. For Hortense, recalling her well-received write-up for the March Hoarfrost meeting, these two novels *were corrugated testaments to the tragedy of being born at once Canadian and woman.* And this girl was calling them fairy tales. Fairy tales! But she also felt a dab of heart-sink at the now-receding possibility of afternoon teas for two. She was accustomed to the superior indifference of the girls who were sent to work in the library—bored, wan AV monitors rejected for yearbook club and making do; pouting painted circulation assistants on the verge of pregnancy whenever they uncrossed their legs in detention hall. Who were always reassigned to Miss Spillway in the best interests of school hygiene and public morality.

But in this girl she saw something else. A wider emptiness and maybe a little ambition, a hungry hollowness that, she thought, might have been an opening, something to be filled in, fed with sophistication and knowledge and other forms of human fineness. The ability to pronounce German words; subscriptions to leading magazines from Toronto and Boston; a taste for salad as the second course; cheese on a plate unto itself.

Hortense stopped herself. She was no elegant womanly mentor, Europe-returned and man-wise. And this girl was no money-swaddled ingenue in want of tutoring in the ways of civilization. This was no budding Henry James story. Hortense was reminded of the where and the what and the who. She was a lonely coat-rack of a high school librarian, talking to a heavy parka of a high school girl.

And while of course in polite company Hortense was just as troubled and outraged by her nation's guilt by geographic association to its elephantine neighbour, in private she had the sense of living in a nowhere corner of a small-town country. History and culture and capital E events happened below the border and across the sea. Her nation was, at best, a cousin by marriage to all of this. But still. Calling its great books fairy tales? That was unnecessary, uncharitable, un-Canadian. Steeping and steaming, she decided someone still had to come to the defence of what goodness this place managed to produce. She fretted the pleats of her skirt until she had enough pluck.

"They're—these are not fairy tales, young lady. You're simply misinformed. If you would open your mind and, yes, your heart enough to read them, I think you'd find that these writers know more about you and where you are and where you come from and where you're probably headed than you do. But in the meantime," she continued, a little breathless and overexcited but recalling her asthma and professional responsibilities, "if it's politics you want, must have, I'll see what we have for you."

Her chip of a chin set at a flinty angle, Hortense glided around her desk and into the stacks. She was satisfied with her performance even if the audience seemed unmoved. Jennifer had listened with the mute patience of a mule at a railway crossing. Her only response was reiteration. "Politics, please."

Waiting for Hortense to come up with some books conducive to her design, Jennifer again shot her voice through the library quiet. "Books on politics, that's what's wanted. Books on politics." She said this with even more force when Hortense slipped behind a bookcase. To make sure she was being heard. The effect on Hortense, in her solemn hushed library, on Hortense, who had been raised to know that one never discussed politics, pregnancy or plumbing in polite company, was of extreme offence.

The librarian found three titles for the girl, one on Churchill, one on the Fathers of Confederation and a third on the American president Lyndon Baines Johnson. A fourth suggestion, *Macbeth*, was turned away as soon as Jennifer recognized the author's name from

English class. The girl waited in stuffed silence as her books were stamped, enduring Hortense's brittle sermon on the many lessons the Elizabethans could teach those willing to listen—about love, friendship, betrayal and, with this play in particular, about women and politics. Hadn't Jennifer seen the production in Centennial Park last summer?

Hortense had thought it very lovely, entirely dark and rather deep, but perhaps a tad much, particularly the actress who had played Lady Macbeth like a malevolent Bea Arthur. But how the woods had moved, what with lit tallow dangling from each stand to light the actors' paths! That, with its symbolic suggestion of new light coming to vanquish the wickedness of Dunsinane, had been, she thought, very well done. She had rubbed these observations into a small humid glow on her walks to and from the grocers that August, in preparation for the first fall meeting of the Hoarfrost Romantics. But when Hortense told all of this to the lone and single and creative man in her book club, he had dismissed her with a sniff, declaring that showy stage props were the opium of the masses while he was of the Brecht school on such matters.

"Which," he continued, snickering to himself so that his thin reed of a moustache seemed to hum and vibrate, "is why I happen to be so bloody estranged from everyone around me in this vaudeville of a township. Estranged, I said. Brecht! Doesn't anyone understand me? Brecht!"

Someone said "Gazoontite" and he was too pleased with himself to catch the sarcasm. He sniffed that he didn't care if no one else around here was as estranged as he was, or could even know what he was talking about.

In the kitchen slicing banana bread later that afternoon, Hortense learned from the hostess, Faye, that Grant had applied and been turned down for the position of stage designer for the *Macbeth* production.

"But then again, between us girls, given my husband's position in this town, George thinks he's just Viking gay is all," the hostess concluded with a shrug as they gathered the teacups and dessert plates and eased their way back into the sitting room.

Hortense made a sour-cherry face. This was the expected and properly ambivalent response among women in town to hearing that an insensitive man like a husband figured that a sensitive one like an older, well-read bachelor had to be that way. The sour-cherry face condemned the evaluation and agreed with it and disapproved of the universal race of men all at once.

The girl's eye-blinking and shut mouth suggested to Hortense that she hadn't seen the play. When they had been stacked in front of her, Jennifer scooped the three books off the counter and made to leave. Staring a moment longer at a spinster face the colour and firm of eggshell, she was off.

Two weeks later, Jennifer was back, marching, her face shaped into expectancy and a smile impressed upon it as if by a baker prettifying a lump of pastry dough by turning a fork around its edges. She had returned to the library to drop off the books, two of them anyway. She had come for another reason as well. Jennifer found Hortense behind a book cart burdened with end-of-the-year returns. To be helpful, she took it from her and started pushing and pulling it across the library on its rickety shrill wheels, trailing Hortense around the shelves. The librarian was glad to have someone else manoeuvre the heaving cart but felt uneasy. Something was hanging in the air.

Her lips opened.

"Miss Spillway. You said women and politics. In that play by Shakespeare, you said. But I never saw it last summer. And I can't read that stuff very well on my own. But you could. Will you talk to me about it maybe sometime, maybe when school's done?" Her white teeth dug into her lower lip as she smiled.

Hortense politely, cautiously, apologetically started to say—but then she agreed, remembering with heart-sink that it was soon to be lonely summer Saturdays and that here was someone who just might be made to understand the terror and beauty of Birnam Wood and the virtues of cloth napkins and other such fancies of the civilized imagination. Jennifer made a date and time and took directions. She left the cart still swaying a little from her twisting and turning.

IV.

During the summer after she graduated from high school, Jennifer visited the librarian on a series of Saturdays and then one Sunday, after which there were no further meetings. She visited Hortense Spillway and her crinkling doilies and porcelain cats and ballerinas and CBC FM always in the background. This was where Jennifer took her lessons about Shakespeare and scones in the time before she started her HR program at a nearby community college. But going to see Miss Spillway, Jennifer liked to think, had not been only for herself. She also went because, she decided, this chalk stick of a woman probably needed another human face to look at now and then. It was well known that Miss Spillway had lost both parents and had only a younger sister left, who lived and married well outside of town. So her going over there was also an act of community service, a response to the needs of the lonely and the alien.

She'd asked for the meetings because reading those books on politics had taught her that anyone who became a Beloved Leader had to have something to do with Shakespeare. The problem was, *she* had never had anything to do with him except read the Coles Notes before her grade ten Christmas final. She wanted clarifications. To know what made it a compliment to say that "Sir John A. was perhaps the only figure for the premiership because he alone inspired hatred from neither the Capulets in Upper Canada nor the Montagues in Lower Canada." To find out what she was supposed to take from "Churchill, who, from a middling mediocrity after his Navy stint, enjoyed a meteoric rise to an historical greatness that made lazy Prince Hal's ascent to valiant King Henry the Fifth seem little more than changing seats on the West Hampstead lorry." She didn't have questions about the book she had held on to well past the due date, which was about that American President from Nowhere, Texas. She didn't care to know why "Johnson had raged across the Oval Office like Lear upon the heath when Party elders told him that they didn't want him to stand for re-election in 1968." She didn't have any questions about that book because it was immediately taken on as something of a saint's life, an exemplar after which to model herself. Johnson's story was one that Jennifer hoped to reflect on, later in life, as resonant. An unremarkable man from an unremarkable place who wanted, needed, had to have at any cost to himself and those around him recognition and admission that he was capable of more than his blood and drawl allowed for. Which could come not from wealth or beauty or fame but only from power, the hard power of ruling others and being feared and loved for it. But it was how Johnson did it that took Jennifer. He never stopped at the getting. She also studied the biography's pictures of Johnson at his business, politicking himself onto others, with his deep lean-ins and collar grabs and extorted promises of support for his programs and slogans. Johnson, she thought, was like a defenceman who couldn't keep up with the snipers, so he turned his bulk into an asset and crushed them along the boards. She found her method there.

Her own parents were not people to ask for help. Their interest in periodicals ran from farming journals to *Reader's Digest* and, after one surprisingly good crop some years earlier, *TV Guide*. Also, the annual

Sears catalogue, and occasional church bulletins whenever Sunday mornings were just too blank to be spent at home waiting for that evening's roast to thaw.

Wanting to bust and slug through mere Thickson expectations, Jennifer visited the librarian at her home in hopes of having these questions about Shakespeare and great men answered. She also sensed that this could be something like "a broadening experience," which, she knew, the richer girls from her school were given as graduation gifts. Weekend shopping excursions to Montreal and even to Toronto; the daughter of the richest man in town—he owned the lone car, truck and RV dealership—was sent for half a summer to some kind of young ladies' camp in New York where, it was rumoured, they had sailing lessons and Jews and other such fancy things. Her own graduation gift had been, in truth, a very nice surprise: a distended encyclopedia set that had sat through the spring thaw in a half-flooded basement. Its age was evidenced by the overwhelming length of an entry on the Lindbergh Baby. Her mother, with gift money granted by her father, had purchased it at significant discount at one of the first May yard sales. But it was also Barb Thickson's attempt to match what seemed to be her daughter's new interest in books. She was worried that Jennifer might fail to attract a husband and leave them with no way to continue the farm. This was certainly possible, what with the girl's overgrown gourd of a body, and with more scrub grass than corn rows on Thickson land these last couple of years. She thought the books, which the seller advertised as "four years at Carleton for forty bucks," might save her. Or at least help a little with what she was looking to do for herself.

The Thickson family, being firmly Middle Canadian, prided itself on permafrost reticence whenever anything close to the inner life came up; this was as much of a virtue for them as sending prompt funeral flowers and filing early tax returns. Which meant that Barb never entirely told her daughter that she was also a little sympathetic with her wanting to go and get for herself something more than just okay in life. Equally, Jennifer, though moved some by the graduation gift, by its implications and the quiet sanctioning for her designs that it suggested, had simply nodded and purse-lipped her mother's cheek and grazed up at her father's neck stubble in thanks. But then she noticed how her mother was lingering nearby as she thumbed through the first few books in the collection while her father pack-muled the rest to her room. Jennifer caught a look at how Barb's fingers were wriggling and her hands hovering around her blouse-flounced waist. Waiting to say, wanting to hear.

"You know, Mum," Jennifer began, her lungs feeling a little more than pinched by the breathing necessary to say something of matter to a near relation, "there's a lot of information in these pages, just an awful lot. Which is, well, pretty good."

"More than that, Jennifer. More than simply information, because that's what's in the phone book, you know. There's knowledge in these books." In answering her daughter, Barb was low-voiced and kitchen-retreat-ready in case she heard Gus's tread on the topmost step. But this was her chance to tell, to tell what she dared to. "And knowledge, they say someone said, well, knowledge is power. And power—" Now this was getting to be too much, so Barb got up to check on their chicken dinner and reread those directions for softening the ice cream cake brought home in honour of Jennifer's graduation. "—power just might do you fine. In fact, it might be worth more to you"—now she was verging on the autobiographical—"than a clammed-up fist of from-the-field flowers and what, well, what he'll probably call a champagne diamond. At least that's what they used to call them."

After this, Barb Thickson almost always mouthed the proper lines about the superior goods of marriage and children to her daughter, and agreed in nodding silence with Gus that politics was like urinals and moustache combs: they were designed for men and God help the woman who tried them out. But that one time, just that once, after giving her daughter the encyclopedia set, Barb wanted her to know that it was okay to look for, and want, more in life than smiling at your husband's news that he found a sale on wiper blades in the middle of January, or accepting that a *Canadian Homemaker*'s report about interesting variations on the butter tart was, in fact, interesting.

Jennifer hadn't openly responded to Barb's words about the encyclopedias and power at the time—this was prevented by simple shock at her mother's capacities, by a little fear in Jennifer about what her mother thought about her own marriage, by Barb's mad dash into the kitchen, and by her father's return downstairs to get the rest of the books and loudly predict a visit to the chiropractor later that week—but they went to work on her even more than the books themselves, pulling and pushing like some Old Testament prophecy. Like double yeast baking in a hot summer kitchen.

v.

At Jennifer's first visit, on a Saturday mid-morning in early July, Miss Spillway served spongy angel food cakes covered in confectioner's sugar that left a fine white dust in the webbing between the thumb and index finger. Nervous, hungry and accustomed to such finery only at funerals and weddings, where meat-handed cousins were always lurking open-mouthed, she ate three off the platter right away. Like they were dressed-up potato chips. Her face went reddish when she saw Hortense pick up a tiny fork and eat her own, her one cake, in moused nibbles, while telling Jennifer the stories of the Henry plays and *Romeo and Juliet* in response to the opening volley of questions. Hortense had noticed without comment what had happened to the other cakes and took this, courageously, as a sign of the magnum opus work-in-progress before her. Meanwhile, Jennifer successfully resisted the urge to suck her hand clean. This was, for her, an indication of how far she'd come already.

"You mean to say, Jennifer, that they don't study at least *Romeo and Juliet* in grade ten English anymore?" Hortense asked, nudging a fork and napkin closer to Jennifer's unused plate and then nestling the final cake onto her doily.

"No, Miss Spillway. Only the one about the Jew who went around asking people about his prick and blood and pound of flesh."

Now Jennifer wanted to show Miss Spillway that she could do like civilization. She went to her task of portioning off just a little corner of the new cake with her fork. Extracting a wedge, she plugged it into her mouth, where it dissolved with Eucharistic solemnity, her jaw clamped for politeness. Meanwhile Miss Spillway was coughing up a cakey hairball at Jennifer's Elizabethan paraphrase. Neither woman was optimistic that this thing would go on. She can only fail at this, each thought of the other. Jennifer decided that she should give up, slam the rest of the cake into her maw and forget about someday addressing Parliament. She should just go home and wait for her father to come in from burning up stalks from this year's fallow field and have supper and dishes and folding the laundry with her mother and maybe a few hands of Hearts before bed if they're feeling like it and then, at most, a Revenue Canada information counter position in accord with the suitable-careers profile her guidance counsellor had given her, which would be but the penultimate stop on her way to an unremarkable, to a regular, to a Canadian death. No.

She passed Hortense a napkin for the cake bits still coming up. With this, an honest, secret look passed between them. Of mutual need. Their schedule of Saturday morning tea and books was thus confirmed as being so necessary to both as to be acceptable beyond crammed mouths and a little spit-up.

As summer in the Ottawa Valley beat on, Jennifer grew to like their weekly two-hour conversations, the cubes of sugar arranged beside stacks of shortbread, the oval platter set on the knee-high table between them. She listened and watched Hortense weave together tea cosies, creative autobiography, marmalade tins, and the storylines and characters of *Middlemarch* and *Anna Karenina*. She was gaining far more than the how and what of fine books here. Because smarts and book knowledge in general she was already getting at night by ploughing the encyclopedia. (She was currently on the Rs, finished with Rasputin, Richelieu, Robespierre, and presently on the second Roosevelt.) Tea with Hortense was, for Jennifer, her face-to-face preparation to be close by the real hard power of the world. Of knowing how many bites should be taken to finish a tea sandwich, the number of times a butter knife could respectably pass over a scone, the proper interval between mouthfuls during an interesting conversation. Of knowing, after more than one attempt, how to dispatch an outraged housefly trapped against a window screen without gucking up one's palm.

She sensed that these tutorials would only help her when she made it to those places that Hortense, in her small quiet rooms, could only puppet. Receiving lines and cocktail hours and drop-ins and dinner parties. Before getting her hands on these, Jennifer needed to practise a more basic human science, the humming at the top of the throat and the anglepoise of head and brow that conveyed interest on the leader's part in the voter's humanity. She had gleaned as much from the politics books. Especially from the pictures of LBJ. With Hortense, Jennifer was developing that sense of when to lean in and ask a further question, when to sit back and ruminate on an observation. Her broad shoulders would crowd everything else out, but the effect, after much practice on Hortense, was less suffocating than beguiling, because Jennifer was fast developing a great blankness of face that was poised to fold into whatever—shared concern, shared excitement, shared outrage, shared admiration—the interlocutor's tone and looks needed. All of which were necessary to the *sine qua non* of her political training, which Bokarie had likewise trafficked in by the time they met: to make those whom she depended on for what success she could get depend on her even more to get theirs.

Jennifer thought she was doing very well, so far, with Miss Spillway, who was made to feel that she was coming into her prime with the girl. Hortense discovered unknown powers of persuasion and instruction as Jennifer was refined over the summer, soon dropping the *s* from *anyways* and eventually remembering to hold back her braids while leaning over the pots of jam to ask a follow-up question. In the near corner of the family pew of a Sunday, Hortense would regret being so cheap with her charity when the poor hulking thing had first come to her in her library, and then she would commend herself on the enhancement she was effecting. Rapturously unaware of what was coming up and around her grandmother's bone china.

Everything was building towards the great unveiling that was to occur that August, when Jennifer was to accompany Hortense to a performance of *The Tempest* that the Community Players were doing in Centennial Park. For which, boldly breaking the summer hiatus, Hortense had written out invitations to members of the Hoarfrost Romantics on her Crème Anglaise stationery. This had been left over from when she had sent notes to friends and family in gratitude for their prayers and casseroles and concerns when her parents had passed on.

> *Please you, draw near. You are cordially invited to un petit déjeuner sur l'herbe with Ms. Hortense Spillway and her blossoming young friend, Miss Jennifer Ursula Thickson. Centennial Park, August 25, 2ish. Tea and The Tempest will be served.*
>
> *RSVP regrets only*

Impressed by the heaviness of the paper and curious about Hortense's new friend, all the members of the reading group called to say they were coming.

To round out Jennifer's training in advance of the performance, they had read the play and discussed it on the previous Saturdays. Hortense further encouraged Jennifer with the pronunciation of certain French cheeses that were to be served, and she helped her practise clever and thoughtful observations for presentation. Their attempt to read aloud particular exchanges from the play, however, was unsuccessful. There had been some disagreement over roles. Over who would be Prospero and who would play Caliban.

On the appointed date, Hortense was feeling like a grand lady of theatre. She had even purchased, from the Bay, no less, an expensively in-season sun hat, whose Upper Canadian austerity she offset by affixing a spray of lilacs to the band. When they met in Centennial Park, Hortense was satisfied and relieved to see Jennifer arrive un-plaited, her hair held round her head by the paisley kerchief the librarian had given her. Which was ostensibly a going-away gift, but was in fact intended to deter that mesmerizing and unseemly habit Jennifer had of twirling her braids when thinking, listening, watching. Which, Hortense knew, would be a judgment on herself when the others descended onto their quilt to consider what she'd created. Forged, of sorts.

Jennifer was feeling top-heavy, waiting in the park as it grew to half full in the hour before the performance. It was because her hair, no longer clamped and braided on either side but bandaged back by the librarian's gift, felt as if it was tugging her face up over her head. But it did make it easier, she would later notice, to smile and raise her eyebrows at the same time, in response, say, to an interesting observation about climate or to a personal story of hardship. When the others arrived, Hortense placed Jennifer in the rough centre of the picnic spread. Like a dressed-up game bird. The tins of cheese and olives and crackers and fruit and bony women and smiling women and nibbling women were schooling around her. Jennifer started feeling all this swirl and attention, and also the tea they were drinking. Hortense had delicately emptied a Niagara Valley VQA into a Thermos in the parking lot. Heart going fast with the scandal of it while pouring out the cups, she had giggled through her nostrils that afternoon tea was courtesy of Stephano and Trinculo.

"Who were responsible for getting the poor monster Caliban drunk didn't they Miss Spillway but then really what man, drunk or otherwise, isn't a monster I wonder. Of an occasion now and then," Jennifer fired on cue, and was pleased with the nodding and murmuring she caught from the women around her. As was Hortense, who was now whispering for approval to Faye, the de facto Hoarfrost hostess because she alone had a husband and a real sitting room. Hopeful of earning a private dinner invitation, Hortense was telling Faye, arrayed as ever in her Timothy Eaton finery, how far Jennifer had come. The poor girl had called sugar cubes "mare candy" a mere eight weeks ago.

Jennifer was watching the librarian talk to this woman. Who seemed, by comparison with Miss Spillway, less straw than stalk. She had more and better meat on her bones, but also a presiding way to her. Jennifer sensed here something suggestive of power. Perhaps it was how she smiled such evident dental coverage and waved at other members of the audience on nearby quilts, who seemed anxious to catch her eye. Who, Jennifer also noticed, whispered among themselves afterwards, a little flushed.

Meanwhile, the little wine she'd taken, along with the gym-sock whiff of the soft cheeses and the general atmosphere—the black-shirted men and women pulling and pushing thrones and canoes across the stage, the Hoarfrost women comparing their summer reading lists and estate sale linen finds—all of this gave off a great swelling and excitement. Bravely, she had breached a new world, and for this, she decided, chewing on a little squishy brie rind, Miss Spillway was to be thanked. But then the performance began.

Good boatswain, have care. Where's the master? Play the men.

That was all she could recall from the first few acts. Because Jennifer spent them studying Faye and resenting Miss Spillway for how she had done the seating, plopping Jennifer in the middle, like an Easter ham or something. So far from her. From Faye. Who sipped her cup and nodded with such relaxed, vacant intelligence while Hortense and the other women bubbled around her with clever observations and curious facts. A woman who could do her better than forks and fairy tales.

She started moving at the intermission, when Stephano exited stage left after his scene-ending declaration, which was received with much Port-A-John-ready applause.

O brave monster! Lead the way.

Hortense could feel the pressure on her hat, her shoulders, and now coming around in front as Jennifer circled and sat down, close in on Faye. Jennifer's blank face was expectant, her nose distending. Everything smelt sweet and low-slung with the flower-busted fullness of Faye's husband-gifted perfume, with this musk of proximate, blooming power. Waiting to be introduced, Jennifer undulated her fork across and beneath and overtop her fingers, which Hortense noticed with middling approval. This, Hortense held, was better than doing it with the braids but seemed a little too close to fancy card-table manners. But still, Hortense thought, the wine opening her up a little, look how far this girl, otherwise consigned to the dustbin of a small-town country's history, had come with her! So she fixed her hat, Dalloway- and Prospero-proud of the absolute masterpiece she had brought off.

"Oh yes, I'm so sorry, Jennifer. What with all the commotion of our little picnic, I didn't introduce the two of you before the play started. Faye, this is Miss Jennifer Ursula Thickson, who promises much. Jennifer, this is Mrs. Faye Gallagher. She's Alderman Gallagher's wife. Speaking of women and politics, perhaps she could—"

The last words anyone of importance ever heard from Hortense Spillway.

ROAD APPLES

I.

Into the bins behind his store, Bokarie tossed the bottles that his new countrymen called recycling. Often they knocked and slid and broke, and this gave him a mixed-up feeling. He didn't like this sound, this having to think again on his past, this incursion from over there.

Mostly children brought the bottles to his counter, and by the armload during the summer months. As instructed by his manager, he dispensed to each clutching, grabby hand a predetermined catch of coins in accord with however many bottles were presented. There was such precise largesse in Canada. Bokarie also thought this while palming the monstrous apples at the grocery store and studying the Bible-thick channels guide for the television.

Some of the bottles that were given to him in his new country had busted-up cigarettes at the bottom; others, the sweet ones, usually had a few ants. There were also muddy bottles, which were brought in by the older boys. Bokarie learned that they had fearlessly gone by Little Caitlin's Creek and snatched them by their floating, idling necks. That's what it was called now. Little Caitlin's Creek. And, encouraged by its reputation, they had even come back once with a rusted-out shopping cart, as they now boasted to Bokarie. But the owner of the greengrocery had been too suspicious of starting an epidemic of theft and recovery to offer anything in return.

A band of town children and a few of the younger teenagers who frequented his store adopted Bokarie as something of a mascot during his first summer in Canada. Having studied his schedule, they would meet him around back in the alley with the Dumpsters and recycling bins when he was tossing the bottles. He had a sense of how it would look if such ice-cream-sticky, mustard-crusted hands got cut up, so he wouldn't let them throw any of the bottles despite their offers of help. Instead, he occasionally made a show of flipping a bottle into a high spinning arc, and received impressed noises in recompense. He liked that.

II.

Bokarie's first Canadian picture, not including his asylum and refugee identification shots, appeared on the front page of the local newspaper on the Monday after the Little Caitlin memorial rally. It was pleasing to carry this stack into his store. The picture was taken just after he concluded his inaugural speech to his new fellow countrymen, and the accompanying caption reprinted what was arguably the most emotive bit of his remarks. *For I desired mercy, and not sacrifice.* Many in the crowd assumed he had been addressing some ancient river god, to whom he was lamenting the unfairness of Little Caitlin's loss. He was smiling and showed jagged teeth and grape-black gums. Large, blond and sort of smiling as well, Jennifer was close beside him. Her presence in the town was growing of late. She was now the mobilizing force behind the successful Little Caitlin Fund. Yet she still received little in the way of further consideration. She remained a Thickson whose heavy ankles and small farm family were reinforcing barriers against greater success.

For Bokarie, however, the newspaper photo was evidence he was becoming one of them.

An African in the Ottawa Valley! This was a sign taken for the wonders of twenty-first-century living, on the same order as city buses that lowered for elderly riders and the availability of cappuccino at the Tim Hortons. These strange, fancy things, previously seen on hockey tournament trips to Toronto and cable television. There was, of course, some resistance, from a few retirees who took their morning news over black coffee and cigarettes, thank you very much. And none of these new buses better treat them like the G-D Holy of Holies, that's for sure. This rheumatic rabble spoke out against Bokarie to their wives and chiropractors. One or two chose the familiar parable of the road apple in the snow to argue for the danger this new fellow posed to the rest of us.

You find a road apple in December and you curse the cow that crapped it but you don't do anything because hell, what's the harm? It's frozen, right? Just stuck there day in and day out—you know you can keep an eye out for it. So what do you do then? Well, you keep clear, of course, shovelling around it, and on the way to get a Christmas tree from the city park with the grandkids, and you tell them to keep clear too and maybe you even toss a pylon in its general vicinity before one of the February storms. Always you got these plans to get rid of it, but not just now, an old Beachcombers is on. Or maybe your arms are full of kindling. But right when you get around to it, you're gonna turf that patty into the woods. Then next thing you know, spring comes up and out you go to take down the Christmas lights and tarp up the snowmobile and maybe put out the cardboard Easter bunny for the squirts and oh yeah, you really should get rid of that old black turd. Now's the time and it's got to be done. But you can't find it, though you catch something right ripe in the air. And you know what that is? That's the smell of everything gone to shit.

Jennifer heard this at Sunday dinner with her parents, a couple of weeks after she first met Bokarie and directed him to speak at the Little Caitlin Event. This was when she first informed Gus and Barb Thickson of her plan to run as an independent in the next federal election. Undaunted by what had happened back at the end of high school and more recently, embarrassingly, against an alderman, she was confident of her chances this time, she explained, having found a potential global dimension for her local drainage security campaign. Think Pink. In addition to Little Caitlin, she could now have Bokarie's children, lost to floods over in Africa. Her mother crimped her face a little at the wording but didn't say anything just yet, not just yet.

"After all," as Jennifer knew from her reading and then informed the table, "FDR distinguished himself by combining the domestic accomplishment of that New Deal with the overseas success of World War II, while LBJ had initiated his Great Society and increased America's intervention against the Communists in Vietnam. In both cases," she had learned, "domestic success wasn't enough to be a beloved leader," and a three-letter acronym was vital.

Her father put his fork down for added effect and warned Jennifer that bookworms hooked no men and that learning from Americans was like lending to Jews. Then, to sum up his case, he told the parable of the road apple in the snow, which had been proclaimed to him by the man who ran the gas station. Having done his fatherly duty, he picked up his fork and went back to his mashed and wondered why it hadn't been a boy. At least that would have made more sense of the shoulders and ambition.

III.

A Spanish priest ran the white-walled orphanage where Bokarie lived until a better possibility came up. After many beds went empty one night and the younger children said men who smelled like smoke and bottles had come into their rooms, the priest had decided to line the orphanage's walls with row on row of cut red and green glass. Father Alvaro gave a soccer ball to the boy who collected the most bottles per month, tallying on each boy's rosary how many were brought back from their excursions to the surrounding town. These bottles were shattered under the priest's supervision, and the shards were collected into the orphanage's red, white and blue camping coolers by children who had more calluses than cavities. The priest would then choose one of the older boys to sink the jigsaw pieces of glass into the mud-and-dung-filled trench that was grooved across the top of the orphanage's white walls.

Using his gravest Ash Wednesday voice, occasional sprays of holy water and flashes of a Santiago de Compostela medal, the priest was able to hold off evening recruitment visits to the front gate by the frequently drunk and always superstitious representatives of the national army, and by the various local rebel groups, and by the occasional roving militia from one of the neighbouring countries. But that wasn't enough to stop those agile and desperate enough from scaling the orphanage wall in the middle of the night. So the glass-shard wall was maintained, at least up to when the blue helmets came. (At which point a quartet of nervous Bangladeshis was stationed in front of the building with a military Jeep loudly donated by the French, who had salvaged it from what was left of their Algiers tackle. The Bangladeshis displayed bayonets on rifles that dated from 1971. They were considered quaint by local warlords.)

Bokarie liked to imagine that the orphanage was a giant shark, having seen a picture in one of the *National Geographics* that had come to the orphanage with the coolers. He thought its walls were like open jaws, with all those sharp teeth ready to snap down. He told this to the younger boys at night under the mosquito nets, and the idea was quickly taken up and spread, with attribution coming his way. He liked that. He wanted more. This was before he was chosen to mount the wall and fix the few teeth pulled out and blotted and flattened every five days or so, according to troop cycles and the state of supply lines and recruitment efforts elsewhere.

The *National Geographics* and the red, white and blue coolers had been donated to the orphanage by an evangelical millionaire from Texas named Bayard Jellyby, who presided over the largest sporting goods and camping equipment chain in the Southwest. He had seen something on one of those television specials they do on empty Sundays after football's done and the spring recruiting camps haven't started up yet, about the modern history of Atwenty, Bokarie's first country.

Jellyby learned from this documentary that the nation's post-independence history was punctured and potholed by corruption and shifts in governance so frequent that the power grids left in place by the exiting English at the end of World War II were long since defunct. As were the basic mannerisms of civil society that the Empire had exported to the dark corners of the Royal Society's maps. Things had turned rather carnal rather quickly.

This wasn't surprising to the nation's last viceroy, a Sir Basil Seal, who was interviewed in his palsied paisley splendour for the documentary. Upon returning to the Home Country after his stint in Africa, he confessed that his time in Africa had killed what merry old Kipling had been in him since boyhood about life in the colonies, and brought him over to that nasty Conrad chap.

One story he especially liked to tell when he was back in London, at sherry receptions and old headmasters' funerals and now for this documentary that Bayard Jellyby was watching, described his last time with the natives. To his always captive audience, Sir Basil explained that before leaving, he had listened to the local bureaucrats, whose colouring and capabilities were modelled after Macaulay's minute fiats for Bombay middle managers, flub those famous lips of theirs to express what a pity it was he and the British were leaving. They were a spot nervous over this exit and what the new power portended for them and their country. This came up during a melancholic farewell reception Sir Basil had held for them in the gingerly upright British barracks, though he knew some of the invitees had bloody well agitated for his going, dancing and clapping alongside the scruffier natives at their passionate, incoherent independence rallies. In response to their doe-sad eyes, he had loudly wished he could just stuff all of them in his steamer trunk and take them home with him, but of course this was right around the time that ugly Enoch Powell and his lot were bloodying up the streets. They were more worrisome, he assured them, than what life under the nation's first homegrown prime minister would be like.

The native mandarins weren't naive; they expected the new Big Man to clean house and bring in assorted cousins-in-law and other village baboons to run the nation, just as the British had done to the French and the French to the Germans and the Germans to the first tribal leaders they had met. The first post-independence leader, a man of the People as they all are, was rather brutish. While he had been educated partially in England as a young man, he had spent more time at Oxford thrusting and grunting as all-school Eight Man and midnight caller for the dons' girlfriends than he had spent studying gunpowder plots and suffrage politics.

Sir Basil knew all of this, as he told the documentary's host, but he also knew that he was only a week's voyage away from trustable clotted cream and the glorious freedom to see a man about a dog without having to check the bowl for a scorpion first. So he did less than his best to buck up the black spirits around him at that goodbye get-together. But he concluded in full Britannic style, of course. On behalf of Her Majesty, he raised a toast to the newly independent nation and to its grand new leadership. To Kong and country! His gin-soaked slip of the tongue was neither copied nor corrected. It was taken as a closing colonial wisecrack and regarded, with false hope, as false prophecy.

As the documentary then recounted, the new man burst through mere expectations of gluttonous vice and implacable incompetence. His inaugural act as prime minister was to neuter the parliamentary system into a self-appointed National Assembly, proclaim a democratic republic, and accept the title of President-for-life. He was the first of many in the decades that followed.

Meanwhile, the majority of the nation's people, including its many orphans, had been in straits since this magnificent independence, rarely provided with light at night or refrigeration for what food they had, both of which compounded already high levels of malnutrition and illiteracy. This juxtaposition, along with a closing photo montage set to an Elton John–Peabo Bryson duet, and a 1-800 number branded on the screen, got Bayard Jellyby to thinking.

"It is just plain un-Christian for these young boys to be without my two favourites way back when I was just a little trigger myself, bedtime reading and ice cream. These things transcend all cultures, all religions and both races, which is why my family and I are sending them along to the African nation of Atwenty. God Bless America, and may theirs bless them."

Jellyby made this speech to the San Antonio news crew he arranged to profile him and his family as they packed up and sent along his personal collection of *National Geographic* back issues to the orphanage. The magazine's famous yellow borders and exciting, informative pictures were bright enough to be read at night regardless of light bulbs, he reasoned, which was important, since young African minds could be more than terrible wastes. He explained all of this at the swelling close to the local NBC affiliate's Community Hero spot for that week.

The Texan knew that it was no good sending over ice cream, let alone refrigerators. Instead, he cleared his Harlingen warehouses of the previous season's Fourth of July Freedom coolers and hired a cargo plane from a private security firm. He added a monetary donation and listed in the cheque's memo "Rocky Road, Tin Roof, etc." He also threw in some soccer balls, having been convinced that baseball bats might be misused and pigskin possibly offensive on religious grounds. Practicalities required the priest to modify the Texan's requests, which were detailed in an accompanying letter. Because ice cream, like red meat and disease-free prostitutes, was only to be found on embassy row in the capital city, Father Alvaro bought some chocolate with what money was left over from the Texan's donation. After, that is, the conversion fees and processing charges and national surtaxes were variously assessed. He also sold most of the coolers that were left after customs and port inspections to the beer bars that squatted around the orphanage. He reserved a couple to hold and haul the broken-up bottles—a far safer method than using doubled-up soiled pillowcases—and also for six to eight quality four-by-six photos of the boys smiling and reaching into the coolers. This had been the only particular request from the Texan. The priest did as best he could to oblige, and a Tucson graphic design firm was later commissioned to airbrush ice cream cones into the little black hands. Pamphlets were eventually available beside in-store credit card applications at registers in each of the Texan's stores.

Father Alvaro gave out a soccer ball for best bottle retrieval once a month. He awarded the yellowy *National Geographic*s and mushy chocolates for best elocution and memorization of a Bible reading from the series he offered every morning after their breakfast of rice pap and mashed banana. When he was eighteen, Bokarie won for both speaking and memory on a selection from Hosea, which the priest had read to the boys in hopes of getting them to forswear violence and the other temptations and dangers outside the orphanage. Bokarie would draw on it again.

> *For this reason have I hewed them by the prophets, I have slain them by the words of my mouth: and thy judgments shall go forth as the light. For I desired mercy, and not sacrifice: and the knowledge of God more than holocausts. But they, like Adam, have transgressed the covenant, there have they dealt treacherously against me. Galaad is a city of workers of idols, supplanted with blood. And like the jaws of highway robbers, they conspire with the priests who murder in the way those that pass out of Sichem: for they have wrought wickedness.*

Because the boy had already won a soccer ball and now had both elocution prizes and was long known to be a voracious, even gluttonous consumer of any Bible passage that came his way, the priest judged Bokarie ready for further advancement. Also, he was more than old enough to be subject to whatever mandatory conscription law seized him if he was found roaming the town's streets with the younger boys.

The priest instructed Bokarie to maintain the broken-bottle perimeter against the government and the rebel recruiters, and also to pick assistants. Bokarie chose his two brothers and his cousin, the only other members of his family to have survived a tribal dispute from a few years earlier, as the government in the capital city had called it. (Alas, there was no time for questions at the press briefing that morning, so no one had to account for why one tribe in this particular conflict had air support and machine-gun-turreted Jeeps, while the other had dull machetes and comparatively unsuccessful chicken-bone curses.) In the aftermath, Bokarie and his brothers had been picked up by Father Alvaro on a pass through the village ruins. He had found them, like so many of their contemporaries, wandering through various heaps in search of food, the odd toy, an interesting bauble, their mothers. They were vaguely feral, shut-mouthed about recent events out of mistrust and sheer incomprehension at the things they had seen and heard and been spattered by. They had gone with him into the van out of boredom and belly pang. Their foraging skills were put to use once they'd been acclimated to the orphanage. When they stopped crying out in their sleep and shitting themselves at half-remembered outrages and relived threats.

Bokarie had been good at the bottle-getting game, but he liked this new duty a great deal more than crawling around behind the canteens for discards and beating the gutter brush for empties tossed from the overcrowded pickup trucks. Teamed up with his blood men, as he took to calling his brothers and cousin from then on, Bokarie would often get chased by bartenders and dishwashers smoking their cigarettes, and by truck drivers and ticket touts on piss breaks, and also by the hungrier and more desperate dogs. He was fast enough to get away from these wheezing, barking predators, and just because he could, he would mock them from a little more than near at hand, by slowing down and fancying up some footwork before catching up with the other boys already hauling back to the orphanage.

But with this promotion, he was now allowed to hang back when the other boys were sent out. After a time he would play soccer with his brothers and cousin, but first there was the unwelcome job of breaking apart cow dung and mixing it up with the water left over from the morning washing, to form the paste that held in place the pieces of glass the younger boys returned with. In those years when he ruled the orphanage wall, Bokarie persuaded the others to do the work, though two were bigger and the other older, while he supervised, the dirt-specked soccer ball cradled under one arm like an Eden apple. The dung-and-mud mixing was not only their duty-bound honour to their fellow orphans, Bokarie suggested, but also a way to get a few kicks at the ball. He liked how well he could bend them.

Bokarie also enjoyed the views and sounds that came his way from both sides of the orphanage walls when he was on top, holding himself above and between these two worlds. His presence up there was unprecedented. Before him, boys would smidge and sweat their way across the wall, purse-lipped and vibrating on their haunches as they leaned in to replace a missing piece of glass. Eventually they would shimmy and dangle back down and get a little rubbing alcohol into the pink cracks that had opened up on their arms and legs, and only then boast to the younger ones about snapping fat dung beetles in half with well-placed stabs and about snatched looks at the working girls on their way to the beer bars.

Now the younger boys, upon returning from their raids, gathered and marvelled at Bokarie's ever more daring dances across the top of the wall. They also listened to him. As he grew longer and lankier and cockier still, a few women on the other side started to notice. They would laugh and clap and make loud predictions of his future talents. The drunker ones, on their way to and from work or the odd public hygiene clinic, would even swing their hips in unison with his move-ments as Bokarie threaded his way along the blocks, darting here and striking there to shove a cracked bottle neck into the trench his blood men had prepared.

From up there, he could see a few cooking fires in what settlements remained after the latest raids. Now and then, he longed to be close by one of them. He could remember one childhood time when someone like a grandmother re-boiling something like sheep bones had given him a palm's worth of the brownish foamy runoff to drink when the others weren't looking. But he stopped himself from remembering like that again. Nothing good could come to him from back there.

But he liked the rest of it, of being so high above the earth, with faces watching him from below, waiting to hear from him. Father Alvaro had encouraged the boys to select a line or two from the Bible as private credos, God's words to them to live by. Bokarie found his in Isaiah. *Thus saith the Lord GOD: Cry out full-throated and unsparingly, lift up your voice like a trumpet blast.* Bokarie did like that from his Hosea passage while stretching his back between glass refittings. He liked how the words bounced and jumped off his tongue, and also that he could make the women below him dance, that he could turn a hip and some would turn theirs. In time there was one girl in particular who started keeping time with him. She had a heavy chest and three friends. She looked riper than the African girls he had come across in those old yellow magazines. Meanwhile, Father Alvaro thought the boy a bit flamboyant in the hips but gifted in the tongue. If he could be made to stay and settle down some, perhaps there was a vocation here.

When Bokarie left the orphanage, he did it by scrambling up and across and down the wall at an opening he had prepared in advance, by sinking some of that week's glass to only a shallow depth. It was not difficult to press the pieces into the still-damp mud and slide across. He had the others go first and smooth out the path, having given effective descriptions of his woman's bouncy friends just waiting with jiggling on the other side. Later their first night out, nervous and aggressive and hungry, they tracked them to one of the beer bars. As rare as it was providential, all were on break. While Bokarie and the girl finally danced up close together, knees and then higher parts knocking and sliding, his brothers and cousin raised up their shirts to the girl's fey friends and plumed for them, arcing their backs to bare the glass specks that had nicked into their skin during their courageous escape from the shark's belly, as they had taken to calling the orphanage. The boys buckled at the waist when their stomachs and points nearby were inspected by the girls' hands, which were nimble and efficient like seamstresses'. Claims of possession, if vaguely conflicting, were quickly and showily established.

It had to be accepted that the girls made what they did for the man who ran the bar by doing and letting have done to them as was required. After being introduced later that first night and assuring the owner that he'd never chased after him before for stealing bottles, Bokarie told Uncle, as he was called, that he and his blood men were looking for any work to be had. They were taken on as bouncers and dishwashers in exchange for a place to sleep and the right to finish any drink left by a man who picked out their girl for a go. They were instructed to keep the red, white and blue iceboxes full of beer and cool with river water. Now and then they thought about the orphanage, even saw a few of the boys around town. Out of guilt and charity and laziness, they would leave empty bottles at the back of the bar's dish hut and turn away when the darting, snatching hands came.

Bokarie soon progressed from dishwasher to whore's tout. Uncle had noticed a surge of interest in Bokarie's girl, Elizabeth, after they had been dancing together on another of her breaks. This, Uncle realized, was a very successful way of advertising particular flexibilities. Uncle had him dance the talent in front of the men who came in each night. Each morning, when the last of the customers had gone off, the girls would limp and laugh over to the river to wash themselves off and the boys would sweep and sponge off the dance floor. Uncle let them sleep and fumble and giggle there together until the first men came in the afternoon from their hangovers, their marching, their surveying, their recruitments, their peacekeeping.

IV.

When Bokarie later returned to the orphanage to liberate its holdings on behalf of the General's National Restitution Campaign, he had men waiting in a nearby and idling truck, which was driven by his cousin. The Bangladeshi quartet lowered their weapons at the sight of so many machine guns and machetes, and Bokarie marched in. Father Alvaro threw holy water in his face while Bokarie finished off a bottle and then broke it over his head. When the current collection of orphans had been assembled in the courtyard, Bokarie pointed at the crack-pate double-bent priest and in the general direction of the Upriver people to the north, the target for the General's National Restitution Campaign. He informed the boys that those were the men responsible for killing their parents and leaving them in this white prison, this shark's belly.

"Like the jaws of highway robbers, they conspire with the priests who murder in the way those that pass out of Sichem: for they have wrought wickedness. And I say to you, my little brothers, suffer an eye for an eye! Make a Father suffer for your fathers!"

Returning outside the orphanage's walls after a few more broken bottles and other such things, Bokarie offered the Bangladeshis certain compensations for maintaining their services. Then the truck chugged and gutted into the orphanage and he had the gate shut after it. The priest's body was wrapped in a bedsheet and left with the rest of the soiled laundry. Bokarie kicked around a soccer ball with the younger boys and added to the force he was leading Upriver for the General, for the nation, for possibilities.

The following year, three U.S. congressmen were empanelled by a special congressional committee to conduct an open, honest, fair and balanced study of the UN's peacekeeping activities in Africa. Among other interests, there were spending cuts to be justified. The troubling actions of the Bangladeshi contingent in the northern province of

Atwenty received special attention. The orphanage there was designated non-sectarian and to be guarded as such. But when Bokarie had taken it for the General and the People, the Bangladeshis had maintained their posts and the international community had guarded a child-soldier training facility for a few weeks, until the Bangladeshis, overcome by the compensation package Bokarie provided them—gin and syphilis—failed to submit one too many weekly action reports to mission headquarters in a timely fashion.

Shock and awe were expressed on behalf of the American people at learning that a series of wholesome Christian picnic coolers, once used by orphans for ice cream, had ended up in brothels. And also that a few had been used by street urchins and scavengers to collect broken gin and beer bottles for a priest reported to have been killed by a local warlord in a drunken brawl. This was a place that needed America's prayers and investment. There were rumoured drilling possibilities. Natural resources were a terrible thing to waste.

v.

In time, the boys from town got their mascot to play soccer with them after his shifts. Bokarie proved to be very quick on the ball and had the footwork of a dancer. They delighted that he could knife between them, faking one way and darting the other, and then score with ease. Their fathers gutted and chugged their way around slo-pitch diamonds with beer coolers for bases. And Bokarie climbed up and over an infamously high retirement-home wall and returned an errant Frisbee one Saturday. He reached summer legend status.

A week after this feat and elevation, Jennifer took Bokarie to tea. He detailed his recent activities. His options for further community involvement were discussed and he was also given an overview of parliamentary democracy and campaign cycles. A soccer workshop was announced after their meeting, to be held in conjunction with a

Little Caitlin Bottle Drive. Jennifer decided that it was still too early, too traumatic, for a full creek cleanup. Better to wait until the coming election date was set and then count back from there. Recycling would be a fit response to the tragedy.

The day was a great success and Jennifer took many pictures of the pink-shirted Bokarie bouncing soccer balls on his knees as he deked and danced the children around the pylons, shouting instructions and adjusting postures. Every child was given a set of pink wristbands for bringing a bottle. Parents wore proud seamed faces and inquired about personal soccer tutorials and cursed themselves for forgetting to charge video camera batteries. Cream soda was served. The town was starting to froth and overflow with its recent excitements. First that little girl, so tragically gone, and now this twisting, this turning, this chocolate-skinned newcomer. Dropped in from nowhere and kicking around town as if he's always been here. A few of the old-timers even conceded that road apples could make for good fertilizer.

LICORICE WHIPS

I.

As instructed, Bokarie raised his hands to the ceiling and waited. Despite prior explanations of what this would entail, he was still a little nervous. He didn't like any of it, especially this strange man asking questions and measuring him up. He had been told that this was the necessary procedure. Searching hands closing in on his body. Professional interest in his height and habits. The outlay of cash. There were other suited men standing immediately outside the room where he was getting measured up. They were watching him and his escort, smiling with force, waiting to be of assistance. He wondered if he had been tricked in being taken here upon first arriving in the capital city, whether he had been made into someone else's turtle.

The surrounding music, muffled and martial, was interrupted by a loud voice charged up with gunpoint enthusiasm. As if, Bokarie thought with private knowledge, the speaker was using prepared notes not his own, and the words had to be delivered with impeccable vigour of voice or its owner would be made to suffer. Even the man writing information about Bokarie on a notepad paused and looked up at the interruption, though he must have been accustomed to such occurrences.

"Attention, please, ladies and gentlemen, ladies and gentlemen, this is a red alert. I repeat: this is a red HOT alert! For the next hour, anyone who wants real savings on already low low prices is directed to visit the Home and Garden Department on the lower level. As part of our end-of-summer sale, all mulch and lawn ornaments on clearance are an additional fifty percent off! Hurry!"

Jennifer was standing outside the tailor's room where Bokarie was getting fitted for a new suit. He needed one for the prominent wedding he had been invited to attend later that summer. The Father of the Bride, who had met Bokarie at the car dealership he owned, had encouraged him to find a cap as well, if possible. Bokarie and Jennifer were going to the wedding together, in a manner of speaking. Since Bokarie had an official capacity in the proceedings, Jennifer would be arriving separately. He was the Driver.

She nodded at the announcement and stomped off, leaving him in the men's section of the department store they had come to as their first stop in Ottawa. This was a few weeks after Jennifer had organized the well-received soccer tutorial that Bokarie had conducted for the town's children. In addition to getting the materials necessary to attend the wedding, Jennifer made this trip so that she could give Bokarie a look at what she had earlier promised to show him, what she was now promising to share with him if he helped her get elected. And also so she could take a few pictures—Bokarie in front of the Peace Tower, Bokarie beside a diversity mural, Bokarie with a seniors' tour group, etc.

But before all of this, he needed a wedding suit and she needed to see about wedding gifts. So Jennifer left Bokarie in the capable hands of Vince, the Italian Canadian who was measuring him. When he finished, Vince chuckled as he noted the figures on the seamstress's card. Twenty-eight-inch waist, 36-inch inseam, black as licorice. He crossed out the last part; the seamstress was new, a Filipino woman, and he wasn't so sure about her yet. Instead he satisfied himself with more immediate amusement.

"Just a quick cut in the back and your pants will be ready. Come by in about twenty minutes or so. Hey there, you like Twizzlers, buddy?" he asked with the xenophobic confidence of a second-generation immigrant. The newcomer didn't seem to hear or understand. Bokarie was fingering through a fantail of neckties in search of something to match his new clothes. But he had heard the question, and was familiar with this item from his shifts at Gary's Milk and Lotto, and had a good enough sense of what was implied. He also knew that a necktie could, in a pinch, serve as a garrotte. But he thought better of it. There were finer opportunities becoming available to him than such easy greasy revenge, so he crooked his back and did his best slinky innocent African instead. This had been working well in his new country. He looked up and smiled and nodded with vacant happiness, like a marionette being tugged around by a cat.

The stub-fingered Calabrian's superiority was thus reinforced, but feeling a little ex–altar boy remorse Vince decided to waive the fee for having the suit pants taken in around the waist. He gave them to the seamstress and went to the Home and Garden Department to spend his break searching for a ceramic owl. Damned squirrels were raiding the birdfeeder every night.

Because he didn't know where Jennifer went, and because he had to kill twenty minutes anyway, Bokarie decided to entertain himself a little. He started wandering through the aisles of the men's section, aware that two sales associates were trailing him with open, friendly suspicion. Bokarie picked up a tie and turned on them. Close on his heels, they hopped back a little, smiling and buckling. He recalled a bit from a song he had heard on the car radio on the drive in. He continued his practice of gaining Canadians' trust with a brand of ancient African wisdom they could easily ingest. Holding the tie up like a limp rope, he explained in his slow, stumpy English way that in his old country, "great hunters and priests killed snakes and dried their skin and painted it just like this. They hung the snakes from their necks. Cobra snake for necktie. Many brave men had these." The associates nodded, respectfully, and pulled back their cuffs to show off their white plastic knowledge of his people's suffering.

When they left the store, Bokarie had a slippery plastic suit bag swinging across his shoulders and Jennifer had a squat grinning garden gnome headlocked under each arm. Their shopping necessities having been filled, the next stop on the expedition to Ottawa was a look at Parliament Hill. At possibilities.

"The eyes, the face, all chipped up," Bokarie observed, a little annoyed as he pointed out the clearance table bruises while Jennifer set the pair down in the back seat. (With part of the proceeds from the Little Caitlin Fund, she had purchased a used Mary Kay car to help raise further awareness, and had also, given her efforts, accepted a modest salary. Whenever someone in town made a fuss about it, she made them a member of the executive board, non-voting. It was during one such exchange, with one of those always-tousled Gallagher daughters, that Jennifer heard about the grand wedding planned for later that summer. Jennifer wasn't invited, but she knew that a good showing with that guest list was crucial to future plans.)

Bokarie was willing to bring her along to the wedding, and pleased that she had agreed to pay for the gift. This seemed a good trade. But he was wary of her promise that the suit "could be written off," whatever that meant. It represented the better part of two weeks' convenience clerk pay, but he was very pleased with it. Professionally dark, black-lined and blended, he was told, from the best Indonesian polycotton. He looked very dignified in it. Unlike the grinning, cracked-up men in loud costumery who ran things back home, or the ones Jennifer had just bought as wedding gifts.

With all the shiny whirring blades and fancy button machines this Canada had, he sourly wondered, why choose such ugliness? The same, he could imagine his dead brothers and cousin pointing out, might be said about his pick for a wedding date. He missed them, now and then, and he regretted what had been done, what the General had made them do to him and also the reverse. He also missed his woman, Elizabeth, though that was another matter. He didn't think as much about the other woman, Marigold. There was no need for any of that to reach him in this here and now.

"You don't understand these ways yet," Jennifer lectured. The calibrated admiration that had been in her voice back when she first brought him under her wing was now chiding and exasperation, as the situation warranted. At other times it held out a little more promise. Speak down to them and they have to look up to you. LBJ in the Senate cloakroom. "This is the type of gift that people of distinction, like the bride and her father and other invited guests, will appreciate. The groom's side won't, but that doesn't matter. They're all about football with no helmets, red necks and blue collars. Plus, they're from a different riding, some mullet town over near Toronto, and they vote whatever the Auto Workers' union says. Such people have no interest in drainage security. Think Pink. But the bride's father, now, he's a man of real influence. His support, for Little Caitlin and our election bid, is necessary for our advance."

Our, Bokarie thought. She had no idea.

"Anyway," she continued, "the salesman said that the chipped ones were a better choice when I described these people to him. These could be considered *objets trouvés,* he told me. That means objects of true vain, only in French, which is even better. I know we can't really understand it, and it seems unfair maybe that you have to buy a brand

new suit and I have to buy older items, but that's just how it's done."
She smiled, her thick lips chapped even in the latish August heat from
all her licking and smacking as she told him her plans for future
success.

Bokarie was stone-faced. He knew a little French from back home,
which was one of the nation's many master tongues, and he was suspicious of Jennifer's gloss on *objets trouvés*. Either she had been duped
or she was trying to dupe him. Regardless, he had to play as long as
was necessary at this *our* business. Until she got him down into the
capital city, where he would do so much, just like he should have once
before. Could have.

The car buckled once and then wheezed a little when she got in.
This woman wouldn't be much for dancing with. He was glad that
they would be arriving at the wedding separately. But the prospect of
having to move around with her later, this was disappointing. He
hadn't danced in a long time, not since his own woman had gone on
from the beer bar to the campaign headquarters and beyond.
Wrapping up with this Canadian woman would be like pressing
against a big boiled yam. But this was what had to be done if he was
to get on, just as had been the case before. Because he had given her
the second of two wedding invitations he had been provided with.
Because this woman, Jennifer, was planning to get elected to the
national parliament and had promised him a position with her in the
capital city, if he performed in a manner conducive to her developing
campaign. So he might have to press up a little against her on the
dance floor. Not the worst thing. After all, his woman Elizabeth had
done pretty much the same, back in Atwenty, when they were taken
to meet the General. Who was a big round laughing man with
jewellery-clotted hands. Who liked dancing. Who had been informed
that Bokarie and his woman danced in a beer bar. Who— Bokarie

clenched against this unnecessary raid from the past. It did no good. But things kept coming together.

The General enjoyed song and dance, as he had explained to Bokarie while they toured the National Restitution Campaign's offices. As future Father of the Nation, he had rights and responsibilities towards his daughters. Once they'd reached the church hall that had been converted into a rally and staging room, the General had had his aide-de-camp turn on a little music and then had cupped Bokarie's woman around the waist while he and his brothers and cousin and the other woman, Marigold, waited. And watched. Soon the General was holding her close to his shuffling thighs, bending her at the waist and twirling round to an American pop song. Bokarie had no choice but to assent to this, that much was plain, but he'd still made a fist while his woman giggled and the General tongued patriotic messages into her ear.

When the General had finished with Bokarie's woman, he brought her back to him, arm in courtly arm, and then squeezed Bokarie's shoulder to draw him close to speak of private matters. The General told him his plans for the northern province and suggested Bokarie's possible role. He could feel the hot hungry breath close in on his neck, the hand vise-gripped on his frame. He kept wondering what the General's other hand was doing. But he knew well enough. Could tell his woman's hips were buckling and turning on the General's gold-ringed fingers while he poured grandeur and governorships into Bokarie's ear.

He spat and put his suit in the trunk.

Getting into the car, he put down this insurrection from over there by thinking instead of the wedding he was going to. Would he remember some of his own hot fast moves from the beer bar? And it was no matter if the cracked-up little men were found dishonourable, he could blame the woman Jennifer anyway. He was smiling again.

The bride, whom he met in passing at her father's car dealership once, was fine in the face and fruit-firm in other places. He hoped he could dance with her if the father and the husband granted it, especially once she, once they all, saw what he could do.

II.

Mr. and Mrs. Glenn Hollerwatty

cordially request the honour of your attendance

at the nuptials of their daughter,

Catherine "Cat" Hollerwatty,

to

Glenn Gary Kane

~

St. Mark's Anglican Church

Saturday, August 27, 2005

2:00 PM

Reception to follow,

Orleans Golf and Country Club

~

Gift information: www.weddings.com/~catandgare

A favour of a reply is requested before July 15.

You steal my sunshine

C&G   XOXO

Many invitees to the wedding thought that Glenn the Engine and his family were showing off with these invitations, which even had blue ink for the Internet part. A few expressed surprise that the bride had successfully resisted her father's request for a Biblical quotation at the bottom of the card, given his love of quoting Scripture when closing car deals.

To the bride's daily logged-in disappointment, most stayed away from the specially designed website. The few who did visit went only in search of hair salon and coffee shop grist, to see the bride's list of things she just absolutely had to have. Which no one could afford to buy her anyway. Instead, the wedding gifts were on the more expensive side of small-town finery, being for the only daughter of the town's richest family: ornate ceramic angel mugs, discontinued French quality cookware collections, various back massage devices, advanced kitchen gadgetry from the As Seen On TV store that had recently opened up in a local strip mall, a set of mermaid-and-seahorse-crowned cheese utensils, a pair of bright splattered garden gnomes.

Bokarie came to be invited to Catherine and Gary's wedding because the town-famous Father of the Bride had a black man for a lawn ornament and didn't want some wet-headed Greek ogling his daughter on her special day as he opened the limo door for her and goosed her onto the seat. During his first summer in Canada, Bokarie went to Prime Mover Ford on Sunday afternoons after his shifts at the convenience store. He liked to visit with the bold-coloured cars lined up row on row unto the horizon. In the July haze they were waxy and shiny and many, like the bright fat candies that lined the lower shelves of his counter. He wanted one very much, having never driven anything in his old country except stolen aid trucks and commandeered school buses.

The first few times he came to the lot, the salesmen, their fat chests heaving and key chains jangling, had taken professionally responsible interest in him. They were following two universal commandments in sales. First, a man always wanted a new one and just needed help admitting as much to himself. Second, an unidentified black male looking at your merchandise was a cup of hot coffee tipping at your crotch. But enough of the salesmen knew something of Bokarie; they had seen him around town or bought smokes and scratch cards from his counter or heard him (via their wives) speak for Little Caitlin at that rally. One even had video footage of him playing soccer with his kids. Poor harmless this and that. So, if with a little disappointment at the lost opportunity for a little Sunday excitement, they accepted him as a vaguely identified black male who thus wasn't subject to the recommendations outlined in a "For Your Eyes Only" pamphlet that the manufacturer had sent on from Detroit. *Customer Satisfaction, Racial Profiling and Loss Prevention: Some Difficult Statistics to Consider.*

So the salesmen returned to their standard Sunday afternoon pursuit of gifting the gloriously plump-assed receptionist with the in-season peaches their wives packed for them and then snickering and aching behind office partitions to watch the late teen bite down and oh how it squirted and then her slurping the dribble up from her chin. Meanwhile, Bokarie was allowed to dip in and out of the rows and peer into windows and under hoods in the repair bay, which is how he met Glenn the Engine, who was in one Sunday to work on the car he was overhauling as a wedding gift to his future son-in-law.

Hollerwatty was the shape and colour of a beefsteak tomato slow-cooking on a barbecue grill. His colouring was especially strong in the summer months, when he spent long stretches at the family place on the St. Lawrence River tinkering with the boat motor so he could drive over to the local sandy beach and grip an afternoon cold one and watch the limber lifeguard girls stretch and yawn. But back at the office, he was always popping and bursting and reddening at monthly sales figures and trade-in overpayments and especially inventive dirty jokes and ethnic nicknames. *Glenn the Engine made his first successful vehicle sale at the age of twelve—a homemade Go Kart outfitted with a lawnmower motor, to a grateful and awed classmate—and he's been the prime mover in this community ever since!* The caption accompanied The Engine's personal portrait, which was placed centre-top in the school portable the dealership used as a sales office and also figured prominently in the advertorial literature regularly placed in the local newspaper. In addition to great deals on late-model Fords and reasonable repair rates, Glenn was widely known and respected for his penchant for quoting the Old Testament. He did this for a variety of reasons—rhetorical flourish, bona fide morality, intervention from on high at a crucial moment in a deal. Glenn's favourite, in this last respect, was Proverbs 31, which he used when he had a suddenly panicked, mortgage-calculating husband and a pro-purchase wife at the pre-point-of-sale moment. Just when things were fully dilated for a new car to drive home.

Who can find a virtuous woman? for her price is far above rubies. The heart of her husband doth safely trust in her, so that he shall have no need of spoil. She will do him good and not evil all the days of her life.

Glenn also drew on the best of Job when agreeing to accept a jalopy rust-bucket trade-in, and the darker tracts of Exodus when a customer made noises about buying Nip or Kraut instead. (If anyone asked, he would explain that his father lost a leg in France, so he had a right to these terms.) He had also been reading Daniel and John of Patmos of late, searching for push-back and righteous anger for when he was asked about that terrible ugliness being born. Hybrids. When pressed, Glenn admitted that he had little interest in the New Testament; there was just no business sense—all those upturned money tables and JC whipping businessmen just trying to get by and those thirty silver pieces with poor returns.

They met under the corrugated ceiling of a 1987 Ford Mustang. Priding himself on knowing all things in advance, The Engine was nonplussed to find Bokarie in his pneumatic garden. He even vaguely recognized the thin black rail of a body from a newspaper picture from a while back. Munificent, he decided to have a chat.

Bokarie was quietly lacerating himself. He was getting just so soft in this new country. He hadn't even noticed the squat round body mashed against the other side of the car when he first came upon it, and he was surprised at how friendly, how unsuspicious, how interested the man seemed, staring at him from across the engine. This seemed too easy from what Bokarie knew of Great Men from his past and about this man specifically, from all the pictures around the compound and in his bunker and also on the full-page back cover of the local newspaper most days. Even the General would be impressed, he thought.

So Bokarie went into full newcomer mode while he tried to figure Glenn. He recalled once again how the other asylum cases had dealt with the trip-tongued Newfoundland immigration officers when they'd first arrived on the tanker. Like the Tamils and Falun Gongs then, he smiled apologetically and curved his back into a pitiable bow in response to the questions about his name, his prior whereabouts, etc. To be extra helpful, Bokarie unhooked the yellow lamp that was hanging above the engine and held it over his interlocutor's plug-twisting, cap-cursing fingers as they worked. This was his great fortune—a *deus ex* machine shop coincidence. The Engine sported a black little livery boy ceramic statue in his landscaped garden. It was the one element that had survived of the Old South motif he had originally wanted for his custom-made executive mansion. His wife had vetoed pillars as "just too paving-contractor Italian," and the building company representative had seconded her opinion and also noted the logistical problems of adding Greco-Roman flourishes to a ranch plan home, however grand it was.

So when Glenn saw his statue come to life, right up in his grille, his juicy eyes grew fat and excited, but he thought better of asking directly about the wedding. Instead, and guessing this might have an effect on the African if he was a down-through-the-ages Ham boy or some new evangelical, he went to Scripture. "Today is the tenth day of the seventh month of the year," he started in, "or thereabouts. I'm no literalist. But do you know Leviticus 16?" He gutted and scraped and spat from his throat, ready to deliver from on high.

"'On this day, the Lord God commanded Moses, you shall deny yourselves and shall do no work, neither the citizen'"—here Glenn pressed a plump hand against his man-busty chest for clarity—"'nor the alien who resides among you'"—then a second hock extended a sausagey finger towards Bokarie. "What do you think? Should I take this as a sign, your coming here to me on this day? That maybe we should sit down for a chat and I should just accept that the Lord deemed it good that the Parts Shop rest on Sunday, which means I can't get a new fan belt for this damned pony?" He back-slap-chuckled Bokarie out of the garage and towards his office. He could tell from the man's shoes and evident lack of dental coverage that this wasn't a walk-on sales opportunity, but there was, Glenn hoped, another possibility here.

When they were seated, The Engine in his ergonomic throne and Bokarie on a cigarette- and coffee-scored customer chair, the young man from far away was invited to tell a little more about himself. Bokarie gave the now-standardized version of his story—Rwanda, etc.—which had the usual effect. The Canadian nodded and exhaled and shook his head and curved his eyebrows empathetically.

Then, because what the hell, Bokarie mentioned how he had for many suns longed to drive one of Mr. Engine's fine chariots. He couldn't have known how consonant this desire was. Sensing that it would strengthen his case with this man, Bokarie recalled lines from his orphanage time, about sharing with others. The priest had taught them to the boys, and they linked up nicely with Glenn's earlier invocation.

"And Mr. Engine, sir, I think you should grant this my humble request. Because as it is written, 'You shall not strip your vineyard bare, or gather the fallen grapes of your vineyard; you shall leave them'"—here both of his hands turned inward, long knifelike fingers pointing at his burnt little birdcage chest—"'for the poor and the alien.'" He paused, hopeful.

Glenn was tempted to finish the sentence, but thought better of it. The implications could compromise his transactional independence.

"Where'd you learn the Bible, son?" he asked.

"From a priest, back when I was an orphan." Bokarie cursed himself. This was his first wrong step since coming to Canada, the first revelation of something from his own past instead of from someone else's, be it the Liberian he strangled by the man's necktie in the tanker, or a snipped story from the International Briefs section of the newspaper, or a retelling of a segment from the Aid to Africa charity programs broadcast late at night that he watched to make his insomniac paranoia useful. He wanted to leave the office; he had lost interest in a chance to drive. It was too much of a risk, too many questions could follow, and even one of those dazzling, juicy Fusions wasn't worth it. He had spent too much time around that Jennifer. He wasn't just becoming soft, he was getting greedy.

To Bokarie's good fortune, however, The Engine was too interested in what this black cord of a new Canadian could do for him in the here and now to wonder about the man's life back then. He parried in plain old folksy car dealer.

"Learning the Bible from a priest? My goodness, that's a surprise. All we got around here are Frenchy Canadian Catholics, and they wouldn't know the Bible if it hit them in their rummy noses!" Bokarie heaved and pulled his shoulders in unison with the chortling Engine, who further explained that he himself subscribed to no particular church but certainly loved his Bible and it did him no small good in getting him to the place where he was today. Grateful for the change in subject, Bokarie made his eyes wide and admiring. He leaned in to hear more about The Engine, who then had little trouble getting himself a bona fide Miss Daisy driver for his daughter's wedding. Glenn even threw in a couple of invites to the wedding proper like they were heated seats.

III.

"Please, can you tell me, what are these things? These butterfly kisses?" Bokarie was watching everyone watch Glenn, the Father, have his dance with Cat, the Bride. He was standing beside Austin, the Best Man, who was chewing gum furiously to mask how drunk he was. Which, by now, was beside the point. At the summit of his toast, he had started advising the Groom on the best possible approach to his pending *primae noctis* only to stop short and shrug, "But you've been there, done that, eh buddy!"

Austin's speech was met with the chill clinking of champagne flutes, the only sound in the hall save the slapping-meat thwack of sweaty high-fives that a fellow drunk-hearty groomsman gave the Best Man as he returned to his seat.

Bokarie and Austin suddenly smiled and posed like old linemates for disposable-camera pictures that the latter's engaged-to-be-engaged girlfriend took before she waddled off in search of a girlfriend, and then the tequila-cracked tuxedo shrugged a conspirational response to Bokarie's question. "Spend a little more time around here, Shaft, and you'll get the way things always are in this town. That dance? The usual world-revolves-around-Glenn-the-Engine bullshit. Which we all have to clap to and agree to, obviously. Because guess what this town and the new married man have in common? They're both totally whipped. Do you get that joke from where you're coming from? Listen hey buddy, that's between us, eh buddy there? Never know when you're going to need a good deal on a half-ton! Speaking of which"—now giggling himself, remembering that hulking shape from high school—"looks like your date's here." He staggered off for another shot and in search of a bridesmaid rumoured to be tight-lipped and on the rebound.

Jennifer had just finished affixing a pink ribbon to the gift table. She was standing beside Bokarie, looking intently at the parquet floor. She wanted to dance, given the prospects. Think Pink. The town's most important man was almost alone out there, and she had already cleared it with the videographer, who agreed that it would make for a beautiful image, the Bride dancing with the town's prominent newcomer, encircled by the smiling citizenry done up in their church socks and feathered hair finery. She had already asked for a copy of the reception dance video.

If her impending campaign for a federal seat were to have any success, she needed the riding's most important endorsement. "Butterfly Kisses" was trailing off and the deejay was mixing in Chubby Checker. It was time to make their move. Standing in the middle of the dance floor to applause and whistles, the Father and Bride posed and mugged for pictures. Such Freudian glee. At the same time Glenn, fairly done in by champagne toasts and a flask that had been emptied during the purgatorial photographer's session after church, gave out choice cuts from Solomon's Song while Cat sweet-mouthed, "You're my best friend never change this will be you someday," with venomed cuteness, to each of her *I can't believe you're not married yet!* bridesmaids. Who were openly crying because they were just so so happy for her.

Jennifer clamped Bokarie's wrist. She explained to her grateful partner what it meant to cut in on someone else's dance and they started marching. She was immense and target ready, as always, only this time squared up in a pink sheet of a dress and sporting a mother-done upturn for which Jennifer had endured a *sotto voce* parable from Barb Thickson, about how many people meet their you-know-whats at weddings, and that a career's one thing but a man can pay the bills *and* put out the trash. It had been Gus Thickson's wording and was delivered with gunpoint enthusiasm.

Bokarie's arm sank into his companion's waist. It had the consistency of day-old oatmeal. He was excited by the prospect of firm and shapely woman-flesh. He wondered what the Bride would think of dancing with her slinky wedding-day Driver as he watched her laughing and teary-eyed swig from a bottle and blush and wave and thump up the crowd with the grace of a small-town princess. Having earlier gone to the parking lot, as instructed, to put some pink bows on the Lincoln he had driven for the bridal party, Bokarie knew that the Groom was not guarding his woman. He was standing with his shift-worker cousins and uncles studying the magnificent wedding gift his father-in-law had given him along with a position as Associate Sales Manager on the lot. In fact, these men would spend nearly an hour outside, theorizing about possible decal motifs for the hood and side panels, though taking expected breaks to return inside, of course, *to the open friggin' bar.* The Bride was, for present purposes, wide open.

Bokarie and Jennifer closed in beside Cat and the Engine and began dancing to stage whispers and elbow jabs and Sea Breeze giggles. Bokarie started twisting and twirling around Jennifer as she bobbed methodically in place. He was enjoying the response—whoops and flashes and the Bride's eyes widening and the Engine yelling something from Ecclesiastes over the music and drawling with Great White Father pride at how far this Boy had already come. From driving Quality to dancing beside it! Turning to cut, Bokarie smiled at the Bride and readied to ask her, this beery mound of chiffon and lace, how she liked her licorice whips.

5

BOTTLE RETURN

I.

Though the speakers were bass throbbing and the older men shouting imprecations and their women shrieking lamentations while they took turns trying to putt putt for a loonie in a corner of the reception hall, Bokarie could still hear it, the bright wet clacking sound of the bottle being blunted against the bride's teeth.

It was interfering, this long-ago sound, interfering as he was trying to enjoy slow-dancing with Glenn's beer-brined, crinoline-crushed daughter in the dreamy steam of the wedding deejay's fog machine. She was squashing her *this is my last one I swear* bottle through her lips, swigging and swallowing and nodding to her dance partner's sad, sad tales. Then she mounted her response.

"Listen, I can't do anything about all the stuff that happened to you over in New Whatchamacallitland, but I can at least say sorry, as a concerned Canadian, as a *fellow* Canadian"—here she pulled back and smiled and nodded and Bokarie immediately responded in kind—"I can say sorry for my dad having you dress up like that and drive us to the wedding. It's like it's the States or something and I swear to God sometimes I think he wishes it was. That wasn't my idea, the whole Miss Daisy thing, and it wasn't ever supposed to be a judgment on you and what you're capable of in your new land though you probably think it is and after all that persecution and shit back wherever and now this."

Bokarie liked this girl. She was more efficient than most in blaring her indignation on his behalf. He nodded for her to say more and asked her to give him the words loudly. So he could hear her better. So that he would not have to bend in and listen to that bottle slide on her teeth.

"Plus I had a friend I never told anyone about when I went to summer camp in Oneonta. That was my high school graduation gift. His name was Jamal, like from *Cosby*, and contrary to what you might have heard he always wore a belt and he had both parents at home but … but …" Here she went a little teary and shook her head, hiccupping a General Arts degree's worth of First World remorse and sucking away at her bottle. Bokarie was enjoying her sweat and pearl-beaded décolletage mashing mournfully against him, but that damned sound, the bottle CLICK-SMACK! against her whites as she sipped and swallowed. It punctuated every other pronouncement. CLICK-SMACK! It was urging him on and bringing him back and screwing up his dance steps.

He thought it best, just now, to unhook his gauze-swaddled pelvis and get away from that bloody noise. He would take some air. He did a deep bow before the gracious bride. Knowing that eyes and apertures were on him, he showily grooved his way out of the hall, leaving anthropological commentaries in his bopping wake from coffee-and-cake-taking onlookers.

"You know how it is. That type always just having that rhythm."

"Must be from all the drumming you see on those documentaries."

Earlier, there had been a few noises about how close the bride seemed to have been dancing with that Thickson girl's African. The more sexually frustrated invitees were openly bitter that the new guy got first crack at every small town's summer grail—the courtly bachelor's allotted four minutes of rhythmic squish against the *bella figura* of the tipsy, hugsy new bride. These Tip Top Tailored Iagos circulated through the tables, loudly wondering whether the next song was going to be "The Jungle Bunny Hop." When this cleverness dissipated, their discussion returned to the relative weights and merits of older, budding and jiggling teenaged cousins for Last Call use, in the aftermath of the pending garter-belt brawl.

Meanwhile the Bride, flush, stumblish, makeup moulting in the African's absence, was primly escorted to the ladies' dressing room by her girlfriends for a little touch-up, and maybe for just a giggly smidge of dish about how it felt, that hard-body black number moving against her. But this request only occasioned new, too-late dirges about the bride's portentous first dance with her new husband, Gary, and also knowing evocations and simulations of his pillow-soft man-flesh and his beat-timed, head-nodding overbite. And so that was to be her future, since she'd gone and married him and all because, well, whatever. It was just total bullshit. The girls agreed her back to happier times and then finished up by bringing out, for the umpteenth time that day, the whole town's necessary fiction. That she wasn't even showing yet.

After the bride had been tanked up with some coffee, she was returned to the festivities, waving and laughing and hiccupping. Those still in the powder room checked each other for dangling slip swatches and spurting thong strings. They were preparing to shriek and claw and present in the pending bouquet toss. After one last check in the mirror for bits of iceberg and peppercorn in their teeth, they took envy and glee in chorusing about their first-trimester girl-friend's fate. Having married in haste, she would repent during labour.

The Father of the Bride missed all of this. Glenn and Jennifer were orbiting far from the bride and Bokarie's double-backed beast waltz. To fill in the cogitating pauses in their conversation, the car dealer and would-be federal candidate passed billowy bon mots back and forth about their friend-in-common.

"Ham couldn't be prouder!"

"Caliban can't compare!"

Eventually they came to agreeable terms for the pending election race and then exchanged offers to be driven home by the eloquent linchpin of the coming campaign.

In the meantime Bokarie had gone outside, intent upon securing some space away from the teeth against the bottle, from that too-recollecting sound. But for such a wide open country, it could be hard at times to find a little patch of one's own. He was immediately surrounded by smoke and barricaded in by the brisk flicks of chin that young men give each other while waiting for the start of the hunt. They were all in their late twenties and early thirties and magnificently single and just looking to have a good time, no head games. They went quiet at Bokarie's appearance. The new African in town. They found him just too hard to figure because he was more than the convenience store counterwork and always smiling at every-one. There was something else there that didn't sit right.

It wasn't so much how he looked or even how he made them feel, but just being here. It was what he did to their place and their stuff. The African wore a heavy chain that attached his wallet to his belt-line, just like the rest of the stylish young men about town. But the brushed steel links clanging against his clover-boned hips gave off something less than transplanted Leeds tough. More Goree Island redux. None of this was ever said or even thought outright, but it was in the air. Bokarie was the one too many.

The older immigrants around town, for all their ripeness and silly sounds, could at least provide linebackers for the high school and cabbage rolls for the church hall. They could rice-paddy over the strip malls with all-in-one dry cleaner and computer stores. They could bindi-dot intersections with their incense-drenched video outlets. But the new guy from Africa? He brought nothing with him except untold suffering embodied, the back pages of the newspaper made flesh.

Bokarie sensed something of this in the suspended air when he walked out. He accepted that Canadian men his own age were tougher marks than their elders and their women. But he was a prac- tised manager of men's passions since his orphanage days, and also a close study of which words and signs mattered in his new land, and of where the stresses should fall with each group. And of picking his moments. This wasn't one, and so he did a perfunctory grin and cut past them. And so the young men left off any further thinking about what it meant for this new African to be in their town, living beside them. This soft collision of incompatible realities. Because more immediate needs presented. This was the last wedding of the summer and it was getting late and more beer goggles were needed before Last Call. They wandered back in, wondering what was left for talent on the dance floor.

II.

Because he could already sense the greatness and power that would come to him after he was named governor of the northern province, Foday had refused to budge from his spot in front of the dance floor when Uncle had sent over the first pair of girls, compliments of the house. Foday, the new area warlord, and Charles, his visiting grandee, had come to Uncle's beer bar to celebrate their recent agreement in

regards to the reorganization of the nearby Upriver lands and saniti-
zation of its swinish peoples. All of which was part of a National
Restitution Campaign quietly being organized by one of the nation's
most patriotic generals. This clientele, Uncle knew, were well above
using the partially converted Port-A-John stalls that were made available for standard customers (left over from a recent NGO reconstruc-
tion effort). He offered them use of his private next-door flat, which
featured both a flower-faded chesterfield that still had a little thrum
in its cushions and a three-position, Union-Made With American
Pride recliner that held self-evident virtues (Left Behind, along with
books by the same title, by a family of Iowa missionaries). But Foday
dismissed this offer with a wave of his hand, dictating over the music
that he would drink his drink and root his root there and then. With
his men and the General's man watching, he had decided that if he
were going to be the future governor of these lands—the promise
given for services rendered in the Upriver—he had better start acting
like it.

The girls initially assumed this was merely a more exaggerated
form of conventional tent-pole impatience, the hungry patron
looking to get a little tasting plate before consulting the full menu or
inquiring about that night's prix fixe. So they stroked a little and
tugged a little and then went farther into their thigh-rubbing, crotch-
cradling cajolery to get the men moving and efficiently processed.
Charles was ready enough to go, feeling mostly tired and looking for
a good draining and then some sleep before returning to the capital
the next morning. But he realized plans were otherwise, and rather
vulgar even for a provincial, when Foday grabbed his mitt by her
bangled wrist and twisted her twiggy arm until she was turned to the
point where an elbow in the small of the back and a categorical shove
from behind suggested his forthcoming plans. At which point the girl
bucked for her dignity.

Finding herself crammed into the ready position for a manful flogging, in front of her few friends and co-workers, and in public no less, was too much, was beyond the furthest limits of respectability and decorum that Foday's girl was willing to ignore for steady meals and pills and a few hours of quiet, man-free earth at the end of every night. Though expecting no Magdalene redemption, Marigold nevertheless wanted to serve notice. She tried to pull away, which Foday found very amusing as he grabbed and squeezed her back to him while his guards, a passel of teenagers floating on bottles of test-market cough syrup they'd liberated from a multinational health clinic, half-consciously cheered him on. At which point Uncle saw Foday rest his palm on his knife hilt, struggling to get the girl back in place. Feeling less intervention-minded than pragmatic, Uncle decided that if Marigold were cut up, she could still go at discount and better that than a spitfire new warlord and his men razing the whole bar in protest at one little request being denied.

Dancing with his Elizabeth and focused on keeping their steps in time with the disco-tangy beats of the Boney M. classic that was playing, Bokarie didn't notice any of this happening. Until he collided with the half-naked body that came shrieking and blundering across the dance floor with its dress pulled up over its head, its arms snared in a bunched-up, sequin-dangling span of rayon and polyester. The new warlord lurched over and knocked her down and flicked his chin at Bokarie, waiting to see if there was to be a challenge. But Bokarie, because what did he care, turned back to his dance partner and to "Ra Ra Rasputin."

But then something happened.

He reached the bouquet-pocked wedding gazebo. He listened to the sound of Canadian summer, the cricket chirps and metronomic crank and triple flick! of the country club's in-ground sprinkler system. Nearby, some preteens were passing a bottle of peach schnapps back and forth and then spinning it around and giggling behind a riding mower. This was a place empty enough to admit it, the something that had happened at the beer bar.

He was feeling undone, incapable of holding everything in check from back then. After so much else, why did this one thing come up in his new country and crack through his winning smiles and long faces for his fellow Canadians? Why did it matter as it did?

The real reason had remained a hard little pit inside of him since then. Ever since he'd killed the local warlord Foday by dancing over to him and elbowing him through the teeth with a CLICK-SMACK! while he drank and rutted on Marigold, and then gutted his prone body with the broken end of the bottle. The men around Bokarie in Uncle's beer bar had made it both easy and necessary for him to conceal the truth of why he'd done it. But now on this gazebo he had nothing but time enough and space to look in on it and then get solidly shut of that past.

Because going after Foday wasn't brave and daring and quick-thinking and all so wonderfully set to music, as the General's man Charles had announced to the bar after Bokarie had finished him off with a final few swipes and shoves with the jagged bottle neck. This account had been conducive to his subsequent rise, since it demonstrated Charles's immediate interest in him as a new recruit to the General's Campaign and also smudged away what trace loyalties the dead warlord's former guards had to their former leader, who hadn't come to his aid in time out of the slouch and sloth endemic to any clump of drugged-out teenagers. Before they were able to shrug themselves into compensatory action, because maybe they should do something since *the boss man, he dead,* Charles had already reformed them into devotees and enthusiasts of Bokarie and his rhythmic mania, and so they became his second catch of action-ready admirers, after the crowds he spoke and danced and won over from on top of the orphanage walls.

But still, Bokarie's going against Foday wasn't so bold and courageous and valiant, or any of the other curlicues and blandishments
that Charles had further devised when he later presented him to the
General at the National Restitution Campaign headquarters in the
capital city. Nor was it out of allegiance to his outraged blood men,
as they boasted to others afterwards, though he knew they had been
standing outside the bar while Foday chased and knocked Marigold
around the dance floor and then started his pelvic pounding at her,
and that they could probably see what was being done to their poor
wailing patch. And it wasn't even in hopes of saving his own woman
from a similar bent-at-the-waist boring. Because he hadn't even
thought of that as a possibility, didn't even notice Foday sip away at
his beer and expansively address his companion and his guards while
making windmill motions with his arms and thrusting away on
Marigold. He had only noticed when his woman, who had been
watching all this from behind his shoulder as they kept dancing,
finally turned in to him hard and he thought this meant she wanted
a swivel so he obliged and then saw it—her. The woman was no
longer struggling but had gone resigned to her fate, bagged up in the
bunches of her upturned dress, cowl-like around the neck and head,
at most hoping this one would at least be a quick finisher.

In time, of course, as Bokarie readied a band of butchers to take
the Upriver for the General and the People, the fable of how he did
away with the wicked warlord Foday became an important recruitment tool, involving all the elements others offered on his behalf.
And to be sure, he eventually cited them himself as explanation
enough for dancing over and shoving the beer bottle through the
other man's teeth with that CLICK-SMACK! and then mashing up
his throat with its cracked crown neck. Though if pressed on the
matter, Bokarie would showily confess that none of the high and fine
reasons the others cited for his killing Foday mattered in the end.

That in truth he had been looking for a way out of the beer bar, a means of making his name heard and felt and feared, and a man with one hand on his beer and another on some hindquarters and the rest of him drunk and all stuffed inside of some mareflesh, well, that was just an easy target for a dancer who could cut like a knife.

But that wasn't it, really, at all.

Now, in Canada, feeling protected by the peacock plumage he showed off as everyone's favourite new refugee, Bokarie went past these easy claims for going against Foday—past the sheer glory and power of it, past salvaging his blood men's property, past protecting his own piece of fur. It was none of this, at core, beneath the many casings it was given, he was given. It wasn't about what had to be done about Foday, or even about what Bokarie wanted to do for himself.

But Marigold. For Marigold. For some mediocre-looking whore who never did much for him before or after, but was, for the four minutes of that song, so wrongly done by, so needlessly ruined, that Bokarie had wanted, had needed, to act. It was when he saw her go limp and pliant while Foday rampaged through her body, treating it like a bottle opener and beer coaster and champagne bucket. At her acceptance, at her just having to endure this. Bokarie had done it to give a moment of decency to a life otherwise meagre, gutter-clad, fated by geography and anatomy to be never more than bow-legged, viral and miscarrying.

It had taken long to come to this because, back when it had first happened, before he could explain himself to anyone or even decide if he wanted to, they were crowding him in with their reasons and praising him for it and inviting him to leave Uncle's beer bar and meet a Great Man in the capital city. Maybe become one himself. Because there was suddenly this trajectory before him, requiring only more fiery moves and fine words, which, he immediately sensed, was how he would get more of the looks and listening that he had first won from dancing and declaring along the orphanage wall.

Plus, his reputation was so quickly solidified in the eyes of others for killing Foday, what would have happened had he explained why he'd really done it? Who would have believed him anyway? And so he told no one what had made him do it, not even Marigold, whom he made sure to avoid thereafter beyond a quick dismissive nod when she came to thank him the next morning. Because by then he'd already started to form himself into a hard shell around the true how and why of his bottle break into the warlord business.

III.

Returning to the wedding in the thick air of late Canadian summer, Bokarie saw the night's first drunken fight break out in the parking lot outside the hall, between a just-joking uncle and a mouthy nephew. The brawling brought nothing back, gratefully. Besides, there was enough currency to play on and move from and lord about in this, his new place. He would stay there.

"There you are! Way up here and away from the action. But I have news to tell you. Plans have been made and you're involved, of course." Jennifer was smiling with unprecedented teeth. As they walked back to the reception hall, she updated him on developments. Glenn was on board for the campaign and already big-skying about Jennifer's election chances and how good a dancer Bokarie was and how important his moves were going to be in the coming campaign, and soon they'd be in the capital city just like she'd promised. Provided they could get a majority of the community to Think Pink and get over the recent sudden and sad Alderman Gallagher's heart attack business, which had pushed poor drowned Little Caitlin into the background. Jennifer predicted they would have to counteract a strong widow push to the ballot box. Mrs. Faye Gallagher, according to reception hall rumours, was going to run for the federal seat in memoriam of her recently departed husband, George. The campaign, in effect, was already under way, and Jennifer needed Bokarie's advice about how the pending funeral should be approached. "Also, um, my parents want to meet you. So dinner at my house in a few days?"

Bokarie shrugged and nodded at all of this as he put on his cap once more, ready to drive Jennifer home and, on the return, drop off her new supporter before taking the Continental back to Glenn's dealership and maybe catching the last bus. Such bliss and power he had gained for his efforts. This was what his talents had brought him so far.

As he was holding the door open for her, Jennifer noticed that Bokarie was a little off. He had a bare face on, vacant even. She was about to ask him if something was wrong—but then he noticed her eyeing him and went back into his head-nodding, smile-cracking kit, which was well matched to the post-wedding shambolics around them, the usual pawing, coaxing, flailing, accusatory denouement to the town's grand doings. So she didn't take this for much, this Bokarie blankness. After all, it was only for a moment, and, for him, so out of character.

6

CASSEROLE INTERVENTIONS

I.

"I don't care what it means back where he's from. I don't! Go ahead and tell me again, Jennifer, that it's the colour of what? Of the dawn, over there in that—that little road apple's African lion safari. Sorry, Barb, I know I shouldn't say it like that, but damn it if your daughter isn't trying her dear old dad these days. Have a look at her! Carrying on like she's going to be the high and mighty Governor General by Boxing Day and she's gone and found herself a fine-talking, spear-chucking footman for her Cinderella ride to Ottawa. Again, Barb, don't make that face, we're family and if I can't speak my mind here then I don't have one to speak of. Because, you know, I've kept my conscience all this long while, but now, as a father, and as a man with a name to consider in this town, I'm doing what needs to be done. And I'm saying what needs to be said.

"This is for our daughter's good. Now, Jennifer, listen to me. This is your dad talking, not some big-words book about Lyndon Bloody Johnson. I said nothing, right, about your setting up the soccer with the kids and the African, though I heard about it at the gas station, that his touching their kids made a few nervous but they had to be polite. And I kept my mouth shut, right, about your going to that hoity-polloi Hollerwatty wedding with him, though again, people's been talking about more than just his rhythm from what I picked up at the Legion the other night. But no matter, really, I have nothing against him. After all, what with dinner last night, your mother and I were doing our part to make him feel welcome and we even tried to get a little company going his way. Because I know it can't be easy for his type, coming here from Lord knows what hellfire and jungle and famine. Surprised at your old dad? Yes, I do know something of that stuff, and also about the hiv going around over there in Africa these days like spring lice in a schoolhouse. Your dad reads the papers every so often and even tunes in his radio to the talking stations when the mood hits him. So what I'm trying to say is this, Jennifer: knowledge isn't a Crown corporation of your very own in this house.

"What I'm saying is because, well, I want for you what you're supposed to get. Jeezum Crow! I even signed my name to your petition about that Little Kristen or Sierra Mist or whatever they call the drowned girl. And fine, I'll tell you that I was, yes, even a little proud of you when I heard from your mother that someone from the bank told her that you got up on a stage over at Centennial Park for that memorial rally and helped with crowd control or some such thing. But this, Jennifer, this is the one too many, this outfit, what you're, what"—changing targets suddenly—"your daughter's wearing right now, Barb, what she's proposing to wear to a funeral, for God's sake!"

Here Gus aimed his gravy-spackled fork at Jennifer's ensemble and then at his wife, who was rewashing dishes at the sink and watching her husband rage on his inscrutable daughter. Who, as it happened, was withstanding her father's grapeshot and bluster by calculating whether they would still be able to get good spots in the receiving line at Gallagher's wake. That is, when the barrage let up. But then Gus drained his milk and reloaded his blunderbuss.

"Jennifer, I don't care what it means in that Bokarie's old country. And to tell you the truth and to save you the breath, I'm not too concerned, either, about what it's going to do to your election chances in a few weeks, though I think in that respect you're looking for a bumper crop where you might find fallow, my dear. Because the late George Gallagher had a name in this town and you'll see that tonight at the Home—that is, after you change out of that heartburn of a dress you're wearing, mind you. And I'd bet my best bush jacket that you'll also see that his wife, Faye, who as I understand it is also running in this election, is going to get plenty of votes as the fresh widow. She's going to get those votes, in fact, just by wearing black. Do you follow what I'm saying?"

Jennifer's face crimped, sensing the rightness of her father's forecast. She started accepting the hard logic of his case against her chosen outfit. Not that he was done.

"But the upcoming election, that's another matter. We're right here, right now, Jennifer, in everyday Canada. Do you hear me? Not look-what-Immigration-dragged-in-this-time Canada, but under-the-radar, regular-people Canada, just-trying-to-get-through-to-the-next-baby-bonus-cheque-and-farm-rebate Canada. Oh, and let me remind you of it, in case you've forgotten about *that* Canada, being too busy at your summit meetings with the Secretary-General of Gary's Milk and Lotto. Just let me take a minute and remind you what Everyday Canada is all about. Because it's in you, Jennifer, to the very marrow, and there's no escaping it.

"Everyday Canada is finding a new coffee can for bacon drip; it's making Canadian Tire money part of your grocery budget; it's watching hockey on the French channel if that's what God and the rabbit ears give you. Everyday Canada's trying to convince your wife that she can't have you strip perfectly good wood panelling from your living-room walls and repaint them something called Summer friggin' Kumquat; it's finding a good someone else to settle down with and then, well, as I still hope you'll see someday, then life becomes deciding to brew an extra fresh pot after breakfast just to get a new can in time for the bacon drip and arguing paint chips to a draw and all the rest of what makes Everyday Canada what it is. Which isn't much, granted, by comparison with the stuff you pull out of those books of yours that your mother ..." Here he let up a second moment, just to send a little wither and shiver his wife's way, because Gus was starting to hold her responsible for all of this since it started, in his mind, with that high school graduation gift of the encyclopedias. "But anyways this Canada has its values and its reasons and its rights and wrongs, and it'll still be here long after anything they come up with to throw at us—including, mind you, your garden-variety-store Africans.

"Which brings me back to my point. I don't care what it means in his country. In this one, in your country, Jennifer, which is Everyday Canada, YOU DON'T WEAR PINK TO A MAN'S FUNERAL. Now get upstairs and change and leave me to my cold supper."

II.

She didn't move, not just yet, because she was still measuring up her father as Riding Everyman. If this was in fact how the median voter responded to her wearing full pink to the late Alderman Gallagher's service, it wasn't in the best interests of the campaign. Jennifer was leaning this way when another intervention, more decisive, took place. Her mother dropped over to the kitchen table like a clipped duck and snatched her father's plate away to reheat it. Flutter-limping back to the counter, Barb offered a sober second to her husband's throaty filibuster. "Yes, go upstairs and change into something more becoming, Jennifer. Something black and proper. Your dad's right—"

Barb almost concluded "this time," but with Gus in such a state, he might have caught it.

After Jennifer had gone upstairs, her father took a long breath and turned to address his wife. Barb was enduring a purgatorial wait for the microwave to ding its appointed conclusion, which would get Gus quiet and eating. Because otherwise, he was fired up and hungry to boot and so he kept at it.

"Barb, you think I'm just trying to save face, but there's more to it than my stopping the girl from wearing a prom dress to pay respect to a man's passing. This Bokarie, I don't like her carrying on with him, even if, as I pray to God you pray to God, there's no heart in it or physicals to speak of. And sure I'm disappointed that I don't think that young man took to her at dinner last night and I don't know why she came in and went straight up to her room after they went for that walk, except maybe he didn't ask her for a second date, but I wasn't exactly hoping for an engagement notice in today's paper, just a little, well, interest on her part in anything other than politics and drownings and Africans. But anyway, Barb, take this … this pledge for what it's worth—"

Here Gus Thickson's voice cracked and he hurt, just a little, his nose tingling and crinkly and his eyes narrowing, levee-hard against the unexpected spillage. Because, leaving aside worries about his name and questions as to why it wasn't a boy born to them, Jennifer was his only child, the flesh of his, and so forth.

"Take it, Barb, this pledge, for what it's worth. Remember, I am the man who took your daughter by the leg when she was a little girl, do you recall that? How I took her and cut that leech off and did it so gentle-like she didn't even scream or cry or hurt. Just stared. Anyhow, I'm trying to do the best I can by Jennifer, Barb, and right now, if that means cutting away another black bloodsucker, well, this time—"

PING!

Desperate, Barb had twisted the microwave's timer to a premature conclusion, hoping fate would smile on her and the food would be hot enough. Though still upset and looking to take some action, Gus settled down at the noise. Fork in hand, he was ready for his daily comfort. His mashed and meat.

He made a few more noises about getting the number for Immigration, but she agreed him back to his crammed mouthfuls by repeating his rightness, that yes, Jennifer's attempt to wear pink to the Gallagher funeral service later that night was simply out of the question. But she also put Gus at ease, and did away with any vigilante plans on the near horizon, by telling him that he had little to worry about, romance-wise, with Jennifer and Bokarie. When Gus asked for evidence, Barb invoked wifely privilege and maternal prerogative.

"A woman just knows these things, Gus, and that's all there is to it. Do you want me to try to explain, really?"

Though she really had little idea of Jennifer's intentions towards Bokarie in the romantic sense, or what she thought of that business herself, Barb was at least able to get Gus away from it. No need to worry about heart stuff, not just yet, not yet, she thought. Let's see where politics and this African take her.

He let it alone, this question of Jennifer and the African, and he perceived suddenly how his wife protected him from that skull-softening world of women's ways. Still waiting for Jennifer to come back down, Gus decided to take a minute with his wife. He went to the sink and nuzzled with her while the last dinner plate was scraped up and scrubbed, his sciatica-ripped hips buffing hers through their dark-toned, heavy-fabric funeral outfits. But it only takes so long to do a dish and put it away and scoop up the sink salad and wipe down the counter. And after all that loving, Jennifer still wasn't ready, and now she was ignoring hollers and threats to present herself so they could get going because parking was going to be torture. Pacing the living room, Gus got all fired up again. Her offer of apple crumble and milk evaded, Barb had to redirect her husband's fire and distract him from whatever was taking Jennifer so long up there. If he didn't want the Summer Kumquat for the living room, she ventured, that colour being her choice and what did she know anyway, what did he think of bringing in one of these interior consultant types you hear about these days? She knew a woman down the street that had a friend whose son was known to be creative and had even done courses for that kind of frill and frippery in Toronto. Maybe they could even see about a discount?

She took heavy artillery, as expected, and it was mission accomplished. A husband's executive powers were invoked and fifty more years of wood-panelled living was declared, which she accepted because it meant Gus forgot his half-forged promise to stop his little girl from tumbling into a big-lipped black hole. Looking ahead to future fronts, Barb was willing to accept this collateral damage. She could do that much for her daughter. Because even if it was never credited, even if Barb Thickson was universally assumed to be capable of little more than carpet-bombing cupboards with fresh contact paper every other spring and calibrating cream of mushroom shots for winter Crock-Pots, she had sense enough to know what kinds of publicity would and would not help her daughter at the polls.

III.

Black-skirted and mauve-bloused in compromise with her father's edict, Jennifer was stalled, unexpectedly. Sitting in her bedroom, she was still thinking. About him, no less. Not Bokarie. He had his marching orders and matériel for the evening's event. But about the other one, from dinner the night before, the one who had courted her by spinning the sugar line that he had a magnet in his pants and bet she had a steel magnolia under her dress. It was around then that she brought up an intervention.

But before that, and before he pulled out the monogrammed flask and before he encouraged her up the barn ladder with a thrusting, feely smack of the palm, she knew that this man her parents had invited over was intended to be an impediment against her future plans. And she'd been tempted.

Initially, Jennifer had been made wary by the sudden and opaque increase in place settings for the meal her parents were giving the Thursday evening after the Hollerwatty wedding. She thought the dinner was for her new friend, Bokarie, but then that night Barb asked Jennifer to set six for dinner, not four, and to take from Grandma's collection no less, and also to be sure to skip plates with chips in them or too many fork scrapes. At these Christmas and Easter instructions, Jennifer had felt a little vault to the heart. At evidence that her parents were intent upon impressing the guest of honour. Little did she know.

Bile came quickly when she realized what really stood behind her parents' unexpected suggestion, the previous week, that she invite *that new friend of yours, Boo Cary, over for a little supper.*

The date was set for one of those rare evenings in the Ottawa Valley between the fever hot of late August and the blouse cling of later September. The end-of-summer wedding itself, in its aftermath, was being recalled and studied around town less for the noblesse oblige of its *open friggin' bar*—hard liquor, too, not just wine and beer—than for what was understood to be the most striking image of the affair. In subsequent representations and re-creations, particularly by those young men who had never had their dance with the lady of the hour, her having gone sleepy and stomach-achy a few songs after "Butterfly Kisses," the bride's four-minute twisty twirl with the town African was the big news. It had looked about as dangerous as a sapling twig dangling a campfire marshmallow, as classy as electric tape patching up a torn milk jug.

But Jennifer's parents knew nothing of this chatter. They had made the dinner invitation in near direct response to her informing them that she was going with Bokarie to the wedding. And because of how freely this offer had come, Jennifer had been warmed by the idea. By her parents wanting to meet the new friend she'd told them about, even if she was feeling edgy at the prospect of these constellations of her life colliding over sweet corn and cider.

In thinking about Bokarie coming to her home, Jennifer was, in truth, as nervous as a fourteen-year-old girl who'd invited over a new friend with better hair and makeup. Upon his meeting her parents, she worried, Bokarie might refuse to help with her campaign, having seen evidence suggesting that her mouth was writing him cheques that her bloodlines couldn't cash.

But she went through with it anyway, giving in to the desire for her parents to see Bokarie and understand what she had grabbed on to, to sense what he could bring her and understand where they could go together. Because then, maybe, she had hoped, Gus and Barb might start to believe a little in the rise of Jennifer Thickson themselves.

She had miscalculated. Profoundly. After asking her mother a second time why six, Jennifer realized that Bokarie was barely on their radar, and then she really understood: *Oh nobody special just a young man also new in town that your dad sort of knows who might share your interests. There's no harm in finding out so we've invited him to have a little supper with us too and when we told him about your friend from Africa the young man said he had someone in mind so there you are Jennifer your dad thought it up.* All along her parents were readying something of a bloodless coup by trying to get her hitched up before she could get her shot at Ottawa.

And worse, she had almost taken them up on it. She could admit this much now, while her father was downstairs yelling at her mother about the eternal virtues of wood panelling.

Soon enough they would drive off to the service, at which point the campaign for the federal seat of Nipissing–Renfrew–Pembroke would effectively open with a eulogy, delivered by her main opponent and one-time mentor Faye Gallagher. The start of six weeks of grieving and vote grubbing in the black widow catbird seat. But before Jennifer left and the battle she'd wanted was fully joined, it was best to make sure, one last time, that she didn't want him instead and what life he had proposed, what he had brought up for her.

IV.

Rick Hopewell taught grade seven and eight gym. He had been Gus's choice. Thickson was getting on, and getting worried about the fate of his farm and daughter. Hopewell came his way on recommendation from the local gas station owner, who understood from cash register chit-chat that the young man was new in town but, unlike some people we know, had politely blended into the background. It was easy enough; he was indistinguishable from a standard national mould—reasonably well-kept goatee, hairline just starting to horseshoe, reflexively anti-American, kidney fat spilling over his cell-phone hip clip. On further inquiry, Gus learned that the young man happened to be freshly single after a long cohabitation elsewhere had failed to take. From Gus's vantage, Rick seemed to have interests that matched his daughter's well enough. Contact sports weren't all that different from government, he figured, and when the gas station man snorted at this observation, Gus decided to use it as a conversation opener at dinner. Through the necessary channels, it was learned that Rick had shrugged some interest at meeting a young lady who had a really great personality and no brothers to speak of on a seasonally productive family farm. Eventually, speaking directly with Gus at a planned run-in at the gas station, Rick even offered to bring along a friend he knew of who might match up pretty well to Jennifer's little buddy, given the specs provided. Gus was looking to do some parallel matchmaking in hopes of simultaneously neutralizing manifold threats. When this possibility was established, he had Barb ask Jennifer to invite Bokarie to break bread with the family.

The soiree itself was slightly below average for the latitude and tax bracket. A stifled-cough, lame-question affair, during which Jennifer played the part of coy catch, if unwittingly. She had bluntly refused to participate, pushing food around her plate in cramped quiet and thus forcing her parents to speak on her behalf whenever Rick asked a friendly question. She had barricaded herself against the suitor's overtures, against her father's touting her like a good used car, this inviting a buyer home to kick the tires and take it for a test drive. She was also embarrassed for Bokarie and more violently anxious that he was going to walk away from the campaign. He was marooned on the far corner of the table beside his dinner partner—a brisket-tongued, enthusiastic educational assistant from Rick's school named Trinh, a Vietnamese Canadian who smiled and nodded and said, "Oh yeah huh really? Well I think that's great and courajust!" to every comment that came her way, including queries about seconds and requests to pass the gravy boat.

When dinner was finally, finally over, and the last of the meringue had been shaved up between the men, Gus sensed things weren't going that well and so he went to straight economics. After the dishes were cleared, he asked Jennifer to help the guests walk off the casserole—after all, Rick had eaten three servings!—by giving them a tour of the barn and the family acres. While this was a time and place self-evidently beyond dowries, Gus Thickson could, at the very least, give the suitor a sense of possibilities.

Meanwhile, Hopewell turned out to be more interesting than he'd planned for. Initially, he'd accepted the invite to dinner with hopes of little more than a non-microwaveable meal and perhaps some no-strings rebound scoring. Sex and casseroles, these were his hungers, given his current situation as a new teacher in a nothing school in a nowhere town northwest of the capital. He had applied for a transfer outside of the Ottawa–Carleton board because he needed distance from a former live-in colleague who had recently dumped him for, as she put it, "forcing me to wait through five years of your shit in case someday I find a diamond in that coal pile." Because they were both gym teachers, this meant many things lost. Twenty-five-cent wing and trivia nights, midnight coed hockey, annual road trips to see the Bills play, and other personally loved, professionally enriching pursuits had grown unworkable. So, having had little of either in the months since his transfer, sex and casseroles were the thing.

Extending his post-prandial exercise at the Thickson place, Rick had climbed up into the barn after Jennifer, allowing himself a view that led to a quick calculation of her presumptive merits, though this was merely the topographical confirmation of what his squash-happy hand had already intimated at lower rungs. There was a lot, space-wise, to work with here. Her uniform silence, before small-talky questions and casual feel-ups and other such magnetic punning and probing, was received as an openness to more intensive business. But Rick could tell she was a little nervous, sitting in the straw beside him and twirling her hair like a little girl, so he prepared for a soft landing and took an oblique approach.

"I think our little global villagers are really hitting it off, eh?" he opened, pointing out the loft window in the general direction of Bokarie and Trinh. Those two had ventured into the cornstalks when Rick broke Jennifer away from the pack and asked her to come see the sunset from up in the barn loft.

"Doesn't surprise me, you know, those two getting along so naturally. Both living here and being from away—she's from the east end of Toronto, originally, and he's from, well, I never caught which one—plus she does ESL, as you can tell, and also"—softening his voice to sensitive potential husband tone—"you know, she's done courses in special ed, and, well, given what your dad said about Bokarie and from what I can tell, I thought that would be a bonus in their getting together."

She was staring, mutely, so he changed tactics.

"Well, you're acting the shy type, but that's not what I hear from your old man. He says you can talk up a storm about politics, which is fine by me, I lived in Ottawa for years. A little loosen on your lips, maybe?"

He brought out one of his hammered steel flasks, the fifth he'd been given the previous summer for having served as groomsman. This streak, which showed no sign of abatement, had in part led to the live-in colleague's *rock or walk* ultimatum and the subsequent breakup. Jennifer immediately grabbed after the rum, which Rick took as a sign that this tractor just needed a little oil to get its gears working.

"Ottawa? You've lived in Ottawa? You know Ottawa?" Jennifer asked this with hot wonder, a little studied, but most immediately brought about by the scorch she'd just sent down her throat with a swig at his flask. But her stomach started gurgling and popping, not so much from the swig as from the suddenly potentially marriageable prospect sitting beside her in the barn, who had just taken the place of the lumpy grabby jackass that her dad had brought to dinner. Jennifer wasn't so resistant to the trajectory laid out before her, all of a sudden. If this man could give her a little entree to Ottawa and, after the vows and the Legion reception and a Thousand Islands bed-and-breakfast honeymoon, if he would take over the farm while she found rooms in the capital and they together oversaw the family's and nation's business, wasn't this both a perfect compromise between Gus's wants and Jennifer's plans and a more reasonable outcome than her drowned and out-of-Africa approach?

But she forgot. He was a gym teacher.

"Yeah, I lived in Ottawa a few years. But I didn't really get it, the whole politics thing. I tried to follow for a while, but the Hill and, well, the entire city, Ottawa, it's about as interesting as licking a phonebook. And that explains why I moved out here, you know, to be with the good people of the country, and maybe, I don't know, you know, to settle down or something." He leaned closer, her face distending in the dusk-light reflection of his wraparound sunglasses.

Having gone some months in monkish isolation, being tummy happy with a mummy-made meal, liking the idea of becoming a gentleman farmer and more so the opportunity to spite his ex with a wedding announcement only a few months after she had dumped him, Rick was mostly serious in his implied proposal. He was looking for no commitments or head games, just some country matter; but if he didn't bother double-bagging and she got pregnant enough, why not?

And though Jennifer knew better, she was, for the moment, considering it herself. Because while she could tell the man was plainly retarded when it came to matters political, he was nice enough looking and clearly had hands for her—which was virtually unprecedented, Jennifer's prior physical experience being limited to games of football Kennedy-style with uncles and cousins when she was just a little too old to present as nose tackle. But also, maybe this man was the better choice. Her chest and stomach heaved a little when she imagined abandoning her design on Ottawa. There was sadness at this, but also relief, exhaustion, ending.

Because Jennifer had been going at it since losing Graduating Class President by acclamation in high school, and she'd thumbed through enough of the encyclopedias and the LBJ book to know that politics never stops, politicians can never stop or else the gills get stuffed up and the lampreys attack and the carcass sinks to an indifferent end. So why not just accept her notch in the Middle Canadian grain, why not take this Rick onto her here and now and keep at it for a few minutes and months and go back to her HR job and gain what acclaim and dignity she could by showing off a new champagne diamond and then register for garden gnomes and push one out a few months after the I do's and then—what? A life of looking forward to casual-wear Fridays at the office and measuring out morning and evening medicines for her parents and waiting for the weekly call from a daughter of her own who was trying to remember how many cups of peas it was for the tuna casserole.

Her lips opened.

v.

After explaining his no-strings rules for dating colleagues and then finding himself a fresh pair of underwear, Rick went to his laundry basket to get Trinh a T-shirt. They started trading stories of what had happened on their respective mini-dates at the Thickson place, the frustrations of which led them to decide on a nightcap at Rick's apartment. After some subtle-like wordplay in the kitchenette, a tour of old hockey trophies in the living room, a little teasing and tickling before a montage of oh so cute pictures of the bachelor as baby, boy and young man carbuncular, and then, climactically, a chin-up demonstration on an iron bar wedged across the bathroom door, it had been a straight shot to the bedroom. And now the couple shared their most immediately available secrets in the body-sapped after-burn of their mushed lovemaking, in hopes of investing the explorations of the previous few minutes with some significance beyond the groans and short shocked cries.

Trinh was especially up for this, having wiped away the tears and redness with as much dignity as allowed by the gulch spot where she lay on Rick's aged futon. Her story from the dinner was comparatively mild: She'd walked the African around the corn and asked him about his homeland. His quick answers were suggestive of a greater cognitive capacity than she'd originally assumed, but he wasn't for her, in the end, being just a little too skinny and smiley. Anyway, she was looking for a manly man. Marvelling at her words, she felt womanly herself, fuller in the hips than she was, someone her mother would refuse to recognize as virginal daughter and her father would disown for no longer being one.

Rick had hip-buckled at the implied compliment and then agreed, explaining that he knew Jennifer wasn't for him either because, after just one little swig from the bottle, she'd thrown up all of her casserole dinner beside them when they were talking up in the barn loft. For all her size, he reflected, she was just a little girl and couldn't hold her drink. To turn this chit-chat more immediately productive, Rick further reasoned that Jennifer had gotten sick because of how nervous she was to be so close to, you know, a manly man, especially one who was treating her like a real woman.

Here he started pressing and moving in again, the conversation-making recharge complete. Trinh flashed a wrinkled smile, feeling a little lost, her eyes tearing up once more as she winced and took stock, winced and took stock, winced and took stock of what she'd done. It was so great and courajust and they could make the necessary wedding plans in the morning and, if necessary, discuss baby names on their second date.

VI.

Even from the back of the funeral home's main showroom, where
Jennifer and her parents were standing along with other latecomers
and last-minute porch smokers and shrewder types who'd planned to
be near the exit so they could beat the traffic on the way out, the noise
was fit to bleed ears. Before the Unitarian-licensed deacon finally,
delicately stepped in to adjust the microphone away from the penultimate speaker's throat, the assembled masses were grimacing their
way through the prologue to the eulogy proper. Which was delivered,
in a manner of speaking, by the late councillor's dearest friend and
former colleague, Blaise Maurier.

Like the rest of the crowd, Jennifer could make nothing of what
Maurier was saying, about the man with whom he'd once shared a
modestly thriving real estate and mortgage consolidation practice in
town. That was before George left the legal profession to take up
his civic duty as an alderman and Blaise was felled, partially, by the
Big C. Partially, because cancer had eaten away at Blaise's famously
honeyed tongue until he had to accept the necessary indignity of an
automated voice box that he held to an incision in his throat to speak.
In the pack-and-a-half-a-day past, many clients had been soothed by
Blaise's mellifluous sounds into agreeing to take on the short-term
cost and long-term benefits of higher fixed rates, or to disregard the
matter of capital gains because now now now was the time to sell. In
time the community had accepted, even come to like, the lawyer's
now-monotonous and corrugated sounds; he continued to practise
part-time, as per doctor's orders.

But in all his post-operative dealings prior to speaking at his
friend's memorial, Blaise had never been in front of a microphone.
Holding the voice box directly in front of it had the unanticipated
effect of garbling and reverberating and chainsawing his considerate
words into a barbarously electrified yawp. His mournful reflections

were lost on the crimping faces before him, though he never knew this. He had started with the universal opening questions of small-town oratory: *Can you all hear me okay? How about at the back?* These were answered with a silence that he took as ready assent.

Her frontal lobe ground down as much as everyone else's by Blaise's speech, Jennifer was nonetheless impressed. Faye had been smart in arranging the order of speakers this way, softening the crowd up like this by force-feeding them the courageous, violently amplified words of the cancer-stricken as a prelude to her own. Jennifer watched how smartly Faye took to the podium at Blaise's buzzing conclusion, how she embraced the speaker and swivelled him back to his seat. How, fully in control of the stage, she then looked up to her audience and readied to end the evening's proceedings. To start the campaign.

The crowd, Jennifer could sense, was keen for this. They wanted to hear from Faye as a respite from Blaise's metalled tonguing, and also because when she was done they could get to the basement reception hall for the sandwiches and pastries and coffee that, the deceased having passed while in office, the Incorporated Town itself had put up for, according to rumours circulating through both of the funeral home's bathrooms. This meant more than the fridge-hard ham rolls and jam-glop Danish offered at plebeian wakes. Jennifer could also feel something more in the hungry crowd, for whom this alderman's passing was an event about as close as they had come to experiencing, from near at hand, one of those fancy celebrity funerals that go on these days, for popes and former sitcom stars and such. The Little Caitlin Event, Jennifer stoically accepted, was for the immediate time forgotten, having happened some months earlier. Like the rest of Middle Western Civilization's members, her fellow citizens' memories were not those of elephants, even if they did move and snuffle for stirring words and tearful embraces and other such emotional pornography like palmfuls of peanuts.

Having checked the program to see what she had missed in addition to the receiving line by coming late to the service, Jennifer knew that George Gallagher's funeral was a properly ecumenical affair. Hymns were selected in equal number from the Wesley brothers and Andrew Lloyd Webber. At one sobbing rise in the service, the Gallagher daughters had together read aloud their personalized version of "Footprints" so as to thank their father now in heaven for having carried them through the hard times. And just before Blaise's speech there had been a slow-fade slideshow montage of Gallagher family imagery, set to a medley of Mendelssohn and *Les Miz* arrangements and projected onto a screen temporarily, respectfully, set up in front of the casket. The funeral home's willingness to grant this request explained the location of the memorial service; no church in town, not even the low Anglican, would agree to audiovisuals in spite of the unprecedented numbers such a prominent passing would have attracted to the pews.

Now it fell to Faye to bring the evening to the right climax. As she readied to speak, Jennifer leaned in, waiting to see how Faye would use the black-draped podium to her advantage at the coming polls. No longer expressly studying, as she once did, her former mentor at work, but now hoping that Faye would go long enough for Jennifer's first rebuttal to take to windshield.

"Family, friends, Mr. Mayor and Deacon Phil, thank you. On behalf of the children, thank you, thank you, thank you. The kind words, cards and casseroles we've been given since George went on— everything's been beautiful, simply beautiful, and just so generous. Many of you knew my late husband as a leader, and much of what we've heard this evening confirms as much. But what I'm about to say, in these brief remarks, which I promise to keep brief"—bathroom- and coffee-ready gratitude spread through the hall—"may surprise you. I have come here today to praise George Gallagher, dear friends, as a follower."

The audience gave up confused murmurs and frustrated growls at this proposal, like black bears searching through trash cans in vain. "Yes, a follower. I know we've come to understand that term as a negative in our culture, and rightly so in most instances, but not in the way I mean it today. George Gallagher was indeed a follower, his entire life. He was a courageous follower of one thing, my friends: Canadian values."

Immediately the crowd released great patriotic drafts of affirmation and exaltation; so many discrete fantasies of what this meant whirled together. Faye looked up, nodding satisfaction at these billows. And then she harnessed the national blow-up doll into her private lodestar.

"Yes, he followed those Canadian values from his time as both altar and paper boy through successful family and legal practices, and then, because he kept following them, a series of terms as this town's most devoted alderman. But, my friends, all of this was merely preparation for what was supposed to have been George's next great search, his plans to run in a federal election."

The crowd gasped and whispered and went collectively downcast at this news, at this bright-light-snuffed-too-early motif. Then they started wondering what Faye would do. Throw herself on her husband's funeral bier? Take up the torch from failing hands?

She'd been so strong through it all, but now she opened up, her mascara running like a drained starfish as she sniffled and sobbed her closing remarks into a tear-drenched declaration for office. "George … he … he was never able to … to follow through on that dream, dear friends. But I stand before you today to make this promise." Her voice quavered its last and then firmed with states-man's resolve before flashing with showman's promise. "My husband, the father of my children, the late George Gallagher, he knew best for all of us. And where he led—sorry, where he had *wanted* to lead—I, Faye Gallagher, I shall follow!"

She turned away from the microphone to pick up a paper and signal to the woman at the Clavinova. She looked up, smiling bravely, and opened her lips.

"Song sheets ready? I know this isn't on the program, but I couldn't imagine ending otherwise. So let's together sing 'Be Not Afraid,' which, I think, is a fitting way for us, as a community, to look to the future, which is to say, together. Because George would have it this way, my fellow Canadians, going before us as he has done, and asking us, as I ask you, my friends, to come, follow me."

Jennifer hadn't noticed the handouts until just then, her focus divided between parsing Faye's eulogy and marking its effects on the crowd. But then she saw the columns of efficient volunteers moving through the aisles, handing out lyrics to what was at once the concluding hymn of the funeral service and, in its refrain, the unveiling of Faye Gallagher's campaign slogan for the federal seat of Nipissing–Renfrew–Pembroke.

> *Be not afraid.*
> *I go before you always;*
> *Come, follow me.*

Mumbling and mourning with the rest, Jennifer had to grant Faye this masterstroke, this blend of religiosity and righteousness so politically pitch-perfect she wondered if her opponent had also been studying the American ways. But no matter, Jennifer decided. Having seen this, the best her opponent could manage, she was confident of her prospects in the race and the more confirmed in her earlier decision to throw up and off her chances at Middle Canadian nuptial bliss.

Because once the singing was done and the crowd, her parents included, had tired of watching close family and various friends embrace Faye and whisper and voice-box their support and admiration for her just-great and courageous plan to run, Jennifer recalled her counter-strike, which was in process. Even if these good Canadians, these everyday people, had been huffing and puffing with Faye at the funeral and singing her tune, Jennifer predicted they'd be thinking pink on the way home. She grinned a little at this cleverness and decided it would be a good conversation opener with Bokarie when next they met. Perhaps to distract him from what paper cuts and wiper blades he might recently have suffered through for the campaign.

STUMP SPEECHES

I.

"Can you all hear me okay? How about at the back?" The speaker didn't get much in the way of response, so he shrugged and leaned over to his cousin to confirm that Bokarie was ready to address the recruits.

The twitchy crowd, which had been gathered across the tee-off strip of the ruined driving range, knew these space-filling sounds. They were usually made before the meal packs and medicine bags came out at the aid centres and AIDS clinics they frequented in the capital as much to break up their days as for the goodies to be had there. So the young men didn't bother responding and kept instead at their afternoon lazing, reclining on each other's shoulders, cadging cigarettes, trading evidence of girlfriends, tattoos, knife wounds. Making predictions of how much this thing they'd agreed to do was going to pay.

Official representatives were moving among them rechecking tribal affiliations before the training session began. This last-minute, extra vetting was a necessity for those leading the General's growing movement, what with the number of informants, false friends, black BBC reporters and other tricky cockroaches clattering around the capital these days.

And so, in response to these very important presences mixing with the crowd, a few strategically earnest types, looking for pay and position bump-ups, blared that they weren't here for the money. They were going Upriver to sink a few of those roundy waists for their family's sunken bellies. Because they were optimistic that an important ear or two might cock at such principled, focused rage. But their voices were laughed at and shouted down by others mimicking toothpaste rhymes and condom jingles, which underscored the pointlessness, the indignity, of such apish pleading. Everyone there knew the *sink a roundy waist for a sunken belly* slogan. In recent weeks it had been a constant on radio stations that broadcast to select bars and slums in the capital. Hotel workers had cleaned pools to it, children jumped rope to it.

Meanwhile, another handful of the recruits styled themselves the cognoscenti among the young and hungry crowd. Showy and knowy, they trafficked in rumours about the fellow who was going to address them. The hard long man who was moving to the centre position in front of them. He was wearing the standard African Big Man sunglasses necessary to ward off the wedged throb of late afternoon sun and conceal bloodshot and leer. But he had something else going on, they sensed, a wide-edged smile and a sharp-cut frame and also a jaunt, even a rhythm in his walk. These were the indicators, weren't they, that this was that new warlord, that Bokarie?

There were always ant lines moving between the northern province and the capital city—refugees and rebels, rustics and random revolutionaries, and with them their assorted wives and goats and children and broken-down elders. Among these travellers, reports had been recently passing back and forth of a dynamo from an outlying village near the Upriver region. Among other things, he was reported to be well spoken and a killer dancer.

He was smiling.

His lips opened.

"Greetings, my new brothers, and on behalf of the General, whose trucks picked you out of your banlieues and boroughs to bring you here today, I offer hearty congratulations on your deciding to join this most worthy mission of ours. Can you guess why we have chosen this place as our training grounds? Look around you. See the flat dead land with the little holes drilled into it everywhere. Once, this was a place thick with huts, trees, animals, fruits. With life! But then someone—and we shall use no names today, in strict obedience to the slander laws that the National Assembly recently appended to the Permanent Emergency Measures—but someone, let us say a certain self-appointed President-for-life who shall go unnamed, had this whole area cut down. Yes, cut down and flattened. And what about those who had lived here? Who had been born and given life and then died on this ground since a time well before even the hungry whites came in their boats and boots? The peoples of this land were swept out like so many husks and feathers, their glories forgotten, my brothers, and for what purpose? For the pinhead Japanese and the loud-mouth Mickey Mouses and the blue-haired UNs that the President is always inviting to his palace for his famous trade and aid summits. This was his gift to them. So that, after a long day of getting their feedbags heavy with our treasure, they could drop their little white balls where they pleased.

"This latest pack of outsiders is gone for now. They've been scared off, terrified like our old French masters of trying to hunt anything that can run in two directions. Because they've heard that the men of this nation have found a great light, that they—that we—are taking courage because we have been granted a new leader, a good and brave and ready man. I have met him, my brothers. The General. He has told me himself that he shall right every wrong, every imprisonment, every evacuation, every marble statue that the great soft sow, our beloved and swollen-bellied President, has birthed in the name of what he calls National Progress!

"We say enough with progress. We say it is time for repairs. The General has decided the hour has come, at last, to do something about the sorry state of our beloved Atwenty. Our country is the sickest man in Africa, or so the Western papers are cawing. And do you know what the General says to this? He says, fine, let's get a little sicker, let's hurt a little more. Because he knows, like we all do, my brothers, that you need to bleed a wound before it can heal."

A voice cried out, raw, blood-lusty and confirming. Almost immediately the rest joined in, their eyes only for a passing moment searching each other's for affirmation that, yes, this was the right response, what was wanted. So they gave back to the man standing before them, their heads swirling with possibilities, their mouths going wider and blacker with want and rage. Like open graves.

It had been a plant, one of Bokarie's brothers, standing in the middle of the now-yawping audience, who had yelled on cue and so brought out of the rest their pledges to the General's National Restitution Campaign. Their howling sounds were taken as positive signs by the men in charge; they also made Bokarie strut some, so he let them rev a little longer. Stalking around, he noticed Charles, the General's chief aide-de-camp, nodding. The man who had discovered Bokarie back in Uncle's beer bar was pleased with himself, with his eye for such talent. He was also impressed at how quick a study the young man, from the outer rim no less, had proven of the rhetoric and premises necessary to get the Upriver mission under way. These had only been shared with him a few days earlier, upon his coming to the capital city in place of the former new warlord of his village,

Foday. He must have been blessed this way, Charles thought, a natural at tongue-twisting men to his purposes.

Bokarie was giving this speech as part of his responsibilities to and from the General. Upon reaching the capital city and meeting him, Bokarie had been informed that it would be in the best interests of various parties, the Nation and the People included, were there something along the lines of a sanitation program implemented in the Upriver lands, since that was where the filth-bathing President hailed from. Such an undertaking would limit the President's support in advance of a *coup d'état c'est moi* that the General, ever hedgy, was considering considering, as he explained to Bokarie in the loud confessional mode he preferred. And then, dangling more sweets before the child's open mouth, the General told the young man that were it a successful cleanup, as new President he would need loyal and capable governors for the nation's various provinces, including the crucial one to the north.

Hearing this offer, Bokarie gorged on what it could mean were he to empty out the Upriver lands of their rutting residents. The possibility became his prime mover, and he focused on it with especial hardness after a little heartbreak came his way. The General had invited his girl Elizabeth—his dance partner, whom Bokarie had brought with him to the capital for a view of the greatness coming his way after his disco beat-job on the old warlord Foday—to be his new policy adviser on women's health and welfare issues. And she accepted.

After telling his cousin and brothers this news over swigs, Bokarie observed that he had every right to go after the General. Cradling his courage and peeling away at its label, he mused openly that he might even do it with a little of his famous bottle work, an idea that was well received.

Swelled as usual from his words, Bokarie's brothers and cousin promised to hold down the General's aides while Bokarie had at the big man. They had added incentive: two were themselves recently abandoned by Marigold, the girl they had long shared, whom Bokarie had saved from Foday but then avoided, because that's what a hard man like Bokarie did. She had also accompanied them, only to start working for some foreign big shot known as Ngo, who, from the name, as far as Bokarie's brother and cousin could figure, was either Kenyan or Japanese. The boys knew they would never have lost Marigold to a bigger man had the General left them all to their beer bar fun back home. They had grudges to work from as well.

But to their surprise Bokarie decided against the move. Instead, he vowed never again to let a woman matter for anything except that fur below her fangs, which was a statement he dragged and pushed off his tongue after taking another swallow at his bottle for ache and numb and guts. Then, drawing his blood men close, he explained that having taken over his girl, the General would be forced to grant Bokarie more power, this being the standard recompense for more flesh. Bokarie invoked the great King David as his historical precedent, noting that after he had bedded Bathsheba, David granted her husband Uriah pride of place in battle. At least, in his rummy swirl and heap of self-pity, that was how Bokarie chose to remember the moral of the story. Because beneath his bravura words and despite more throat-bulging swigs, there was something hurt here, from how she had smiled at him from down below the orphanage wall a few years earlier and pulled him out of that life and been warm and firm to sleep beside afterwards. All of which was enough to make Bokarie want to go against him. But then again, the General had mostly gold teeth and they weren't going to be knocked out so easily and there were those other possibilities to consider, to take as consolation.

The next morning, after cleaning some vomit from his shoes and draining a few coconuts to soothe his head, he presented himself with hot readiness, spotlessly ignoring his old girl setting the tea service while he volunteered, declared to the General that he was the man to lead the first recruitment drive for the National Restitution Campaign. He would supervise the gathering up and training of the gaggles of young men to be found around the capital city, would play a little soccer to bend them his way. His fine words would tempt them away from their roughshod blank lives, because he knew how to shine up promises of money and meals and mayhem. And before heading Upriver, he further guaranteed, he would supplement these forces by grabbing extra fighters. Not just the men he had recently come to rule in his old village, but also boys waiting to be liberated from a nearby orphanage. He knew how to scale the wall, if necessary, or to sweet-talk the good Father.

Listening to this pitch, the General decided to be only partway convinced. He was a bit bitter at Bokarie because the previous night the girl he'd picked off the young man's arm hadn't brought him to nearly as much release as he had expected. He crossed arms and went silent at Bokarie's opening volley. His teeth a little grit, Bokarie bent forward and gave more. He tried out the speech he was planning to give to the recruits, at least what he was going to say to them about the wonder-leader, the peace hawk, the man coming soon who held the nation's salvation in his hands.

Satisfied and reminding Bokarie once more not to use his actual name because of complicated issues best not delved into just yet, the General happily signalled his assent with a kingly flick of his ringed fingers, and then, remembering he wasn't there yet, not yet, gave the boy an immoderate embrace. He awarded Bokarie full command over the Upriver operation, which was to begin immediately with a discreet, hush-hush recruitment drive in the capital. The General also promised to send missives to the other warlords in the northern province, directing them to answer to Bokarie alone. At this further expansion of his power, the young man swooned. While Bokarie sucked away at a sugar cube and marvelled at himself, the General enjoyed the absolution he'd just won in giving the young man this commission. Such a statesman's decision, he thought—the boy was like an overgrown fingernail, something useful for digging out ear and nose dirt, which could be clipped and tossed away. This new girl, the General decided as he slurped up the spillage from his saucer and concluded the meeting, was about the same. A tea bag not worth a second dipping.

II.

Their yelling died down to a happy angry buzz, by which time Bokarie had returned to his front-and-centre position before the recruits. He was ready to continue his address, this time with a prop, a nervous chicken fluttering in a crate at his feet. The rest of the recruiting team, arrayed across the driving range in front of the crowd, were also, to a man, standing before nervous chickens in crates. They'd decided to use chickens as part of training exercises and morale building when, earlier that day, Bokarie's cousin had recalled a popular bachelor's sport from their village wedding feasts and applied its logic to their present purposes. Persuaded, Bokarie waved his arm at his brothers and fowl were liberated from a passing truck on its way to market. Unharmed, the driver was indifferent at the loss. It was just another gunpoint intervention by patriots looking after the greater good, the People, etc.

"But the General can't save our nation alone," Bokarie continued, "or, as yet, with the army he commands, since many of its officers are fellow tribesmen of the President himself. Like a grub-filled slab of meat, the army crawls with so many greedy little beasts that would only try to take away what belongs to us, and this is why, he has told me, the General cannot look there for support. But to bring our cause to its proper end, for now, he needs to be seen as supporting the government and the rule of law. For now. On this, brothers, we must believe him."

Which they did, feeling the fresh tug on the heart and trill in the blood that comes from a touch, a promise, a chance to be part of something finer, greater, firmer, fuller than one's cracked little self. This General the speaker was describing was undoubtedly a Great Man. He would be, at last, a proper father for the nation, for each and for all of them. Or so they were expecting, needing, hoping. Because this audience was young enough, sons left fatherless by war and disease and indifference, to still want a good man to watch over them, and also too young, as citizens of a status quo African country stuck with the bruises and bust-ups of its post-independence life, to know any better.

He was persuasive, he knew, but he wanted to be sure they would have no other possibilities to tempt them. He also wanted to let his tongue keep at its business a little longer. So he kept at them.

"As for bringing about some kind of good change for ourselves through 'blessed are the peacemakers and their peacekeepers,' we should know by now that this will never come. What we render to all those Caesars that feed on us just makes them want more. And from the outside? The Americans only look our way when their cars need gas or when they want to find the Mohammeds and Alis who steal their planes. And the rest of the world? Any money they send just goes to more brass toilets and German washing machines for the People's Palace.

"As for the inside, do I really need to explain this? You already know about the men we have chosen from our own villages and families to take our case to the capital, how they leave us promising to battle the evildoers and then become their perfume merchants and diamond jockeys. Who never return home, only hole up in the capital and come out to pose for pictures with the rock gods and beg for adoption by the tit-flaring movie stars that jet in every other week. They have not helped you yet, and they never will. And they won't help the General either, to pick that scab off the People's throne. Because what if then they lose their airplane vouchers and hot plates and their daily rations of whoreflesh? But they don't matter. Their support isn't wanted anyway, nor does the General need it. But he needs you, he needs all of us, because what must be done to bring healing and peace to our nation only ends with a justice done in the palace! It begins, everything begins, my brothers, Upriver!"

No plant was needed to get them roaring this time. Bokarie let them go on awhile, enjoying it, enjoying what it let him forget and who it let him replace as the grounds for his goodness, his greatness. He bent down to the box and took the chicken by its wing joints, bending them backwards enough to keep the bird from moving but without snapping its breastbone. He had learned this hold as a boy, had watched others do it, others who had talked and laughed and read together from a book at night while he was lying beside them, officially sleeping. They were gone now. Had been for a long while. But this was no time to be thinking of back then. He brought the good hard rage around him back under his spell and readied it for action.

"No doubt you've noticed the chicken I have here. And you've seen the others with them up and down the line. In a few moments we're going to release these onto the plain behind me, and as your first act of training and a taste of your future rewards, you will try to catch them and kill them. I needn't tell you which of our beloved national leaders this chicken most resembles, but we couldn't find pigs fat and wheezy enough to do the part, so this is the next best thing!"

By this point the young men had gone delirious with the wreck and wildness they were soon to make, and Bokarie was himself inebriated with the sound of so many cheering and gnashing at his words.

"All of you, in some way or another, have suffered under the President's rule because you were not fated, thank your stars, to be born into his pig trough of a tribe. And this is why you were chosen to come here today. Like your fathers and mothers and sisters and brothers, you have all gone hungry on this our native land because of the chicken cock that sits high and mighty above us, a man who has let his own tribe, for oh so very long, peck away on maize and fatten up on mealy soil while we've dug at dry dirt and found only vipers and dead seed. And so"—here he gave a signal to his men to get ready with their birds—"as a flavour of what's to come, my brothers, go after these chickens. Any man who returns with one of them limp in his hands will be toasted for glory and honour and praise by myself and his mates. He will also get the bird, all of it, roasted for his dinner. My brothers, my patriots, this begins your mission to the nation! Catch them, kill them, catch them and kill them, catch them kill them, catchthemkillthem catchthemkillthem catchthemkillthem catchthemcatchthemkillthemcatchthemkillthem!"

They chanted along and sprinted past him, their stomachs and throats growling as they poured out across the abandoned golf course. The chickens squawked in terror and darted around in confusion, losing a few feathers with their every duck and dive, and then a few more, and then a few more, with each pass under all the mad hungry hands.

III.

"When a dog has gone and shat where he's not supposed to, what's to be done with the stupid beast?"

The phone connection was shot through with static, so Bokarie asked the speaker to repeat himself. He refused to believe that this was how the General was advising him after receiving news of the first raid. Their opening incursion into the Upriver region, to take a border village, had been a poor showing. The boys had enthusiastically, straightforwardly applied their on-the-links training, which meant that they raided the village's chicken coops and copped and groped for grabs of its women and girls until their men came at them swinging rifle butts and drove them off. This choice of defence cut Bokarie to the marrow—that this first group of Upriver men were so little scared of his fighters that they didn't even bother wasting bullets on what they regarded as a bunch of teeny bashers. Only one straggler, who turned up a day later at their makeshift camp downriver, returned with harder evidence of the lesson the rest were meant to have about challenging the mighty Upriver people. His ears were a little dog-chewed and his foot had been clubbed against a cinder block. Also, an arm had been machete-dropped into a burlap bag and hung round his bashful neck.

"I don't know, Monsieur le Général, do you give the dog a kick in the ribs?"

On the other end the General laughed, his tongue rich with rue and, it being late in the afternoon, maybe a daub of rum. The static of the poor connection syncopated the sound into something like a song, one that Bokarie might have been dancing to these days, had he kept his elbows to himself. He clenched at this warm gurring, wondering whether the General was laughing at him for being such a dunce as to not know how to deal with a dog, let alone a collection of men, or laughing at himself for believing that Bokarie was capable of the duties and capacities he'd been granted.

"If you kick a dog in the ribs, my boy, the dog will slink away, but that doesn't tell it where it's supposed to shit or why. So it'll do it again and again, shitting the wrong way, because it can only learn from what you put in front of it. Which is why, when a dog has gone and shat, as I said, you don't just kick the dog and hope it does better next time. You bag the shit and shove its face in it and then it'll know, it'll learn, it'll feel, what it means to make such a mistake. Men are the same way, Bokarie. When they dirty something, shove their faces in it, roll their noses around in it for a while, make them smell and touch their wrong. And I tell you, it won't happen a second time. Do you understand my meaning now? Yes? Then get to work. Chop-chop!"

Of course he understood the General's meaning, though he jumped a little at the General's bark. Or at least Bokarie told him he understood, at which point he was floridly reassured of the General's absolute faith in him and his men. Then Bokarie was reminded, once more, of the roles to be had in the future, were present events to go as originally planned. The General wished him luck and Godspeed in advance of the next progress report he was to give, which was to occur after they had another go at the first village and then, immediately afterwards, a push farther north along the river. It was vital to keep to schedule, Bokarie was reminded. The General had deadlines of his own in mind.

Thinking of which, he cut Bokarie off, midway through a striving rehearsal of the remarks he was planning to give to any survivors of their next, their *sure to be more successful* second effort to take the border village. Looking too far ahead in our country usually gets your head cut off, the General warned. Bokarie just needed to get his dogs shitting in the right places and leave it at that for now. "Because," the General said, draining his tumbler, "then all would be right as rain, good as gold, red as red as red can be."

He then thanked Bokarie once more for his support and guaranteed the young man that he still had much confidence in him. He clicked the receiver down and harrumphed, looking out his window across the stumpy baobabs and over at the paint-peeled grandeur of the People's Palace. All of his plans were as straw, the General thought, if this jitterbugging butcher boy turned out to be nothing more than a one-hit wonder.

IV.

"For now at least, your name will be Jesse, is that understood?"

The man shrugged and asked for more pills and then clutched once more at the scabrous knob where his arm had recently been. Phantom pain. What was left felt like an avocado seed, hard and slippery smooth and dangling some pulpy bits of blacked-up meat. A long day after his chat with the General, Bokarie hit upon a plan to prepare his men for a second putsch, which he drew in part from Foday and Father Alvaro, in addition to the Almighty. His arm-twisting tactics and stump-pumping word spinning proved successful, though they seeded doubt in his cousin and brothers, for the very first time, about their head man. Who, since the time he had had them line the orphanage wall's trench for his bottle-shard thrusts, was always, if nothing else, a dazzling original. They had basked, by devoted association, in his singular talents. But with the first raid a failure and now Bokarie stealing material from others, they questioned their loyalty and his ability to get them the DVDs and local virgins he kept promising once the General named him governor. But was he even worthy of such a title? In time, because one of them was responsible for communications operations, they started sharing these concerns, via a static phone connection, with a generous would-be benefactor in the capital city. Quietly of course. Very hush-hush.

At present, though, they followed Bokarie's order and reassembled the recruits so something could be said about their recent showing. The boys were almost all still there, nervous and bored, moping and limping around the temporary camp they'd struck. They remained because the General had only given Bokarie one big juicy rainbow bundle of cash to wave in front of the eye-wide audience, back at the golf range, as an indication of the promised payment. None of them understood inflation. And regardless, the promised remainder of the first instalment had yet to arrive in camp. Supply line problems, some thought; a hijacked courier, others had heard; just a miscommunication about location, the optimists predicted. But they were all starting to feel it in their bones. No money was coming for what they were doing, but for now it was all they could cite as a reason to stay, it being a many days' walk from here to the capital city, with more whack-happy Upriver types to face along the route.

Of the two fighters who had deserted, one was an ex-orphan of the former Father Alvaro's. Knowing no alternative, he headed towards his old village, but his bearings were off and he went in the opposite direction, reaching another Upriver village around the time Bokarie's force was hitting its stride. The village elder stuffed his ears against the man's explanations and disavowals, and an hour later the remains were tossed near the chipped beef tins that collected behind the local canteen for area scavengers to take care of. This was done in case the Grin Reaper, as Bokarie came to be known around Upriver because of how he brought them death and destruction with a smile, found evidence that one of his men had died in the village, which might inspire his men to seek more than just their vengeant brands of peace and justice and redistribution. The other deserter wasn't heard from for some time, but when he turned up again, he was well received, mostly for the fancy company he brought with him.

The rest were grouped together as they had been on the driving range, but this time the mood was glum and low and the faces long with callow. They were a band of sour teenagers little different from any other, showing in their looks the expectation of punishment for their versions of broken curfews and busted tail lights, and not

wanting to grant their fathers the pleasure of their *mea culpas*. Bokarie
stalked out in front of them, hoping he could summon the right
passage when the time came and that his words would rally the listeners to the cause of a carved-up comrade. Shaking his head, he began
to pace and bop before their down-turned faces. He kept at this for a
long while, building enough tension to make the whole lot jump
when he barked his first words.

"Chop-chop!" he opened. "Do you know what this means, any of
you? Chop-chop!" They jumped again, their birdcage chests pounding with the possibilities being laid out for them. "Do you know that
the General said this to me when I spoke with him by phone yesterday, when I had to tell him what happened on our first mission? He
said this because he wanted me to make an example of one of you, to
teach the others what happens to patriots when they don't conduct
themselves honourably while on their country's business. Because he
was ashamed, as was I, as should you be, at what happened. After all
the trust placed in us, in you, this is the result? Going after chickens
and women and then running and screaming like chickens and
women when the Upriver pigs come at you waving their sticks? So, to
remind you of the bravery and honour you've agreed to, the General
ordered me—*chop-chop!*" This third time they heard the words, they
turned in to each other a little, quivering.

Bokarie let up a moment and motioned for his cousin to bring him
the burlap bag. Then he beckoned the man he was calling Jesse to join
him. Various shudders and whispers went through the crowd. Some
knew this had happened to the boy in the border village. Others
wondered, with the altruism of private relief, if this poor sap had
already received punishment on behalf of the rest.

"The Upriver pigs obeyed the General's orders before I could,"
Bokarie continued, after embracing the cowering boy and then gripping him by his good shoulder. The boy kept reaching, in vain, for

the other. "They sent this brother, Jesse is his name, back to us like this, with his arm in this sack, as a warning, as a reminder to us that they are stronger, harder, madder than we are. And so I ask, do you agree?" Bokarie knew a plant wouldn't work this time; the crowd had grown familiar with his entourage. His stomach fell some as they slouched in tacit answer to his question and then seemed, as lectured teenagers are wont to do, to go away for a while. They were fondly recalling their old easy useless lives in the slums of the capital city. Each to himself, they were sniffing and sniffling that they didn't care about any fat stack of money or the stupid General or his stupid campaign anymore. They were longing for a return home, but then Bokarie whistled and brought them back, a frustrated coach, job on the line, trying to redeem a failing pep talk.

"So then, yes, you do agree? You're that weak, that soft, that womanish? If so, then why don't you give up on the General and suck at the President's milk bags? Go ahead and leave, there's no room on this squad for such types. You're acting like his children anyways." Bokarie spat out this last line, flung it at them like a skein of phlegm. But the insult was also a gamble, he knew, with the dejected air hanging over the camp since their bashed-up return. If even a few were to break away now, he realized, the rest would follow. And he would be left holding a bag of arm, of shit, of his prospects. But before this could happen to him, Bokarie started smiling, forced confidence turning up the corners of his mouth. Everything he had said, they would see, had been mere preparation. Having scorched them with the righteous flame of his anger, he had some lamb words ready.

"I don't believe that about any of you. I know you have strength within you, that you need more than the tasks given to you to bring it out. As if running after chickens was enough to suggest your talent! This is why I have Jesse beside me today, whose suffering, my brothers, shall be our inspiration. And so I promise to all of you that when we return to that village tomorrow, the spirit of the Lord will rest upon us, a spirit of strength that will put fear in other men's hearts, and you, in revenge for our brother and for oh so many others, you shall strike the ruthless you will find with your rods and slay the wicked who lay up there with your knives, and justice shall be wrapped around your waist and patriotism a belt upon your hips. Because"—here he guided the distracted boy forward, who, being actually named Philip and shot through with codeine, had little awareness of or interest in the part he was playing in Bokarie's speech as it reached its climax—"many shoots shall sprout from the stump of Jesse, my brothers. For our General, our nation, our Jesse!"

On cue, rusty rifles were distributed to the recruits to supplement their machetes. East German surplus that hadn't arrived in time for the first raid. They would all jam with the first firings.

The reaction, the lack of one, to Bokarie's rousing address surprised him. He had been expecting, if not a chocolate prize for his fine scriptural elocution and creative memory, at least another rush of voices at his phrases, as had happened on the golf course and, before then, whenever he described how he took down his opponent Foday and, before that, from below the orphanage wall. But the boys hadn't throated up, as expected, at his grand ending. This was indifference to his words, to him. He didn't like it. He would work up some new material for next time, he decided, though he was worried that maybe the Bible had outgrown its usefulness.

But even if his speech didn't get them going, Bokarie noticed with some relief that the timely gun distribution was having a good effect anyway. Most were clamouring after them and then, like children on Christmas morning, sliding around the parts of their new toys and imaging scenarios for their use. As some paired off and exchanged slow-motion re-creations of the rifle butt punishments that the Upriver men had given them, Bokarie accepted that his current prop, the renamed amputee, and his words, the punched-up bit from Isaiah, and even himself—that none of this was so crucial all of a sudden. Next time, yes, he'd do better. For now he had to consider the matter at hand, and he began to think that perhaps the first defeat had been worth something. Because at least his fighters now had some smack of memory to feed from and private desires for future reckonings. Which meant, most importantly, that they were still movable to his plans and the General's directives.

But still, his tongue felt like a cramped eel. His mouth was crammed full with good writ. He couldn't resist. He decided the boys needed more convincing. A touch more.

"You are remembering, I can see, what's been done to you and now you have in your hands the way to return the favour." They looked up at him, semi-interested. "But we will fail, brothers, if we act each for himself. This is why I want you to feel another memory before we go back to give them some of their own. Tomorrow you will spring and shoot out, victoriously, at the Upriver swine. But first you will know, each man for himself, what's been done to one of your own, and what's to be done to them in revenge. Bellies for bellies, yes, and now arms for arms!" This got at least some snorts of agreement. He ordered a line to form and file forward.

They processed past, their rifles low slung, and casually saluted and hailed him. Bokarie tolerated their swaggering because of what was then happening to each when he had them reach into the riper and riper bag to feel and wince at and study the mushy pointlessness of a chopped limb. (Jesse died from infection a few days later, a vague martyr.)

None of the men complained when their rifles failed to fire at pinkish dawn the following morning, because this let them swing away and chop instead. True to newly inspired and recently corrected form, they ignored the chicken coops this time and simply knocked down the women they passed as they went at the village's men, whose pride in their prior victory left them surprised at how fast and hard this second effort came. They were quickly dispatched, pate-cracked and machete-dealt. Eventually the jouncy leader of these hack-hardy teenagers arrived, having hung back because he felt this was conducive to the image he was rubbing into a fine glow, of a leader above the fray who provided a concluding flourish to the proceedings. So, as the bound-up prisoners and back-slapping victors together watched, Bokarie was driven into the village by one of his brothers. He danced a little victory jig on the jawbone of the ass-sprawled village elder. The man's dog came out and growled and whimpered and Bokarie loosely shot at it, tearing out the side of its belly. It slumped away. Then he pronounced the area officially claimed as part of the National Restitution Campaign and offered terms for peace and reconciliation to the next eldest survivor.

Judging the evidence around him, the man accepted immediately and Bokarie embraced him, whispering in his ear what would happen if the man didn't do likewise. They had to demonstrate their healing and friendship before those gathered. As instructed, Bokarie then invited himself to a burial ceremony for the recently passed elder and did likewise with his family there, emphasizing sympathy on behalf of the General and reminding each of the grieving that justice took great pains to get done. The clenched were stunned, as much by the hack and ruin around them as by the audacity of this grinning reaper's response to what he'd just brought off, his whispering what were to them sweet nothings from the Psalms about bones being crushed so that spirits could be revived. They could do little more than go limp in Bokarie's arms and wonder where the rest of the bodies were and hope they could make it to a refugee camp before they heard that chanting come up the road again.

Meanwhile, Bokarie's men cheered lustily at their own success and with his encouragement did a little more dancing and reconciling of their own. They swept through the last of the huts, turning them into private commissaries and, as opportunities kicked and screamed and were forced to present, occasional bordellos. Soon enough, though, the hoarding and humping had emptied out all the huts and groins, but there was still nervous, vicious energy to be spent, as if they knew that to stop now was either to go back to their glum, waiting-around lives or to invite a reckoning with what they'd chosen to do to avoid them. So things intensified. Clay braziers, like the old people slumped around them, were kicked over and cracked. Children were chased down and tossed around like teddy bears while mothers bartered their shrunken paps to retrieve them. Then someone hit upon the idea of tearing up a shirt to pick a lump of coal from a broken brazier and drop it down a woman's top. They watched her shriek and dance to get it out and chanted and clapped to help her move. There were multiple encores.

Eventually Bokarie broke up the festivities with the promise of more to come. There was a timetable to keep to. He left a few of the squadron leaders in place as constables and sent word to allied neighbouring tribes that there was fertile land newly freed for their use.

Stumps sprouted and limbs sprung across the Upriver lands that spring, and word started moving around. It eventually buzzed down to the capital city's barracks and an unmarked campaign headquarters and then to the People's Palace and inevitably into the hotel press rooms.

A BBC man had an early scoop on the developing story. While interviewing a fresh set of migrants headed to the capital, he came across a deserter from some previously unknown rebel movement that had recently tried to take a border village in the Upriver region. For a squishy bar of Fruit & Nut, the limping callow youth told the reporter about the golfing range training and the first raid. En route to Upriver, having convinced the boy he'd be known as a friend to the world if he helped track down his old mates, the BBC man and his techie speculated whether this thing might have enough legs for an extended piece, or even, if they could just get rid of the damned static on the satellite phone, a live-feed interview on *Newshour*. Auntie's interest had been piqued by their initial proposal, which included a clip of the youth telling about a deadly chicken-catching ritual. Voodoo rites always played well to the home audience. He also spoke of the man leading the new charge into the President's tribal lands. He was apparently a bit of a fine-words-and-fancy-footwork warlord, that one.

When the reporter reached Bokarie and first let the young men roving around him play for a while in front of a lens-capped camera, he interviewed the dapper-tongued leader in an exclusive. This was during a heat-induced lull in the Restitution drive, and Bokarie whiled away the sun-beat afternoon by fencing with the reporter about rumours of a disco bar bottle drive to an early challenger's neck. Impressed by the demure way the warlord responded to an account of his own legend, while his entourage crowded into the frame to confirm and embroider it, the BBC man decided he'd stick around and see what came of this. As a result, he had occasion to record the only extant footage of Bokarie making his most famous speech.

The reporter had it confiscated during an army checkpoint search when he returned to the capital. Labelling it stock wildlife footage didn't convince them. The video, he learned upon later inquiry through one of his sources in military affairs, would not be going to England as intended. And if its owner tried to figure out which General it mentioned, he wouldn't be either.

There will always be growing pains when a great nation is reborn! If a few sandals fall into the fire, or a little woman blood mixes into the ashes, what great loss is this? My brothers, it is no loss. My own mother, my own woman, my own child – they have fled, have starved, have been killed in the first wars of the new history, after the British and the French and the Germans left us to fight amongst ourselves for the right to tend our own fires. Meanwhile, the tribes Upriver have guns and electric and water and maize. They have as many goats in their fields as we have vultures above our huts. Do you wonder why? They worship the swine that squeals in the capital city, our self-appointed President-for-life, who sells our wives and daughters to Nike Red Cross U.S. of A. Who protects the Upriver villagers and fills their troughs because they are all of that snub-nosed, mongrel tribe.

There is one man who can put an end to this. The General. And he has told me that only the eldest and purest people of our beloved home-land can help him cleanse what has been soiled. This is why he has asked us to reclaim our ancient lands as part of his National Restitution Campaign. This is why we must crush the chirping locusts that sing of the President's greatness and slaughter the dancing baboons that step to his orders. This is why we will at last greet rosy pink morning from the moist earth that your fathers' fathers left to you. Brothers! When they desire mercy, you shall make of them a sacrifice! For our sons, for our General, for our nation!

After a few deliveries, Bokarie found his stump speech banal. He gave it from the flatbeds of derelict aid trucks to cap off pre-raid rallies on the outskirts of various Upriver settlements, before he sent the men off chanting their *catch them kill them* and *sunken belly* songs. The stump speech had become his standard because of the guaranteed response it gave. Though trite by comparison with the oratories he knew he had in him if only given the right ears to trumpet into, it proved to be the easiest way to keep his men pushing towards their final target. Which was officially known, by decree of the President's office, as the World-Famous Village of Our Beloved President's Glorious Birth, with Actual Manger in Which He Was Born Preserved to This Day and Recently Restored to Its Golden Humble Majesty.

While supervising the recomposing of the Upriver lands, Bokarie had no choice but to give up, eventually, on the Bible as an aid to his own great and terrible words, save a snippet from Hosea. It just didn't get a rise out of people anymore. He had tried a few more portions after his Jesse bits had flopped—of Isaiah, then some of the harsher Psalms, even a little Judith when a few women joined up—but to little success. They just wanted the regular lines; the veterans enjoyed mouthing along, the new recruits demanded the speech because they had heard tell of it and wanted to experience it in person. Most of the Bible-fed orphans he'd taken from Father Alvaro's, who at least could have appreciated his scriptural brio, had been cut down in the early going. That was unfortunate. Not even his brothers and cousin were sympathetic to his complaints of soul sap from saying the same thing again and again, only the more distracted as they were by their little conversations with each other. And so that stumpy speech would stay with him afterwards, until he finally found occasion for new listeners and new material.

After a few months, Bokarie was growing impatient for his mission to finish, so that he could be called down in glory to the capital and receive his reward, an address to the National Assembly as the newly appointed governor. Such a reception he would get then! His only happiness in those bloody Upriver days was that the General was cramming him with promises in every satellite chat they had along the route to the President's village. This kept him driving his men towards that destination and reciting the same old same old every time he was introduced and stalked out in front to whip them up for another run. But while enduring this boredom for the coming reward, he became disgusted with his audiences, with their easy chanting and cheering and roiling at his words, at how easily he held them with such vulgar jingles and then sent them off to the General's business, to their hacking and hollering and exterminating. The brutes.

8

EXODUS POLLS

I.

Faye Gallagher held herself above responding to the garish campaign ploy her opponent had unleashed on her beloved's memorial. Muckraking, after all, was for farm girls. Impartial observers, family members and campaign supporters alike marvelled at this restraint over their crullers and multivitamins the morning after the moving Gallagher affair. At not just the restraint but the courage Faye had shown when she left the funeral home to find a hot pink flyer crammed into the windshield of her husband-gifted, now widow-driven SUV. Faye had removed it so gracefully, so unflinchingly, like Jackie O or something, they had thought. Without even unfolding it to confirm its contents, she climbed up and into her lady truck and drove off, followed by a solemn procession of late-model sedans, extended-cab trucks and pine-freshened vans full of Faye's pining children and theirs.

One woman in the half moon of supporters who saw the widow and her family out to their cars had started humming "Be Not Afraid" when Faye had been, momentarily, stopped short by the pink blot on her windshield. This had been in hopes of encouraging her to endure and prevail over this provocation, but Faye had left before the others remembered the melody. This left them in that half-humming, half-mumbling condition they were reduced to elsewhere in their lives, as when grin-hardened wait staff clapped Happy Birthday ditties at nearby tables in family restaurants, or when parts of the national anthem were sung in French.

Only Blaise Maurier, electric with outrage, lingered in the canopied car lane that fronted the funeral home. From there he held forth, buzz-throated, for any and all ear-covering passersby who processed out thereafter.

Not knowing what evil Blaise was inveighing against, the rest of the townspeople were surprised upon reaching their cars to find the same pink sheet caught up in their wiper blades or, occasionally, crumpled around them, a condition owing to Bokarie eventually growing tired and somewhat distasteful of the so-called mission Jennifer had sent him on while the rest of the community attended heart-attacked George Gallagher's memorial. He enjoyed this feeling rightfully offended, since sharing pain with others was one of his strong suits, and he could easily have worked up something from Lamentations and gone in for an elegant embrace of the bombazine bereaved. But Jennifer had refused him, explaining that the campaign needed him in the field for now, that his time to return to the stage was coming. He'd started crushing the papers against the windshields because it kept cutting at him. How familiar Jennifer's promise had sounded.

The flyers were received with mutterings at the sloth and greediness of the tactic, of letter-bombing the town's cars because they were mostly parked in the same area and during a mourning service no less. Everyone, not just the high Anglicans, clucked at the poor taste of it. But they all pocketed and pursed the sheets, adding them to the napkin-smashed croissants and crumbly date bars that had been palmed and scooped from the refreshment table on the way out. The townspeople kept the papers so they would remember to mark their calendars when they got home. As instructed. Remember the Date. For Little Caitlin. Think, etc.

Meanwhile, Faye was driving home alone, against the insistence of others. Being an always-Christmas-and-usually-Easter Catholic, she had chosen this solitude because she felt the need for a little purging and penance about what she'd just done to her husband's memory, done with his funeral. For her practical and creative use of both, she thought she deserved a private reckoning with the fifty-first Psalm. She hadn't been to confession proper in years, of course, and she had no intentions of going now—not merely because of the self-evident impracticalities of a rising small-town politician confessing to sins of pride and un-charity towards her deceased husband en route to electoral glory, but because of the sheer pointlessness the sacrament had become. It was administered at St. Anne's these days by smiling bearded Father Joseph, an Indian-born cleric. He was an import from Babel-proud Toronto, an enthusiastic little man with an advanced degree in systematic theology. He was also, as anyone leaving Mass could confirm, ripe with spices Old and otherwise. The former was familiar, being a standard odour for parishioners because of its yearly emanating from the toes of Christmas stockings. The latter were usually described, for lack of a better term, as, *well, you know, ethnick.*

Father Joseph was less than well received, however, not because of his hues—this community had recently come to terms with a real-time African, after all—or for his smelly exotica, or even for his backward Third World conservatisms about the prescription needs of young women about town, but because he spoke that nerved-up tongue-tying high-pitched dizzy English of the displaced subcontinent. Which made it near-impossible for any of his current parishioners—

many of whom went to Sunday Mass as religiously as they went out for brunch afterwards—to make bobbling head or shuffling tail of anything he said about interfaith harmony back home in Cochin or the exemplary work of Blessed Teresa of Calcutta. Which made it plain silly, Faye had decided, to bother trying him out for a confession. And so she had planned to self-administer purgation and absolution on the ride home from the service.

As the initial examination of conscience, Faye decided that George had been a good husband—prominent and providing, open to two children, no more no less, willing to do Rock, Paper, Scissors to see who'd get their tubing tied, but also prone in later years to golfing, dock painting, the television in the garage, the more elaborate perfume gift packages with every successive birthday. Prone to these and many of the other polite demonstrations of spousal indifference available to twenty-first-century Western man, except of course during re-election campaigns and holiday photo shoots and children's graduations. But then, before she could watch enough daytime television and so muster up enough self-worth to call Blaise and file the necessary papers for divorce, there had come those unexpected gifts: first, her devastating management of George's re-election campaign against young Jennifer Thickson, and second, the gift he gave her in recognition of the tactics she had employed.

Driving in it now, Faye could still remember the words that had framed the purchase as George signed the papers, from the French-Canadian sales manager orgasmic to have someone this prominent buying off his lot instead of from his English rival's one town over.

Faye had been shocked not so much at George's largesse—after all, she'd eliminated his only challenger well before election day, and an all-inclusive week to Cuba with in-room rum dispenser would only have been acceptable were she a younger and thus stupider wife—but at how he had gone about it. He did the doubly unthinkable, first opting to buy from a lot outside town, after it turned out that Holler-watty couldn't promise that Detroit had anything in champagne (which Faye had requested in honour of the gift's celebratory signifi-cance), and second, buying an import. And while the jelly-roll stomach and dimpled thigh diminishments of middle age had reduced their sex life to little more than the touchy affection of preteen second cousins, she'd given up a little gasp and sigh at such evidence of her husband's persistent manhood, at his brawny dismissal of the backbiting and character assassination that they both knew Hollerwatty would be sending his way come the next poll, in vengeance for such a notable lost sale. This was no bother, George had assured her, and then explained that he didn't care anyway, because this was what his wife deserved and he wanted for her.

So, Faye decided, he was all in all pretty good as a husband, taking more than he gave, of course, but leaving her with a paid-off house and a car still under warranty. From trading notes during her morning power walks with fellow prominent town wives—of doctors, the police chief, the Junior A hockey coach—she concluded this was a *very* penitential thing for a wife in her fifties to admit. Having reached this insight, Faye thought she could now leave behind her spiritual exercise for a more exacting estimation of her late husband's political ambitions. Which were smallish. Being many times returned to an alderman's municipal seat was about as ambitious as his requests, in later years, that she buy him only khakis with elasticized waistbands. Now, driving down Albert Avenue, the town's main thoroughfare, Faye gave a passing glance at the bloated Victorian dollhouse where her husband had worked for years. The building was *circa* 1900 and the town, like its counterparts across the nation, proudly called it Historic City Hall in its tri-annual tourist brochure. The paint-peeled, nail-pocked walls were updated as necessary with new plaques from the Rotary Club and the Optimists, oak and oil portraits of recently deceased town fathers, and, now and then, federal commendations with airbrushed ribbons for support of handicapped children's bowling leagues, elderly meal services and other such civic sanctifications that tended to count more attendants than attendees in their attendance.

Faye gave City Hall cut-eye as she drove past it, feeling that, from her perfect teeth through her new widow status and beyond, she was capable of better than this. She had decided that nothing less than the algae green grandeur of Parliament Hill was to be hers—that is, once she revved through the pending federal election.

Her victory had been all but assured by the other mainline candidates dropping out when they heard about her plans to run. The story arc of the dead husband was enough for the established right- and left-wing party candidates to cancel their races and not have to make public their respective platforms, which were little more than bric-a-brac borrowings from Nordic dandies (on the left) and K Street juggernauts (on the right), some *u*'s added to words here and there to suggest the native origins of their respective political positions. The presumptive competitors had been happy to avoid the predictable returns and instead come off as valiantly sacrificial in allowing Faye and her party, the PRI of the North, that bald-treaded spare tire of the comfy frumpy Canadian middle, to slouch on triumphant. (The incumbent for the seat, of the same party, had decided not to run for re-election after some decimal point confusions were noticed in his discretionary budget. He was immediately named ambassador to a non-extradition country.)

Faye scaled her driveway before anyone else got home, which meant she had a little more time to herself before the latest stack of Tupperware comfort was opened up. But not wanting to go into the house alone, she finally read the pink sheet that had been shoved into her grieving windshield. She had hoped, cheaply, that the colour was a coincidence, that this was just another ad for discount duct or dry cleaning. But no. It was what she expected, and Faye accepted now that she definitely would have competition for the riding seat, from the young woman who had once run against her husband for city council and whom Faye had mentored, no less, if briefly. She further noticed that Glenn the Engine Hollerwatty's dealership was sponsoring the Little Caitlin Creek Cleanup that candidate Thickson, running as an independent, was organizing for the Sunday that happened to fall before election day. This coming campaign wasn't going to be a widow's cakewalk.

But Faye was glad, on further reflection, that they'd done this, Jennifer and Glenn and whoever had put the papers on everyone's cars, because now she could justifiably put off the real matter of what she had wanted to self-confess on the drive home—how she'd lied and implied and hinted during her eulogy that George had been planning to make a run at the federal seat before his heart attack struck him down and that now, in loving memory, the town should make it hers.

She could skip any further spiritual housecleaning and instead go righteous and persecuted at the ugliness of her competitor's campaign. In fact, to be true to George's memory and win the race he never ran, Faye had to forget her Jesuitical play with George's unspoken ambitions and instead concentrate on the matter at hand: making sure the people of town would rather Be Not Afraid than Think Pink. She recalled the joke George had made back at the dealership, just before she'd driven off in her new gift, about the prospect of what a spurned Hollerwatty could do to his incumbency. He had dismissed the worry. After all, George reminded his wife, it wouldn't be the first time he'd have a raging bull on his hands who was angry because they weren't buying American. At least this one wouldn't be twirling ponytails and talking about LBJ all the time.

She smiled at that, recalling it in the driveway. Later, she cried in her bed, her now big and empty bed, after the others had hugged her just one last time and then gone home in their pairs and after her own children and their entourages made do with old sleeping bags and twin mattresses. She cried not so much from the shock of realizing, once more, how cold the sheets were and how far, out of habit and in vain, she could spread her legs in search of his hard shin bones and hairy veiny calves and *God will you cut those toenails already?*, but because the riding seat, the mourning balm she had chosen for losing George—which, she had no doubt, he would want for her because it was the chance finally to be something more than a supportive and devoted and admiring Em Are Ess—was imperilled by the rising power of that bullish young woman she'd first met over sparkling wine and Shakespeare ten summers before.

II.

Faye's voice ran up yet another scale, this time across an "Okay then," to signal that their conversation had reached a reasonable end. She was standing in front of her Mercury wagon with Miss Jennifer Ursula Thickson, the two having been introduced by an intermediary during the intermission of the Community Playhouse's summer Shakespeare offering, *The Tempest*. They were together because one was interested in politics and the other was married to it. At least that was how Faye put it to Jennifer, at first, in the mock-confidential tone she used with identifiably lesser women to make them feel comfortable in her orbit. But it hadn't provided the polite fiction of equilibrium as usual, Faye noticed, because this girl didn't seem so curious about what it was like to make coffee and buy new socks for power. She had wanted to hear more about politics itself. Period.

Faye had been pulled in by such attention from a younger, weaker admirer, like a ladybird Sam Rayburn. It was so unlike the standard fawning she received from the Hoarfrost women. Who, after the encore applause smattered out at the end of *The Tempest*, brushed grass and cracker bits from their frowsy finery and spoke, to no one in particular, of course, but in showy loud tones, of recent arts and letters gossip. This was in permanent hope that Faye would cock an interested ear at one of them and accept a private dinner invitation to hear more or even extend the offer to that lucky lonely old girl to share her bon mots with Husband Alderman George.

Having all read the same column in a recent issue of the town newspaper, they compared rumours that Robertson Davies—himself!— might take in a performance of *The Tempest* in Centennial Park before the set was struck. He was a great fan of the Bard, of course, one woman observed; he had tread the boards himself at the Old Vic, a second casually noted; he was probably curious about whether we Canuck Calibans could ever prosper at playing Prospero, a third smartly trilled off her tongue. All for naught. Faye was already walking away with Jennifer.

She had ignored all of the women so straining for her approval with the Davies dish because she had been taken, instead, with Jennifer's insistence on hearing—from her—about politics. Not about being married to it, Faye sensed, but about the thing itself, as if Jennifer had divined that there was more to Alderman Gallagher's wife than an MRS with specializations in canapés and hugging the elderly. And so she had liked it, this notion of a young woman to teach, to mould, to remake in her own image, even if Faye was a little put off by how hard-charging the girl had been when she first came at her, at the play's intermission, leaning in and down and pawing what's her name out of the way. And then afterwards, back again to ask about the pending municipal campaign and whether any help was needed.

Faye agreed to allow young Miss Thickson to be her shadow during her husband George's coming re-election campaign for alderman. Her own daughters, too busy stealing foundation from her makeup drawer to hide fresh hickies every Saturday morning, never looked for anything of this sort from their mother, and so she accepted Jennifer as her protegé in spite of obvious limitations of breeding. In spite of her uninsured teeth and the shoes she'd chosen for a summer picnic. Faye liked the idea of a willing second, of this recognition that she had a little political smarts of her own. Because George had only ever wanted her to bake before, to wave after and to nod during his stump speeches. It was agreed that before Miss Thickson went off to study human resource management the following month, she could join the campaign for a couple of weeks. The girl had nodded and promised, unbidden, to present herself in Alderman Gallagher's office the next morning ready to learn and to help and to shadow. Then she marched off, leaving Faye to writhe and blunder through her purse for sunglasses against the late afternoon glare of eastern Ontario summer sunlight which, until then, the young woman had been blocking, had in fact blotted out.

After feeling as if a waterlogged sleeping bag kept wrapping itself around her during the early days of the campaign, Faye praised Jennifer's self-starting energy and took the executive decision to let her canvass on her own. The phone calls started a few days later.

George went apoplectic and Jennifer was invited to leave the team, *your enthusiasm for campaigning being frankly too American for these polite parts even if, as you've told us all many times, the cajoling and coaxing and plain intimidation worked for President Johnson. But as we tried reminding you more than once, this isn't Texas, Jennifer, it's not even Alberta, and so a little more humanity is needed in our politics, which is why we will no longer require your services, appreciated though they were.*

As explained in a note mailed to the Thickson house. Jennifer didn't reply, not immediately.

George was re-elected nonetheless, and guffawed during the victory party, and with Faye obviously close enough to hear, that he'd done it all in spite of his wife's political smarts and staff picks. Which had cut. Six years later, Faye gave up the supportive smiles to become George's icy-veined campaign manager, something she had insisted on when news came that Jennifer had declared for vengeance, for his seat.

Outwardly, he neither cared nor quailed about it, declaring that the twenty-five-year-old who lived with her parents on a rural route outside town posed less of a threat as a competitor than she had as a supporter the last time. But still, there was something in the girl that made both George and Faye nervous. Like being stuck in a cottage bathroom with a deer fly. But this was where Faye found motive. Dealing with this challenge was precisely what she wanted. She demanded to be named campaign manager, and with Blaise in his first round of chemo anyway, George okayed it and Faye hit upon the idea of using the death of the family dog as the centrepiece of the campaign. Having taken from Jennifer, unacknowledged, a lesson about how Lyndon Baines Johnson had so easily won the 1964 U.S. presidential election, Faye understood that sudden, tragic loss was a sure guarantee of electoral gains.

The Gallagher family dog, Melville, had had to be put down out of compassion shortly before the municipal election. Extreme diabetes. The dog had consumed summer upon summer's worth of squishy chocolate bars dropped during the frenzy of Capture the Flag games that the younger children played once all the day's tennis balls had been roofed and jawbreakers cracked and spitting contests concluded. Among the older set that the dog trailed—cranberry-cheeked boys who stole the family Sears catalogues for the ladies' intimates section and nub-chested girls willing to experiment with lip gloss and cigarettes and hickies—it also ate what sweets were forgotten during the giggles and fumbling of Truth or Dare.

And so, as the centrepiece of the Gallagher campaign, the alderman went on a speaking and listening tour to local elementary schools. The sombre topic was pet diabetes and preventative measures. Faye sent children home to their parents with candidate information pamphlets that featured a warming montage of photos: Melville as *so cute puppy*, Melville reclining lion regal with the family in their snowflake sweaters for the annual holiday card, Melville *about to take the big plunge!* on the floating dock up at the cottage. These pamphlets also provided what had to be regarded as a fair and balanced account of the alderman's challenger, though there was a little chicanery involved here. A freelance graphic designer from Cornwall had been commissioned to airbrush crumpled chocolate bar wrappers into a funeral wreath for inclusion in the pamphlet. It was intended to be received as a socially responsible, artistic flourish. But due to an oversight or perhaps a minor miscommunication, the wreath happened to appear around the inset box that featured information on "My Opponent." This was only discovered after the pamphlets had been widely dispersed. The implications for the alderman's youngish and heavy-set challenger were many and unfortunate. She had had no choice but to withdraw from the race. During his acceptance speech, Alderman Gallagher publicly apologized for the printer's error, which had produced such unsubstantiated allegations regarding Miss Thickson. He applauded her gracious decision to remove herself from contention nonetheless, and he was sure that she loved animals and chocolates as responsibly as any other child in town. Even the most partisan of supporters had thought this portion of Gallagher's otherwise gracious remarks a little too harsh. Damn near cruelty to animals, others snorted.

And now Faye had the prospect of facing Jennifer herself, in a federal election, no less, since the semi-annual pageant rite of a minority government fall in Ottawa had coincided with her husband's passing. Her opportunity to do more with the remainder of her days than ward off divorced bankers while on senior singles' cruises through Alaska. Only first she had to get past this pink-charging opponent armed with car dealer dollars and drainage security bills and drowned-pigtail tales and also that smiling slinky African that she'd been coiling and uncoiling around town all that spring and summer.

III.

He was breathing hard, frustrated, dismayed, nearing disgust with the campaign in its closing days, or at least with its leader's lack of imagination, vision, awareness of the talent so near at hand and so ready, aching to do what he could to bring this off, to send them both, finally, to the capital city. But Bokarie was also wincing at the very real pain these feelings were causing. High autumn in the Ottawa Valley was a new season for him, and its gunmetal-cold air shot up his nostrils and across his forehead with every angry intake, and he wanted it to stop, this sharp crack across the skull, like a long swallow direct from the Slushie machine. No longer suspicious of Canadian sunlight, he was confronted now with still another season, the third so far since he had arrived. And before he could even come to terms with the slow death it brought to the trees and the grass, there was chatter already of a fourth en route which was even harsher. This was according to countertop chuckles from his customers at the convenience store about what weather he had coming to him next in his new country.

With this latest one, fall, came slippery walking at first light when he had opening shift, and also a taut empty air, the warmth gone out of it, leaving him with tingling ears and a chill deadness dangling against his thighs while he was waiting for the bus. And also all this random sniffling and phlegmy bolus—like one of his old orphan recruits wandering around camp in between raids or some other such pointless weakness.

Not that she noticed this suffering of his, he thought, enjoying the wounded feeling this gave him as he looked at Jennifer's billboard blank of a face. Because as they walked together along the path they were scouting for the next day's event, she was ignoring his suggestions for the speech she was to give. And she had already dismissed his offers to make remarks to the gathered on her behalf, having forgotten, apparently, her earlier promise to let him back onstage when the opportunity presented.

Instead, Jennifer was entirely focused on the murky thick of the leaf-strewn creek beside them, nervous that there weren't going to be enough coffee cups and night-crawler cartons and distended shopping bags to keep people sloshing around for an entire afternoon's cleanup effort, and, more to the point, that this would undermine the combination re-memorial, increased awareness and pre-election rally she had planned. Bokarie's business of the right words for the right moment just wasn't a priority, even if he kept at her with missionary zeal.

"Do you even know Exodus? Do you know that it would make such good sense in this place right now, as a way to make you the great leader of these people?" he asked, even spat at her, feeling tired and proprietary from the weeks he had been working on her campaign. This had included not just the door-to-doors but also the strategizing while restocking potato chips and the damage control when Faye Gallagher showily traded in her champagne import for a more patriotic and practical domestic model off Hollerwatty's lot, at which point Glenn suddenly became impossible for Jennifer to reach. There was also the straw polling Bokarie conducted in line at the grocery store, though this was no terrible chore. Actually, he had liked asking his new compatriots to open up about their political leanings for the pending election while they queued up in checkout lines. He did this with the vacant enthusiasm of an incontinent department store greeter and elicited a muddle of guilt and pity and horror in response, the spillover of which blotted out the shared indignity of such breaches and also squeezed out an answer. He had perfected his method: first draw their attention away from the celebrity smut rags and *Eat lighter, live righter this holiday* recipe guides garishly dangling from the magazine racks; then exclaim how wonderful it was to be part of a country, finally, where turkey, not the ballot box, was stuffed. This cheap cuteness, like a terrier barking in time with a Christmas carol, was well received as innocent cleverness, especially in the time around Thanksgiving.

Having softened them up this way, Bokarie would then ask how they were planning to vote in the coming election—*whether for the Libel Party's candidate or for the Independent and Little Caitlin?* He was rarely corrected for his new-immigrant stumble on the ruling party's name, which Jennifer had helped him to, and so Bokarie had little trouble extracting the desired information before reminding his interlocutor of the pending rally down at the creek where, so tragically, months ago, Little Caitlin had first gone to her death and into our hearts. Vigorous nods and promises of attendance, and maybe a little suspicion about just getting gamed by the town African—who was known to associate with the Thickson girl—but he didn't know any better and she'd never had any friends anyway so that was an understandable match. Poor things. And so the shoppers exited feeling inspired about their participation in a little clump of grassroots politics, their arms crooked and straining and creasing and crinkling their paper or plastic shopping bags. Then Bokarie, taking his time packing up his weekly cache of dried noodle cups at the end of the adjacent conveyor, turned to the next in line and worked up his words and gobble-gobbled them all over again.

He liked the immediate gratification of it, like the chocolate bars he tore through at work, feeding on their stares and nods and admissions and then, having swallowed them all down, politely casting off for more. In time he would follow them into the windy parking lot and, before going off to the bus stop, watch their bright seasonal jackets blow and tumble around the cars like discarded wrappers and unraked leaves while they tried to remember where they parked. He duly reported the findings from his grocery store polling to Jennifer. She was even with her opponent going into the final weekend.

This closeness, Bokarie thought, made more vital his suggestions for how to end the campaign with maximum success. Which required more than some zealous group cleanup effort and a grander notion than a drowned little girl behind it to secure victory, especially against such driven competition. There was, of course, always a cheap willingness in people to work on. To make them drudge through a creek, or machete through a village, or carve up a brother's back, or vote against a fresh widow in a new Ford. Any of this could be had, provided their ears could be pricked, which, in the present case, meant leading them to feel that their deed—their vote for Jennifer and Little Caitlin and drainage security—would sound down through the ages, from the Red Sea to the old crick behind RR #2. And Bokarie was absolutely convicted about how to bring this about. The words, recalled from when they first went unused, in the final days of the National Restitution Campaign, when the General had become impossible to reach and then his blood men tried to carve him up, were massing along the ridge of his tongue. After so much waiting and wanting, the readiness was all, and he had it. But again, denied.

"Yes, Bokarie, I know something about Exodus. I've seen that long show about it with Ben-Hur from *Planet of the Apes*. But the problem is, where it's coming from isn't exactly the movies. The polls are close, as you know from your self-starter work in the grocery store, and this is our final opportunity to get a hearing for my proposals, and I have to tell you"—here her tone lost its immediate strain for the more comforting sound she generally adopted with him, the mellifluous drone of an automated customer care attendant—"that as always I appreciate your support, and your time and input is invaluable to us."

But she was too tired to keep it up and turned a little harsher. "But still, you're on thin ice with this idea of yours"—and, more than sick of having to keep Bokarie at bay like this, harsher still—"because, yeah, I know, I know." She held her hand up to batten him down. She had spoken to Bokarie enough by now to recognize him preparing a volley of poor suffering this and a fillip of long hurting that.

"I know that back in your old place they did ancient rituals and all, and probably something like the old religion fired people up, but, well"—finally Jennifer gave in and went Daddy's girl on him—"over here it only gets you two minutes in the sin bin for mentioning it unless it's a funeral song and then a campaign slogan, and, well, it's too late in the third period to go down short-handed for a hot dog move like quoting the Bible at a political rally.

"Listen, that explanation might have been a little culturally exclusive for you, so let me try again. Between you and me, I lost the first race I ever ran in, to None of the Above. And that was a lesson I learned early in this game—that less is more around here, because everyday Canadians don't ever want to get too excited or too offended or too frightened or too inspired, which was what I was trying to do back then, and I think you're suggesting more of the same. And I had to pull out of the second race I ever ran in because my opponent had a campaign manager who made the town see me for a monster before

I could even open my mouth. So I'm not going to let *my* campaign manager put words in my mouth now that will make me into another kind of monster. You're asking me to come off as a Christian politician. God, that's even worse than a chocolate-addicted pet abuser. Do you get my meaning?"

Bokarie was a little confused but more unimpressed by her low ambitions, by her commitment to mediocrity as the sure way to victory. This was why he was being denied the opportunity to speak at her final rally. His very talent was becoming something of a liability for the campaign. There was consolation in this, but more than that, something else, which was harder to admit.

It was, unexpectedly, respect. Respect for how hard-bore she was about getting to Ottawa herself. In the past he had wrongly, stupidly, near-fatally underestimated the hunger of others. No more. He even felt sheepish, now, for how he'd felt when watching Jennifer go up into the barn two months earlier with that casserole hog right behind her shoving his nose and rubbing his goatee at steep incline. Bokarie felt sheepish about how this had made him pause and wonder whether he had hitched up to the wrong horse. Not from jealousy, of course, certainly not, there were always standards; Bokarie had declined advances from the smiley Vietnamese girl walking beside him after dinner at the Thickson place, even while she was giving him crescent-moon eyes and looked ready to be thrown down among the cornstalks and husked and shucked while the barnyard animals rolled around in their oats. But having learned his lesson long ago, Bokarie had rejected this chance at a little defanged fur and instead gone worried that Jennifer would emerge from the hay a few minutes later and invite him to put his driver's cap on again and make sure there were enough ribbons tied to her own wedding-night getaway car. And not even care if they were pink.

Only she hadn't; the stud her father brought in must have been limp or been shot down, Bokarie had assumed, watching him stomp down the barn stairs and scoop up the Vietnamese and drive off. Emerging a little crumpled, Jennifer had gone back to the house in haste, calling out that they would talk about the flyers for the Gallagher funeral the next day. The father then came to the screen door and gave him shotgun eyes. Bokarie didn't bother asking for a ride back to town. But a long walk was fine. Because at least he left knowing that her ears, like his, were stuffed against sweet nothings and that all that mattered for her was to get from here to wherever was better.

"Bokarie? You must be thinking about the rivers back in your home again, and I understand, but not right now, okay? Try to stay in the here and now with me. Are we clear about how we're operating? Can I trust that you're going to follow through with your responsibilities?"

He nodded, but the familiarity of this question was too much. Because the General had asked the same in one of their last conversations. Just before he'd decided Bokarie had achieved enough restitution in the Upriver and that his services were no longer required. Had become a liability, in fact.

But what was the worst she could do, if *she* wanted to get rid of him? Because obviously Jennifer wasn't about to arrange for his assassination through intermediaries. There were no nights with long knives over here. And even if she wanted to, his pack of Judases were already long dead and bloated along the banks of the Upriver and she, well, she didn't seem to have anyone else in this town but a dead little girl and him. So really, what was it, the worst that could be done?

Would she ship him back east for further training at new Canadian living? That would be just more pamphlets to read and videos to watch and songs to sing from the Department of Immigration on the

ADJUST ME to My New Country program. He remembered this as his first smack of Canada, remembered how, with a musky toothy Turk Cypriot as his partner back at the St. John's holding pen and much encouragement from a Haitian woman in a bright confident pantsuit who wasn't just session leader but session graduate, he had patty-caked the acrostic until it was down rote. *A*l-ways SMACK *D*emand *J*us-tice CLAP *U*ntil *S*ociety SMACK *T*reats *M*e CLAP with *E*quality CRACK SMACK CLAP CLAP *encore s'il vous plaît.* He had been presented with a pencil engraved with this magical thinking in a mini-graduation ceremony to landed immigrant status before being shipped northwest of Ottawa. But thinking about how to fit into his new scene in his apartment at night, Bokarie had chewed through the letters soon after arriving. And so now he was wondering, what punishment could there be? More about how vital and welcome and fundable it was for him to bring his old traditions and recipes to his new country?

Thicking up the accent to make it seem to her as if she misheard him, he had a little extra fun with the fungible fantasy of this Canadian life, and so he continued, in a manner of speaking, from where he'd earlier left off.

"As you suggest, *mon Jenniferal,* I will continue the campaign as you wish and leave the higher planning to you."

"Okay, good—glad to know you're fully on board. So let's drop the Bible stuff and concentrate on what we're finding in the creek—is there enough garbage here to keep people busy? What do you think? And was that French you just did a little? That's interesting, doing a little FSL alongside your ESL. It might help if you did some *parlez-vous* with some of the older RC voters, that is, if you wouldn't mind doing a walk around that new subdivision, Bethlehem Meadows, which we haven't gone to yet. Maybe tomorrow afternoon, during the rally? It's a good time to go, I think, in case there's any stragglers, holdouts, resistance to the program over there. I won't need you here then, but I'll send your best to everyone, I promise."

She didn't want him there, he thought, in case he got up onstage and did a better job of frothing them up than she ever could. Then maybe they'd cross her out and put him into the ballot box and carry him down to the capital. So she was cutting him off from them, after he'd brought them to her. He realized that this was how the Jennifers and the Generals of his northern provinces worked him. Only he would be a step ahead this time. He could oblige Jennifer's request and slouch off to the last neighbourhood the next day with his demotic French and his brimstone wonders and leave her to spin gold from garbage. But he'd be coming back.

IV.

Her lips, trembling from the moment of it, opened.

"The waters beside us, my fellow countrypersons, flow out from our little community and they leave us today strong and clear, thanks to your cleanup efforts in this special place. These waters will carry with them many things, including memories of a little girl taken too young, but also hopes that this will never happen again. As for the beloved water spiders that she'd first tried to catch, they'll be back too, next spring, hopping and dancing along the water, which, no doubt, will again be brimming from the thaw. And we should take their return and the high water as reminders about the danger and power of Nature itself, which can never be stopped, only controlled.

"These waters flow southeast, as you all know, and they join up with the Ottawa River, and from there they make their way into the mighty St. Lawrence and from there they go out to the Atlantic Ocean and from there, my friends, from there they reach the rest of the world! And this symbolizes the way that everyday Canadians, people like you and me, can touch people across the planet with our actions."

The audience nodded, pleased they were somewhat familiar with these ideas, which was owing to the recent proliferation of little booklets tied with gold twine to their purchases explaining how this particular salad dressing or that specific soap bar was helping to combat the sex slave trade in India and the depleted lemur population on Madagascar. Or vice versa. The moral was the same. They listened on.

"I promise that if elected, I will journey down this river to Ottawa and tell them about you, and about Little Caitlin, and about our pink ribbon campaign and about the need for raising awareness about the dangers of rising creeks. And because I'm running as an independent, I won't—be afraid—to speak your mind and I'm not—wedded—to any single party and, most importantly, I won't be—trading in—the gifts this community has given me for anything new they're trying to sell down there." Having thus dashed the widow Gallagher, Jennifer went in for a clear majority.

"But I'll do more than carry this covenant for you. As we all know these days, the world touches us too, and it has, very recently, with our new addition to this community, I mean Bokarie, who brought with him memories and hopes of his own. Many of you might have noticed that he's not with us today, and you're probably wondering why, you're maybe remembering the eloquent speech he gave back in the spring, so courageously coming forward to embrace our tragedy and share his feelings and his ancient wisdom with us. You know, I was walking with him by this very creek just yesterday, and he was telling me about where he's coming from, about how his people were driven out of their lands, men on horses chucking spears and chasing after them and burning bushes around them until they were forced to cross a river bottom that was dry before the next monsoon and flood came, and that was how they were sent into a bitter banishment far from their home. That's all I heard"—or all she could remember from the last time she'd seen *The Ten Commandments* and from flipping through the African climate section of her encyclopedia set the unsleeping night before—"because he started breathing hard at that point in the conversation and couldn't go on, couldn't come back to be with us today even though he wanted to, because he couldn't wade up and down the creek and face such memories. He didn't want to confront what had happened to his loved ones. But we all have cable these days. We can picture what must have happened." Nods to this and also quiet gladness that Bokarie wasn't there with them interfering with their respective imaginings of his tragic humanity.

"And so"—here she left behind DeMille and *Britannica* for some lines she had copied down, years earlier, from a speech printed in a biography long overdue from her high school library—"he came here an exile, a stranger, brave but frightened, to find a place where he could be his own man. And how has he been treated since getting here? Well, you know as well as I, we live in a world in terror, where terrific dangers and troubles that we once called foreign now live and catch planes among us. And some, though I shall name no names, but some deal … and trade in … jokes about a road apple rolling into our town." A few wife jabs to husband ribs, but Thickson's ellipses were enough to let the rest recall Glenn Hollerwatty's awful trafficking in good ethnic jokes and make the necessary ascription. His sales dipped in the months after the election. "Yes, calling him a road apple rolling into our town and bringing dangers and troubles that we once called foreign with him. Is this the Canadian way? I say no!"

Applause they were giving her, Jennifer Ursula Thickson, applause at this, at her. But no time to wallow in it, she thought. Get more.

"I say it's too black and white an attitude for my Canada and yours. Ours is a nation that's proud to be open to new worlds, to blending, to mixing, to bringing things together. And so that's what I've been doing this afternoon and what I'll do for you in Ottawa if I'm fortunate enough to service you from there. You know, if I can get personal for a moment, I lost the very first election race I ran, back in high school. I lost to None of the Above. I found in this my first lesson about what it means to be a leader. People can surprise you, things can happen that you don't expect, and I want you to consider that lesson yourselves when you think about who you are voting for tomorrow, and why. And if you vote for me, that means I'll go down to Ottawa where I'll bring together Little Caitlin's story with Bokarie's, and I know, I have to believe, that you're with me on this. My friends"—here she leaned forward on her lectern, loomed over it, came down at them, and they were transformed into so many back-bending Hubert Humphreys—"I'm telling you, there's no need to be not afraid since I might go before you always, like my opponent suggests. Instead, I'm telling you there's no need to be afraid because we go forward *together*, as a community, as just a really great society. That's how we'll conquer our fears of the unknown!"

The crowd's not knowing what these unknowns were made the message the more convincing.

"We'll do it by being true to the standard we hang above us, the place where our values really fly, our glorious red and white!" She almost added blue, which would have been immediately fatal and perhaps God's retribution upon her for borrowing so much from Johnson's 1965 inaugural, but she was spared, for now.

Jennifer unveiled in a flourish a flag that she'd had Barb Thickson run through the wash that morning a few times to make the colours bleed just right, while they both ignored Gus's grumps about this unpatriotism and also his questions about why all their garbage bags had gone missing the day before. "And so, if I'm your member of Parliament, I pledge to you that we'll keep bringing things together, we'll do what Canadians do best: we'll blend, we'll mix, we'll think pink! We'll blend, we'll mix, we'll think pink! We'll blend— OH!"

Bokarie cut in just then. He had parted the foaming crowd like an ignited oil slick and made his way to the stage. Having hung back behind a tree during her remarks, now he hopped up and took her at her word. He grabbed Jennifer by the hand and started waving and jiving and got up a good rhythm from the people from their chanting the candidate's end phrase. He smiled at her and she forced a smile back and they turned to look again at their listeners, beribboned in pink and each presuming to play Moses to the other's Aaron.

Jennifer had to grant the optics of this even if she hadn't wanted to share the stage with Bokarie again and even though she was wincing at the force with which their hands were locked together. Because he was holding on hard, serving notice that he was going with her. Wherever. Which was fine. She would make good on her promise to bring him with her to Ottawa. He'd play well in the capital, Jennifer thought. They'd be hungrier for his hardship than this place ever was. And then maybe Bokarie could bring her elsewhere in turn. Africa was very hot these days. Third World nations and First World peacekeepers went together like newborns and diapers.

And so she squeezed back harder, matching him, their arms swinging like bullwhips, their hands intent like Vise-Grips, their fingers mashed like slow-mating slugs, their knuckles and notions and nations gloriously popping together in the brusque October air, their Promised Land a poll vault and widow's loss away.

QUID PRO QUO

I.

She won. Over an opponent no less. The widow Gallagher responded graciously and swiftly by sending a congratulatory e-mail and then forming a non-profit concern committed to memorializing as much public land as possible in her husband's name. Which Jennifer supported, even if she was still feeling warlike and wanted to tie Faye by the ankle to the back of her father's riding mower and circle the town limits to show off her vanquishing. But she knew that was neither lady- nor sportsman- nor statesmanlike.

The race itself was notable for the higher than normal interest it had generated, the sixty-percent turnout nearly double the national average. The rest of the country had simply continued their low-intensity citizenship, treating another federal election like little more than a rush hour bus; it didn't matter if they missed this one, the next would chug along before they could finish muttering about all the noxious fumes left in the air by the last.

Jennifer hadn't planned a victory party, though her mother did send her father out for an ice-cream cake later that night. But no victory party because, because, well, the very idea of her actually winning an election, any election, *this* election, was, for all of her ready hunger and brute politicking, something she hadn't really thought through. And this meant that she was suddenly faced with the lashing, taunting words that come after every newly elected leader.

What now?

Trying to hold them off for a bit, the new MP, after receiving the news of her victory in her mother's sewing room, which had doubled as her campaign headquarters, excused herself upstairs. Sitting on her bed, her fingers still too sore from Bokarie's to wrap around her braids, she tried to settle what this was she was feeling. It was no longer the ragged raw taste in the mouth as when she lost in high school and then against George Gallagher and always the desire for more. There was a newness here.

Some pride, of course. She'd started her trajectory now, finally, and at an impressive height, no less—victory as an independent against the fresh widow of a beloved town father running for the incumbent party. This was fine and well and to be marvelled at and only the beginning. But that wasn't all. There was also a sense of recognition, more of that than of pride. She could tell that her mother was pleased from the ice-cream-cake order to her father, and she wondered if her father was too. But strangely, the lording, the tribute, the gloating, though all rightly hers, weren't what she was feeling, or even what she wanted in the immediate after-burn of the election. Nor was it dealing with What Now, which, at least provisionally, Little Caitlin's memory and drainage security and her African angle were enough to hold off. If lacking further specifics, she could at least assure people, based on this array of concerns, that she was for a lot of things and against very little. It had worked for LBJ. Finally, if cornered, she could always tether herself to Canadian values and float away to safety. That worked for everyone else.

Jennifer looked out her bedroom window at the sullen cornstalks of her family's fields, at the thicket mush where she had gone as a child to watch and learn from the birds and the slugs, at the line of leafy water that ran near it, and then over to the road that led past the gas station where she liked the smell and the squat high school where she had her first loss and the town proper where she had her second loss before she figured out what to do with its car dealership and convenience store and the chunky blocky fantail of new housing developments that seemed to spread out from it unto eternity. All of which was now, finally, under her name, while beyond, in the south-east violet light of late fall, there was Ottawa, waiting to receive her. Looking out at this, Jennifer felt a crinkle in her nose, as if she would weep. Only she didn't, because she was—and this was what the new feeling came to—content. There seemed to be nothing more to conquer. She didn't want another go at the buffet. At least not yet.

It was enough to have it, finally, the riding, the power, the glory. The problem now was that she hadn't ever really thought much past the getting. She had never had reason to do so. Of course Jennifer didn't need any Bible to know the nature of the beast: getting begat more getting. That was how it worked, and if she stopped, extinction. And she would be ready when the next bell rang, but she thought that taking a moment before going on wouldn't do any harm.

The strange fullness she was feeling became a temptation—to decline the seat. Not for spite, per se, but Jennifer didn't really want to go to Ottawa. She wanted others to want her to go. Sitting in her bedroom and thinking back over years of fever-dreams about becoming a Great Leader, she realized now that what she had always desired more than anything else was the evidence that only their electing her could provide. Admission, affirmation. That she was capable of going further, of doing more, than her teeth, her ankles, her farm, allowed for. That *others* thought she warranted a higher position, a wider prominence than being Gus Thickson's heavy-set unmarried daughter vouchsafed. But something else still. That while the rest were all wrapped up with each other and thought the cosmic drama of it all started and ended with them, she could open her lips and swoop down and swallow them up.

Only she wasn't allowed to be satisfied. She knew this much and also that she had to go get more and keep getting more to hold on to any of it. Because, having proven everyone wrong, now she had to keep up the electorate's publicly stated belief that they had done right in sending her to the Hill.

This was maintained openly when Jennifer's elevation was discussed at greasy spoons and in pharmacy-scrip lineups around town in the weeks thereafter, though not without some wonder from citizens at what they'd just done to themselves. Like signing up for a credit card because they were sick of getting the blaring bulging offers in their mailboxes and hoped that would put a stop to it. Most had already lost or pulled off their pink bracelets and forgotten why they had pink-ribbon stickers stuck on their trunks. The difficulty of peeling them off left a small streaked mess, gummy stains, a permanent semi-blank space waiting for the next vital imprint. These residuals of twenty-first-century political involvement.

While sitting in her bedroom in the immediate afterwards, Jennifer felt drowsy, drained from the campaign, from all the back-and-forths with Bokarie these past few months, and from everything before she stumbled onto him in the convenience store and let him join onto her and became his host and entree to Little Caitlin and wider Canada. She liked this little pause before she climbed onward and upward. Before the leech on the leg grew thicker and bolder with blood as by its very nature it had to. She was tired from the campaign and from all the campaigns and from all the readings and longings, but more than anything else, Jennifer realized, she was tired with the future.

With knowing suddenly how much more there was she had to want and go after and gain.

That was when the bell went. The phone started ringing and her father hollered for her to come down and take it because it was long-distance and from Ottawa and this was doubly alarming to him. She dropped the curtains back in front of the window and went down-stairs and accepted that she was in a new kind of race now. Answering, she rejoined the hunt, no longer as predator alone, but also as prey, pursued as she'd never been before. What Now meant the three Rs of politics.

The Reporters: *Good evening, Mizz Thickson, I'm calling from* The Ottawa Citizen *to speak with you about your election victory. Incidentally, I did a piece on your Little Caitlin tragedy a few months back, but I've moved on to Canada–U.S. relations since then while remaining interested in local events such as yours. I understand this drowned little girl was a plank in your platform. So can you tell me your views, please, on softwood lumber?*

The Requesters: *Hi Jennifer, this is Joan from church. We're so proud of you. Congratulations. This is so exciting. Of course we know you'll be very busy in Ottawa, but incidentally, do you know that my husband Phil's trying to get on workers' comp? His file is over at one of the govern-ment buildings taking forever to get processed and Marie is the girl we've been talking to. Nice, but French, you know what I mean? Shall I run over some coffee cake and the chiropractor's report?*

The Rasputins: (1) *Listen, you don't know who this is and this isn't for outside talking and I shouldn't even be using the phone like this given my involvements elsewhere, but I'm taking this chance for you and this community. Let me tell you what you need to do when you get to Ottawa. Let bygones be bygones from this campaign in terms of who was with you and who was against you and do your best for all concerned. And be prepared for everybody and his brother looking to give you advice about how you should vote and what you should support on the Hill, but listen to no one other than yourself and always feel free to call me if you need any sober second thoughts on that. You remember the number at the dealership. Have you thought about your vehicle options for the trip down? I hope you're not thinking about going to Ottawa of all places in that pink grapefruit of yours. A lovely vehicle for town and country driving and also, yes, a symbol of the moving tragedy of that little girl and all, but still. You can think pink but you don't need to drive it anymore! I have a beauty SUV on the lot, incidentally. Import and I know you like those. Low kilometres and lady-driven. Want to come down for a test drive? (2) Mon Jenniferal, I can only talk one moment because I'm on break and tomorrow's milk is coming soon. So please call me soon so we can discuss our plans from here. But congratulations on your glory, which the radio has just announced. You have run the race well and I have been honoured to be there as your every step. But before I go, tell me, when do we leave for the capital city?*

The phone kept going like that and then came the knocks at the door, and things stayed this way right up until Jennifer left for Ottawa a couple of weeks later, crammed in the cab beside Bokarie with her father on the other side. Gus rented a U-Haul to take her down, along with her encyclopedia set, her African, and her desk, bed and dresser. After seeing a lease that in fact confirmed Bokarie was keeping separate quarters, he agreed to let him put his few bags in the back and join them in the cab. Jennifer had kept her promise and invited him along. When she had called him back and told him that, yes, he would be going with her to the capital when the new Parliament was called to order, she had been confused by his immediate response. But Bokarie quickly explained that saying *finally* had meant he could at last quit his job. He had grown tired of all the countertop chit-chat and cherry syrup.

II.

Barb Thickson had stayed back from this first trip, promising to come later and bring Dad and drive the Mary Kay car separately. To see Jennifer's first speech in the Commons. But before the U-Haul left, she pulled Jennifer to the side, while Bokarie easily followed Gus's lead and made up the empty time they had together by scrutinizing the trailer. The two traded man noises about the strength of particular knots and the virtues of never having enough twine and then each muttered compliments on certain angle choices for furniture pieces that the other had suggested and thus they reached a reasonable accommodation. Only if Jennifer came home in a few months showing anything more than some pictures with the prime minister, Gus told Bokarie before letting him into the truck, he reserved himself the right to do what needed to be done with a shotgun wedding—hold the wedding. Bokarie nodded respectfully and told Gus not to worry. His interest in Jennifer was purely political.

Gus thought he had misheard the fellow. Must have said purely *platonic.* He knew this term to mean "just friends," as his buddy the gas station man explained it to him a while back, when Gus mumbled to find out about that gym teacher's type of interest in Jennifer, after that one dinner party. He hadn't called for another date. Platonic friends, the gas station man explained, plus, the poor bastard, he had a baby on the way with some girl he worked with. What with Bokarie's accent and all, Gus decided, it wasn't his fault, the misfire on the word. Gus could grant that much charity—he even felt a little progressive in coming to think of it on his own without prodding from Barb or a television movie.

Meanwhile, by the passenger door, Barb put her hands up on Jennifer's shoulders. She knew what she wanted to say to her daughter, about what winning this election meant for her, for them, for all women like them. She didn't like that first go. This was no women's lib silliness, Barb wanted Jennifer to understand, just something like a not unhappy feeling, that Jennifer had done what others perhaps had wanted, had denied themselves even trying at, from fear and always that next load of laundry to get to. But that was all Barb would say. A crinkle in the nose coming and Gus calling out from the cab that he still needed to gas up before the highway and the price had probably gone up another quarter a litre while they traded sewing secrets made her give a squeeze and send her off.

But Jennifer wanted to say something too, something that reached past casseroles and even ice cream cakes and went all the way back to *Britannica*. To let her mother know that, that— Her face, always so blank and ready to be formed as others wanted it, was close to crumple at this. But genetics being genetics, Barb didn't need *that* to know what it meant between them, and so she nodded with harsh Protestant love and told her daughter to wear extra dress shields her first day in the House so she wouldn't show them any fear.

There wasn't any such fear when Jennifer made her maiden speech in the Commons, at least after she changed her tactics. She had thought having Little Caitlin's family in the gallery, wearing solemn salmon hues and ribbons and wristbands, would be an immediate and great success as her entry onto the national stage. She gestured up to them in the gallery at a key moment in her drainage security plea. While they, exhausted with thanking Miss Thickson again and again for all she'd done for them and their beloved daughter, rose again and nodded and gripped each other's shoulders and sat down and hoped this would be the last of it.

Only this came off as rather banal, since the House of Commons visitors' gallery, Jennifer learned her first day, was chockablock with sad courageous stories waiting to be recognized and redeemed into legislation. Recovering child brides from Vancouver, recovering male ringette players from Flin Flon, recovering real estate agents from

Montreal. The drowned little girl's family from Nipissing–Renfrew–Pembroke was just one more occasion for golf applause. The independent member's proposal for a free vote on a drainage security bill, with a codicil for public safety concerns to be set up across the country during the spring thaw, was duly noted, remanded to committee and sent to an unremarkable death in an unmarked file folder.

Not that she minded, in the end. Because she saw her father, boiled in his Sunday best suit and wearing a new shirt to boot, get up from his perch in the gallery and exit, looking irritated when Jennifer was cut off and thanked for her contribution to the day's business. It was only later that afternoon, while giving her parents a tour of Centre Block, during which time Gus and Barb managed to touch absolutely nothing, that Jennifer learned that Gus had been afflicted by pricks from a missed pin in the collar of the fancy button-down shirt Barb had bought him for the occasion of their daughter's parliamentary debut. And this she took as *finally* evidence of her father's love: that he'd endured the little pricks and pocks into his neck-flesh so he could hear his little girl say her piece in the country's fine proceedings, and he only got up to leave when she looked to be done, so he could see about the nicks.

But when Gus got up, Jennifer saw that Bokarie was seated behind him, had been blocked out by his navy blue bulk. Watching, waiting to be unfurled. She had forgotten him for a moment or two, but when she caught his face it came back to her, what she'd been thinking at her rally about Africa, and also from her recent reading in the parliamentary library about the fragile mystique of immigrants' homelands and the necessary importance Canadians placed on hearing their stories. This was material she had been waiting to use at the Governor General's tea for new MPs that she had been invited to attend a couple of weeks later. But why wait? There had already been a few speeches about peacekeepers that afternoon and a few non-partisan crescendos about the need to start a discussion about how to do more than simply talk about Africa. She had material to work with in spades. So she didn't sit down. She cut Mr. Speaker off mid-sentence like the glorified middle school hall monitor he was and then told the House about Bokarie and the pink dawn of his home-land, and there was some real listening in the chamber for a minute or so and then hole-in-one applause when Bokarie, asked to stand and smile and wave, gazed down on them all from the gallery, so beatific and blessed to be part of this little pageant.

III.

She was feeling a little light in the head, like back when she was a child and would go with her father to gas up the truck. She liked the plastic bubble with the fuzzy red balls. These, her father told her, were gas station Adam's apples, and when they were moving, it meant the pump was feeding. Like a bird, she had thought then, swallowing something. She had wanted a touch, a taste of them badly, but then Gus Thickson would come out from paying and she would go with him back into the cab, already gorged on the sweet low-slung smell of the pumps at their business. In Ottawa now, this was what she did— not thinking about home, but thinking from home. To make sense of things while adjusting to these surroundings, to have no newness to deal with, to face only recall.

She was, at present, fumed up by being in Rideau Hall for the first time, with its sprawling, sweetish fragrance of fresh carnations and thick, figured carpets and pinkish, high-browed butlers and, more than anything else, by waiting to meet the Governor General. But also by the aftershave and breath mints and new-suit smell squirming beside her.

To avoid charges from the West and from Quebec about Ontario MPs monopolizing the premium face time, the Bytown mandarins had made a point of shuffling geography in arranging the place cards for this year's Governor General's New MP Tea, which took place shortly after the opening of Parliament. Accordingly, Jennifer had been placed beside a short, loud, toothy Nova Scotia lawyer and part-time boxing promoter. He had a special interest in juvenile delinquents with violent streaks. George Damariscotta Jr., QC, MP for Pictou–Antigonish–Guysborough. He had been elected by a riding split between satisfied clients and outraged opponents, who were now collectively hopeful that he would do in Ottawa what he had done for and to them. The closest thing to a challenger had been a divorced lady high school vice-principal who ran on the old pro-Native/anti-casino platform. She had received Christian applause during debates.

Listening to him thump on a table and list his community service awards and Rotarian spheres of influence, Jennifer studied his crackling cockscomb. It looked like a greasy grill done over in powdered milk. And he couldn't keep still, shifting back and forth as his tongue grooved on and the polycotton pinstripes of his pants went swish and swoosh against his bellied thighs. He wasn't worth much, she decided. Small fry. Baitfish. Jennifer wondered if everyone from Down East was just this way. With rapid-fire monologue and much jostling and jigging and *come here and listen to this, buy,* and *just between you and me* and compulsively wiping the nose. She couldn't think of anybody like that back in the riding, except Judas Hollerwatty or maybe that gym teacher Romeo. The comparison did little for any of them, and anyway, now wasn't the time to be thinking about anything other than the great flutter coming her way.

Madame GG, as she was known to Rideau Hall staff and assorted colleagues and admirers, was a birdish and precise woman in both official languages. She was fond of Persian shawls and Madison Avenue saucer hats and First Nations peoples and outfitted herself accordingly. Watching her work the line, Jennifer was impressed. To each new MP she gave a cocked head at the interesting story about the local riding followed by a syncopated eyebrow-raising smile at the personal anecdote and then a gushing nod *yes indeed how very exciting all of this was* to the fumbled admission of nerves and now the clipboarded Ojibwa stepped in *oh too bad it was time to move on but let's talk some more when you're settled into Ottawa.* Leaving them all wriggling and flush in her wake. Effective. Jennifer was ready for some of it and long waiting to give back a little herself.

But when Madame GG finally introduced herself and congratulated each of them, Nova Scotia came out ready and hard and loud. His hand clutching his teacup with antic violence, he right away started in on a peaty story about how he and his brothers "used to take tea and toast at 2 a.m. before loadin' up the smelt and goin' out on the trawlers with our pops and his brothers back oh way back when we were growin' up in God's country as we call it out there you really should come visit us. So this was something"—tears in the wheel wells, a hard swallow and then vigorous, then thoughtful nodding—"this was *some thing*, drinkin' this tea in this grand room so many years later with the grand likes of you, Madame. If only me pops and brothers"—but there had been a bad storm and heart disease in the family and Coast Guard cutbacks—"could see us now," etc.

With the intelligent vacancy of an experienced public figure, Madame GG went through her prix fixe of responses to George Jr.'s spray before finishing up with "A few 2 a.m. sessions of toast and tea just might keep you up in this coming session of Parliament!" Winking, impish sagacity, vouchsafed by the totemic status of her office. Sensing a clever joke that he was included in, Damariscotta Jr. slapped himself on the knees and reared up, ululating in his briny brogue, his blue eyes bulging, throat pulsing, rum nose reddening.

Madame GG banked over to Jennifer. Jaunty George Jr., squirming and searching in vain for something else to say, had no choice but to stall. He backhanded a slice of quiche into his mouth like a puck of fried cod. Jennifer was waiting, issues and topics loaded, her fork ready with much twisting and turning in her fingers. Leaning in and down to engage the Governor General, Jennifer inhaled the sweet eau of Anglican girls' school and honorary degrees and husband money and ladies' golf and hospital foundations that was variously swabbed and daubed around the golden neck and lobes. Jennifer was ready for this, for all of this. In immediate preparation, she had balanced two buttery fiddleheads on the tips of the tines. When Madame GG looked up into her, how well Jennifer guided the fork and its freight into her mouth! That librarian with her doilies and Shakespeare, that Miss Spill-something would have been pleased. But Jennifer had to stop going back to her beginnings like this. If she was going to get anything more, she had to stay in the moment of this Ottawa reception hall. Her latest getting place. The best so far.

The Governor General was relieved to be nearer again civilization, but just as she started up with Jennifer, she was forced to adjust her hat and shield herself from George Jr.'s volley of crust flakes, broccoli bits, Gruyère shreds and piped-up questions about "An East Coast visit sometime soon for Madame?"

When little came in the way of response, he broke out the top-shelf stuff: his explanation of the native son who'd recently moved to Ottawa for work, the one-time middleweight champion of Eastern Canada don't you know, Antigonish's very own Ricky Rhinehart. Whose nickname, on account of his unfortunate mixed-race background, "was Zebra Muscles, but also this is a political statement about the understudied state of the freshwater fisheries back home, speakin' of which if you'd like to meet him or talk sturgeon I can arrange …"

Madame GG's face gripped at its rouged corners from these rising, trilling decibels, but she remained target on, head cocked and eyebrows set on Jennifer's round and empty and expectant face. She did break away for a moment, to signal to her attendant, who quickly bivouacked before George Jr. and held him back with a good Gananoque glare.

Madame GG refocused on Jennifer, looming above her. She asked the fork-fine young woman about the striking pink sash that she had wrapped over one of her arms and about the fabulously matching pink scarf tied round her hair. Who swallowed decisively and then mobilized her explanation. A little girl, the rising creek, a sudden African. Think Pink.

"Oh wait, wait now, you want to talk 'bout drownin'? Nowhere this side of Labrador got as many men lost in the full fathom deep dark blue than we do! And hey, we got *them* too! From way long back! From slave times come up from down in the States there! I even got my boxing boy Ricky, the one I just was mentioning, I got him a job over at Parks and Rec, if you want to come see him with me!" So Antigonish had tried, one last time, squirting round the attendant. But it was in vain. Jennifer was in control, shaking Madame GG's hand and broadening her shoulders to wedge herself in front of the mint-fresh gill-blown Aqua Velva flop from God's Country. Now forgotten.

Gripping the Governor General's rosehipped fingers, Jennifer said she knew and hoped they would have cause to see each other again. She offered to introduce Her Excellency to the courageous African. Madame GG immediately assured her that, having heard good and interesting things about Jennifer's inaugural speech and visual presentation in the Commons, she would be honoured to meet such a sad, uplifting story.

Feeling large with the idea that she was already gaining a reputation in this town, Jennifer went after and caught another brow cock as the Governor General and her assistants readied to push on to their next pair—a teeth-bearing Albertan bursting around the stitches of his corset-tight Stampede vest with statistics about federal transfers, and a self-medicating, fair-trading Vancouverite who had successfully run on the platform of handing over his own riding to Aboriginal self-governance. Jennifer noted that the African couldn't be with them today because he had gone on a skating excursion along the canal with some schoolchildren from the riding.

"Don't worry, my dear, I know," Madame GG said, departing. "You promise much. Think Pink."

"Yes, that's right," Jennifer answered, greedy to hear such a one as this say her phrase. Which was why she kept going for more and more, calling out as the shawl-clad shoulders turned away, "But do you know that, in Africa, pink means the colour of the dawn? So beautiful and yet so sad given all the problems over there, where a Canadian presence is clearly lacking. So yes, Think Pink, Madam, and think about where that—where we could go with that."

The Governor General made a note of this young woman from the outer regions and of her intriguing appendage as possible add-ons for her proposed junket to Africa, which was pending prime ministerial approval. The government was in fact very willing to send her to a donors' conference on behalf of the national interest. The Governor General's office was ideal for what was wanted from a Canadian mission to Africa. The thin power of a photogenic figurehead. A pliable young MP with a ductile connection to the homeland would be a nice touch, Madame GG decided, and being nice to an independent never hurt a minority government. She would include all this in her final pitch to the PMO. Plus, Think Pink, with its ancient folkloric fullness thus explained, was grander and a little punchier than the rather cumbersome slogan her staff had worked up for the trade and aid conference she was hoping and planning to lead that winter. *Quid Pro Quo: The Third World Needs More Canada!*

10

CROSSOVERS

I.

The blades slung over his shoulder, he ducked into the metal hut. Inside was the man he'd been instructed to seek out. His back was turned to him; he was hunched over a table studying something; perhaps it was a map of the river outside the door. With all the yelling and shrieking and bodies thudding to the ground, the man at the table didn't seem to notice his visitor come in. He didn't turn around at the boot-crunching sound of the approach, the blades swinging down into the hands. But he must have recognized the sound, old steel rasping against old steel. He twisted and looked up and smiled and Bokarie's face went slack, dumbfounded, the colour draining. At who, at what, was standing in front of him in this shed.

"Want to get your skates sharpened? Sorry, buddy, I didn't hear you come in, I was just checking today's ice report, you know, to see how much of the canal is frozen through and through. Looks pretty good, incidentally—feels like January around here already and it's only November! What's wrong there, cat got your tongue? Or is it that you don't speak English? No offence intended, of course.

166

Anyways, it looks like the girl at the rental desk gave you some pretty rusty blades there! Not her fault—it's not often we get adults who show up without their own, so what we have on hand are usually pretty old. Yours look like they're from Original Six days or something though! But that's probably why she sent you in here. Nobody sharpens skates better along the Rideau Canal than yours truly, Ricky Rhinehart, ex–middleweight champion of Eastern Canada. Perhaps you've heard of me by my ring name, Zebra Muscles. I was even the under undercard for a few late night boxing shows on the Sports Channel a while back. You might know that, depending what channels you get.

"But it doesn't seem like you're picking up what I'm putting down, so let's just get to business then. If this is your first time out on the ice, you're not going to get too far on the canal with your steel in that shape. Especially with the school buses coming in today, all the kiddies out there leaving the ice about as smooth as a Québécois girl's legs in February. You didn't get that one neither, huh? Kay-Beck-Kwa. Nothing? Well, that's okay too in point of fact, you know, you're probably lucky that you didn't. Still nothing, eh? All right, be the silent type and just hand 'em over and I'll see what we can do ya for with the old whetting machine."

This was as long as Bokarie had been quiet before a fellow—well, a fellow what?—since coming to Canada. Too much was getting blended and mashed together and he wasn't in control of it, not just yet at least. First there was the sound of the man's talking: it was that saltwater singsong, the same *so forth* and *so on* that the immigration men had done in that deliciously named Newfoundland, back when they'd first flashed their torches on him extravagantly cowering in the bottom of the tanker with the rest of the asylum seekers. But then there was also the look of this man, which didn't make sense with that sound. And something else about it too. The face didn't look exactly like one of his brothers or his cousin, but close enough, given present standards, just with a little more meat on the bone. Bokarie himself had added a little flub around the waist and some chub in the small of the back and a bit of thrum to his thighs since coming to Canada. But he hadn't really noticed it much, being little bulge by comparison with the jut and girth of the host bodies around him. His own weight gain, however, made it plausible that this could be one of them, even if he knew—*no, he knew*—it couldn't be one of his blood men from back home.

Still, this reaching back there to explain away this man standing here, in front of him, was evidence of how puzzled Bokarie had become. He didn't know how to proceed and couldn't exactly call anyone for fresh coordinates. Because, except for bathroom mirrors and the music and sports channels of the television, he had never seen one in Canada before. And for the first time he could remember, ever, he couldn't find any words to come back with, to subdue, to take over.

"I—I—they—they—" was as much as he could manage as he handed the skates over. He didn't know what to say to another black man, or, better still, how to say to another black man. Over here. He was unclear as to what behaviour was expected, required, what codes were to be followed.

So he made a tactical retreat to the corner of the hut while the man went to work on the skates. He started thinking about how much faster things would have proceeded back in the Upriver region had they had such a machine to keep their blades sharp. Yes, he liked that, it was reassuring to juxtapose, to laugh at two places while hovering between them, lording himself over his nations past and present. But the suspension didn't hold for long. The idea insisted on playing itself out.

Maybe if his men had been more efficient in their machete work during the last stages of the National Restitution Campaign, the General wouldn't have lost his patience and stopped taking his calls.

And maybe then the General wouldn't have made that deal with the President to take care of the evildoers to the north butchering innocents of that noble tribe. And maybe then the General and President wouldn't have agreed to the terms the visiting pink-meaty American senator had proposed for reconciliation between the executive and military branches of the government in exchange for freedom and defence contracts. And maybe then the General wouldn't have tried to cover his tracks by buying Bokarie's blood men with Canadian passports so they would come carve at him. And maybe then Bokarie wouldn't have had to do to them what they required of him to do, when the first came into the shed and cut him and the second protested he had nothing to do with it and was unconvincing, and the third helped him across the river without mentioning the men he'd arranged to be waiting on the other side. And maybe then— But stop this! Stop this! What good was there in going on like this? That past was another country. It had to be.

Yes, that's right, Bokarie thought, he wasn't back-bloody scrambling through underbrush to get away from the just-in-case execution squad his cousin had arranged to greet them when they made it over the river into a neighbouring country. His current difficulties were a too-long lineup for hot chocolate and doing something about rusty skate blades, since the children visiting Ottawa from town had insisted on his joining them on the ice, where they would return the favour of his soccer lessons the summer before. All of which meant he didn't need to wield and whip around all those old *maybes*; he wasn't confined to thinking from and about there. He also wasn't confined to keeping it all at bay at all times, either, as he'd realized by the creek that day before Jennifer's successful close to her campaign. That, *this*, was the gift of immigration. The adjustment of memory into identity. Selectively. Because in the weeks since, he'd moved to Ottawa to take up his position as aide-de-camp for MP Thickson and was successfully mixing up and blending this and that together, and liking what and where it was getting him.

Only now, what to make of a black man already here in the capital city when he had presumed to be the only one, to be the lone coffee bean in the flour bin capable of brewing something up among all the blandness? Was this skate sharpener someone who'd beaten him to it? How was he to respond? Tribute? Alliance? Appeal for advice? Bottle to the face? Skate to the neck?

Bokarie's every previous encounter since coming to Canada suddenly seemed so effortless. There was the quick pull at the heart-strings by nodding with shame and pain at the cable-cobbled stories they gave him, his letting them console away any need to say who and what he really was by showing just a little extra meekness and grin-ning here and showy inferiority and incapacity there. To pacify and empower and overpower.

This was a method he'd plied with much success back in his old town and more so since moving to a studio apartment even higher above the earth in the capital. To lull everyone he met into continu-ing to take him for what they wanted him to be, from Jennifer down. Because he needed this time, this space, to figure out what magic he'd need to make things work to his advantage in Ottawa. Because beyond the statues of dead British people and the outrage that American politicians inspired and the fawning that American busi-nessmen brought out in the natives whenever they swooped into town, Ottawa wasn't really that much like the capital city back home in Atwenty. Not that he knew very much of that place anyway, only reports on the transistor and the one visit, when he met the General, who had judged his brimstone and bottle-work talent enough to lead the cleanup effort in the Upriver region and then gave him all those fine promises along the route, of a victorious return to the capital. As governor, no less. But why was he still going on about all of that when there was so much waiting for him here and now? Probably because he was watching a black man sharpen a blade and the bastard at his business kept sending him back there. He stepped outside the hut for a moment, bracing his nose against the constant shock of Canadian winter and then taking short breaths to calm down, and tried to recall his recent progress. Recollect what he could get if he played this right.

He had accepted that he wasn't going to be a governor here. He wasn't even sure they had such things in Canada. But this was no defeat, since Bokarie had quickly decided upon reaching Ottawa that he had no interest in ever jumping into that bucket of crabs Jennifer had joined in going to Parliament. There was just no appreciation for fine speech making in the national politics. He had sat in on a couple of sessions and even been a stage prop for Jennifer's first speech. Which, admittedly, he had enjoyed, looming above an adoring crowd for a few moments, waving and smiling down at them. Only there was no style in any of it, the applause was cheaply won and then he was forgotten and the circus went on at maximum tilt. Just Mr. Speaker this and Mr. Speaker that and point of parliamentary procedure this and would the respectable that, and all the while the rest of them screeching and howling and gesturing and jumping up and down like three hundred minor primates in permanent heat and hunger.

Sharing his confusion about how Parliament heard or did anything with the office manager for another MP, Bokarie had been told in tones earnest and teacherly that even if it looked and sounded like nursery school chaos, Canadian politics was about passionately constructive dialogue and mutual accountability. Unlike less advanced places—and here a finger distinctly pointed south—politics wasn't all rabble-rousing and back-stabbing and throat-cutting and thundering invocations from the Bible to make everything all right. Bokarie nodded and felt a little tempted by the latter description, but not enough to try getting across that border. Instead, he decided to be done with working his audiences into raging and rampaging and ready fear and undying adoration for now. If he ever wanted a fix, he could coach youth soccer.

Giving up on his path to such glory was no cause for despair. An alternative had presented itself and he had worked up a way of describing it that made it acceptable to him. He had heard many intriguing things in staff cafeterias and office supply depots about where the real power resided in Ottawa. It was in something called a bureaucrat. It sounded like an ideal set-up. The bureaucrat ruled a region already subdued and his alone, with any number of seconds and thirds and fourths and so on beneath him. And having met some of these young men and women, young and blond and bland and taking weekend courses in French and PowerPoint to get ahead, Bokarie could tell that he wouldn't have to promise any DVDs or local virgins for *their* loyalty. Nor would he have any betrayals on his hands. These types were simply too content with what they called making a difference to be tempted to a takedown.

There were many bureaucrats in Ottawa, he had discovered from further inquiries, amazed once again at how much there was to be had here, how impossible and unnecessary it would be for any one person to try to hoard it all, which explained the easy peace that held among them. Apparently there wasn't much speech making involved in the position, though he wasn't as disappointed by this as he might have been. By all accounts one's mouth was always too full to talk. That was more than acceptable to him, after he'd finally determined he would never find a refined-enough hearing for his words. And anyway it was time he grew past the clever limber boy on the orphanage wall doing his fancy words and fine moves for a few passing whores. After all, the General and the President rarely said much from their respective thrones, and they sported barrel chests and cannonball bellies much like the bureaucrats he'd seen around

Ottawa, a juxtaposition suggesting that this was the universal stuff and stuffing of Great Men. And finally, most gloriously, Bokarie had discovered that bureaucrats outlived popes and elephants. There were no revolutions or alliances to worry over, no betrayals and broken promises, just a working group to expand via new initiatives, committees to strike, breakout sessions to generate, and revision and renewal and revitalization when in doubt. The words weren't worthy of Job, Bokarie allowed, but the life was certainly easier.

It was just a matter of biding his time until the opportunity for such an elevation came about, and he was willing to do this by greeting schoolchildren from the riding on behalf of Miss Thickson as they made their field trips to Ottawa for ice-skating, among other duties.

But now there was this dark complication to his plans, who had just switched off his machine and called Bokarie back into the hut, where he was holding the blades ready for him. They gleamed and Bokarie wondered how it would feel to have such contraptions tied to his feet while he did a little dance. He readied to ask the oh so innocent worried question about cutting through ice with knife boots. This would bring the native to a pitying smile and tender explanation, which would in turn let him maintain the space apart for himself that he'd come to enjoy while his various homegrown respondents jerked and danced around to his words and slinks, all the while thinking they were in control. Only he didn't think he was the one in command this time. Because Bokarie wasn't sure what it meant for this black man standing across from him to be homegrown.

The man hadn't even given him anything much of the Look when he first turned around to find Bokarie waiting for him, blades in hand. As if he didn't care about the where and the what and the how and the why of an African standing in a skate-sharpening hut beside the Rideau Canal. And Bokarie was a little offended by this, but more than that, nervous. Because the real difficulty with this briny-tongued black man was that he didn't fit the terms Bokarie had devised for playing with the new and the old.

II.

"Thank you for these. And here is your payment. But before I go, may I ask you a question?" he ventured, accepting the heavy boots and holding the sharp bottoms away from him, his voice tinny and empty because he still didn't know what the filling should be this time.

"You just did, chief!"

Well played. He wondered what it meant that this man was calling him chief. Simple sarcasm, like when the doughy teenagers back home used it on him at his old job? But now *that* was back home, he was thinking from there? Things were confusing, breaking down, his gyring ascent turning to tailspin. Truths needed to be established, identities determined, understandings reached.

"Yes, that was a question. Now let me ask you another. Where are you from?"

"You're assuming I'm not from around here, aren't ya?"

"Yes."

"From what, my accent?"

"Yes, and other things."

"Like what? Or no, wait, let me ask you a question. Are *you* from around here?"

"No. Can't you tell that?"

"Sure. From your accent and from other things. So where are you from, then?"

"A land far away from here."

"That sounds nice. Hey, me too, chief!"

"Please, why did you just call me chief?"

"Because that's what we call people back where I'm from."

"Which is where?"

"Back east."

"How far back east?"

"About as far back east as it gets!"

"So yes, you mean—you mean Africa?"

"Jesus, Mary and Joseph, no! I mean Antigonish! But then again, in a sense, yes, aren't we all, when you go back far enough and think deep enough about it, from Africa?"

"Yes, indeed, we are all from Africa in the end. You are very wise."

Ah, a philosopher. Bokarie liked this. He could dismiss it with gratitude and admiration. He'd had *everything's out of Africa* conversations a few times since coming to Ottawa, usually with natty students from the university who approached him in coffee shops to tell of their multiple readings of *Things Fall Apart*.

He commended and thanked them and wondered if this book people kept mentioning was part of the movie he'd heard about from other Canadians when they wanted to share their African cultural experience with him. It made sense, from the title. What else would a Coke bottle do when it fell from the sky? But still, they were simply better-educated variations on his usual marks, and this skate sharpener wasn't. He didn't even seem concerned about their being two black men here in the hut together. This nettled him. He wanted, had, to know what *he* made of this, and so Bokarie broke with precedent and didn't just nod at the deep thought and happy huff about Africa and move on to his next Canadian. He needed more out of this exchange. Seeing a grin on the black man's face, Bokarie wondered if he was getting a little of his own game here, by someone better at it, no less. No, not possible.

"Yes, you're right, we're all from Africa, this is true, and also wise by the depths of the ages. But you say you are from a place called Antigone Fish, Mr. ..., Mr. ..."

"It's Antigonish, and say it Annie-gone-ish if you want to sound local by the by, and anyway call me Ricky, Ricky Rhinehart. Some folks called me Zebra Muscles back when I was still boxing, even if there was no sign yet they'd gone through the St. Lawrence seaward into the salt water, but still, it worked background-wise, which is why we went with it. But that's a little Down East shop talk, sorry, and anyway I suspect you won't be doing that, calling me Zebra Muscles, and not because you're a marine biologist and stickler for the details. Am I right?"

An opening. An implication. Some awareness of something not being right. Bokarie attacked, ignorant of the damage a rope-a-dope could do.

"Why not? Why wouldn't I call you Zebra Muscles? Do you think it would make me uncomfortable to use such a term?" Bokarie was surprised at how much force he brought in saying this. There was challenge and even hurt in his voice, and a little more than he wanted, even if he was happy Rhinehart had committed the magical cardinal sin and made a reference to African wildlife as a means of understanding him. He also sensed, with little pride, that his behaviour in response was all very Canadian, just like his choosing the life of a bureaucrat over a Great Man career. Comfortable, fully funded. Very Canadian. He thought about his options. When his first inclination was to file a discrimination complaint with an ombudsperson, he shuddered and cringed at this successful adjustment to national life. Then he went defiant and wanted to recover his once-grand anger. He showily laughed and started wondering how sharp these blades were and whether he could summon a good passage from Ezekiel to bring down fury and hard cold steel on this his foe. After which he spat and stamped and readied to charge, but the man could sense this anger and squared his shoulders and beat him there too. Big shoulders.

"Okay now, calms yourself down a little there—no reason to get worked up. That was just a joke, a little icebreaker, if you understand. But if you're thinking of throwing down, I should probably tell you that 32-22-15 aren't my measurements but my fights record, if you catch my drift, unless you'd rather catch my left hook if that's how you'd like to finish this conversation. Your call. Chief."

He could tell from the tone of the man's talking and the size behind it that smudging his foot over the plug of phlegm he'd just left on the hut floor was the right thing to do. At which point he dropped his skates and slumped down against the wall and winced at the cold comfort and the everywhere hardness of it. If this Rhinehart fellow took a swing at him now and things ended, so be it.

He'd had a good run, but he was tired of the game of it, this life-long desire to climb up and get noticed and always stay in front of the rest. Only to find someone else ahead of him to overcome with his willingness to moult as they wanted—Father Alvaro, Uncle, the General, Hollerwatty, the immigration officers and the Haitian lady and his fellow graduates from that weekend's ADJUST ME program, the old ladies who came to him at the convenience store. Jennifer. And there were all the living and the dead—his brothers and cousin, the others at the orphanage, his ex-girl Elizabeth, the warlord Foday, that Marigold whom he'd saved, the boys he'd led into the Upriver region, the men and women and children busted through and burned up and buried shallow while his freedom fighters were moving through there, then that Liberian he befriended to choke in the belly of the tanker, Little Caitlin and the adoring crowd at that first rally, the sticky-fingered kids and their mums at his soccer clinic, the beery busty bride and her wedding guests, the Vietnamese girl and the casserole king, the probable voters in the grocery store lineups and the cheering chanting supporters at that rally the night before the election. And now all the fresh easy meat to be had in Ottawa. So many audiences, all dying for more from him, but he was done, finally, emptied out, kaput, dropped to the floor by someone too strong, too sharp to take on and win over with his windbag of tricks.

A few moments later the man bent beside him, a cup of hot chocolate held forth, a bright red hockey helmet cradled under one arm. Like an Eden apple with a built-in mouthguard.

"Listen, my old pastor told me that every man comes to a Samaritan moment in his life. I've had plenty, but most I passed on by just knocking a fellow out. But it looks to me like you could use a little help, so let's just drop our little bout of sparring and come to it. You're not sure what to make of the fact that we're a couple of coal lumps in a snowbank, right? And I knew this all along, could tell from the look on your face when you first come in—it's a look I'm used to because most folks don't expect to find the likes of me working in a place like this. And I'm guessing you're probably in the same boat, pardon the expression—they just don't know what to make of you, which makes it hard on a man because eventually even an ex-boxer, mind you, gets to thinking what he's to make of himself too. And believe you me, I've tried all the options they give you. So let me take a minute here and tell you about it just so you don't go wasting the middle rounds of your life doing the same. Take all this for what it's worth, it's the sum total of my wisdom. Well, that and how to get past the line for hot chocolate. But that's a tale for another day." He winked and made grabby and squeezy motions with his big hands for a few moments, and Bokarie could imagine the counter girl's anatomy well enough, but then the man started talking again, in the blustery twang of a folk philosopher.

"The problem with existence, see, is this here: it gets mighty confusing being black in this place. Because you're always seeing the world three different ways. First, there's just how you look out your peepers in the morning. Second, there's how you know white folks think you're looking out. Third, there's how they think you *should* be looking out. By the by, it's okay for me to say 'they' since I'm one of them too. My mum's people are mutt French Scottish. Though it's always my dad's side that's considered all-important. He's black Acadian. They moved up north and settled in the late 1700s, not so much to stay under the Crown as to get away from all the bullwhips that came with the Declaration of Independence. But let me tell you why I know all this, since that's getting closer to what I think of as the three-eye thing that goes on in Canada, so far as I can see.

"I know my black history because back when I was in seventh grade, me and the other two black kids got pulled out of class one time by a guidance counsellor. Before that, I didn't think too much about anything other than regular twelve-year-old-boy stuff—lifting bottles of communion wine from the vestry, practising tongue-kissing against my palms, convincing Dad to let me stay up past the second period of the hockey game—but then I was told that I had to start thinking about who and what I was. And how to do it, too.

"The guidance counsellor who pulled us out of class says to us how important it is to know our history. I get smart and says shouldn't we get back to our lesson about old Nellie McClung, then? She smiles and says no no *your* history, and then she gives us all some books about black people in Canada and America and apologizes. She says someday these will be accepted as part of the standard—what do you call—curriculum and story of our nation, but until then they were ours to learn from and there was no need to attend the regular history class anymore.

"And so I'm no idiot, I do the math and figure there's something sweet in having a little black magic to play with, and I start thinking it's a pot of gold being Afro-Canadian, even if I wear my hair close-cropped. Soon enough I don't bother much with the books she gave me, but I start working with what I see on the television. O'course everyone else was doing the same back then, the white kids and the black kids and the Natives who came to school regular enough, but I was a big boy and the talking with my fingers shaped like guns and shoving pencils and picks into my grown-out hair—it all just fit better on me than on the rest of them. And so I started talking that way too, all barky and referring to myself in the third person. *Yo Ricky won't be playing this* and *Yo Ricky ain't down with that.* Meanwhile, though, I was standing behind it all, you know what I mean, just giggling at how teachers were suddenly nervous about me coming down the hall when they were alone and at girls boasting that they weren't scared of doing the seven-in-heaven closet game with me at the basement parties that single-parent kids got to throw *even* if their dads found out. Which I took them up on, of course. Soon my classmates were calling me Yoricky, which stuck until I started boxing and my manager decided we'd get more wagers on our side if I had something more patriotic but still a little wink-wink about the race stuff too, so that's where Zebra Muscles come from, and I'm hoping by now even if you know nothing about the fisheries you've at least figured something out about why a kid with parents like mine gets a nickname like that.

"Speaking of which, you know my dad used to cuff me good on the head when I went all big black and bad and he kept asking who the hell was running that school if it let me go on pretending I'm some Uncle Sambo and then he said that if I keep that up instead of my grades he'll just toss me down into the melting pot. Mum just didn't know what to make of me anymore, poor girl, and I didn't help matters much when we'd go over to her side's for Boxing Day break-fast and I'd call Granny my nigger when she made those butter tarts I liked with the chocolate chips in 'em instead of raisins. And even if Granny couldn't even hear me, I knew everyone else could.

"School wasn't going so hot around then. The papers and tests I handed in were whiter and whiter the blacker I got, but I'm not going to sit here and say it gotta be the shoes that made me flunk tenth grade science. Problem was, I was too happy just yessing along with the guidance counsellors and the music videos. They just set it all up and I could walk right into a pretty good situation easy enough. But after a while it starts to get to me, because soon I can tell that, sure, while I'm getting away with everything I want by playing the roles they give me, like the Underserved Youth, that's *all* I'm getting, you know? My every move already explained and taken care of and excused away. So I start hitting out at it, in a manner of speaking, trying to make a break with it all, but it's no better than a few rounds of shadow boxing. Because they got me there too, saying that Black Male Rage is also culturally understandable. This gets me even more pissed off, and eventually I get into a little ugliness at a mall one day and now I'm a Troubled Youth and eventually it's a Hip-Hop skip school and jump an old man to your standard Unidentified Black Male. That's when I meet my court-appointed buddy Mr. Damariscotta Jr., who tells me that if I want to go on embracing my heritage, I should make a little money doing it and stay out of jail to boot, and the best way was to take up boxing, which I did under his management after he got me off on the assault charges.

"And I'm not about to bore you with all my fights stories from the Maritimes circuit, but suffice to say I'm not doing commercials for orange juice and french fries like the really successful athletes in this country, and when the gloves didn't work no more I did what the rest of the East Coast does at least once in each life. Like the Muslims to their Mecca, I came west looking for work and damned near got trampled by everybody else doing the same. Actually, my situation was easier than that, truth be told, since I'm telling the rest anyway. My old lawyer and boxing manager, Mr. Damariscotta, he just got some work up on Parliament and he made some calls to Parks and Rec for me, which is how I got set up here. But anyway, I know I've been going on and I apologize, but it's rare you get to talk shop like this, if you're catching what I'm throwing.

"But before I let you go, I will tell you one more thing I've figured out. It has to do with something in common between years in the ring and a lifetime looking at yourself three ways. They both make you punch-drunk. Because after all the fighting you tend to forget things, and then when you go to figure out, say, which one of Yoricky and Zebra Muscles and Uncle Sambo and the Underserved and the Unidentified you really are when the rounds are up and the decision comes in, you get right dizzy just from the trying and all the masks become part of the actor's face, as the old saying goes. You need to sit down and take a sip of water and some smelling salts and then you wonder why you ever went into the ring in the first place. You ask whether it really was worth it to get out of second-period history to spend the rest of your time working away at this lead punching bag they keep in front of us. Identity."

Then he held up the hockey helmet, gazed on it.

"Alas, poor Yoricky, mediocre Zebra Muscles and the mixed-up rest, not to mention sad yours truly, Ricky Rhinehart. If only we had some kind of helmet to get through all this jiving and infinite jesting we've been doing, it might have made it easier to get past all the stories this place wants to give me about myself. Because all the court jestering I did for others and all the giggling it gave me just left me feeling socked in the gut and worked over on the ribs, and that's why I wanted done with it. That's why nowadays I'm just another regular Ottawa guy, working hard and living in a basement apartment, nice and invisible. But I wish I had one of these helmets a while back. And I'm giving it to you right now, not to keep in who knows how many stories they've already given you, but to keep out as many more as you can.

"Because—and stay with me if you can because I'm really talking about life here—when you're out skating and you got your helmet on, nobody's gonna see you for what they want to see you as, which means nobody's gonna tell you what you should see yourself as. And more important, when you hit some bumpy ice and you go down—and everybody, buddy, everybody goes down at some point, don't forget that—this way you won't crack your head open. So here you go and good luck to you out there. It can feel mighty crowded some-times and everybody knows what they're doing and they're going to want to give you pointers on this and advice on that because that's what polite Canadians do, but do your best to duck and weave and remember that you didn't sign no papers saying you had to spend the rest of your life figuring out who and what you are. End of the day, it don't really matter, does it? Because"—here he stood up and his face recomposed into its grinning easygoing mask—"you know as well as I do, we're all from Africa. Right, chief?"

Bokarie finished the rest of his hot chocolate and then accepted the helmet and shook hands and let himself be pulled up. He smiled awkwardly, nodded jerkily. He had nothing to say. And gratefully so.

He left the hut, the skates dangling once more from a shoulder and the blades now sharp and scissoring against each other. He enjoyed how his boots, grinding for tread into the snow, made a backbeat. He liked the back-and-forth music of it, for itself. His head was free territory as he stepped over to a bench to lace up. He would try this ice-skating.

III.

Before he had his boots off, he was surrounded, jammed in with the schoolchildren from the riding, who had been looking for him all this time and wondering, in between games of tag and pantsing each other on the ice, why he was gone so long at the rental counter. There were little ice picks of snot freeze-dried and hanging down and flash-smeared across their upper lips. He didn't say much in response, but that was no matter—they were delirious with anticipation at getting their African onto the ice and teaching and pulling him around with the beginner's rope they'd found. One of the bigger boys was dangling it in front of him, the bulbous knotted end in his face. Waiting for him. As Bokarie tightened the skates and then waited while they were tested and tightened by a succession of the waist-high experts, things grew heavier. All the while the children argued back and forth loudly about who was going to pull him around first and what was the best approach to teaching him how to stop and whether he should be expected to do crossovers his first time out and what was fairer, culturally speaking, expecting him to be able to do crossovers this first time out or not. Some of them were in intermediate social studies.

For all manner of safety Bokarie donned the helmet and readied to move. The crowd around him slumped a little at the concealment and banality, knowing that he had done the right thing in wearing the headgear but feeling a little underwhelmed by this evident lack of daring from their beloved summer mascot, the mad tosser of empty bottles, the flashy climber of retirement home walls, the quicksilver footman of the soccer ball. All this, but now, standing up and moving, he was teetering towards the ice like a baby sister. The disappointment was corrected for very quickly when a weight of fluttering hands came to his rescue, landing on his wrists and taking him at the small of the back, urging and encouraging and compelling him forward.

Crouched at the edge of the ice, his haunches balanced on the heels of his skates and gripping the rope and feeling a little tug across his old scar from this strange low tight posture, Bokarie waited on as the children continued to debate the *who first* and the *how exactly* of their plan to tug him around a little corner of the Rideau Canal. He didn't like the vinegar smell inside the cage of his helmet and couldn't understand why he was sweating around his temples in the whip and rack of Canadian winter. But still, he was enjoying this just-waiting-to-be-moved, watching the others out there bump and tumble along while the long-legged daddies and mommies loped and looped around, laughing and coming to ice-shaving stops in front of their bawling icebound bundles.

Of course, if he wanted to, he could be bitter at Jennifer for getting to attend some fancy reception for new members of Parliament that afternoon while he meeted and greeted these riding visitors, but after chatting with that confident man Rhinehart, Bokarie knew he'd rather not be there smiling and thanking them for any number of their attempts to adjust his vision.

Instead, he was looking forward to what skating was going to be like. He could find no precedent for it in the treks and trudges and wading and climbing and dancing he'd done in his prior life. Which made it the better. A free moment, perhaps a time to decide things about what that sharp boxer had said. The question was what now to do with this knowledge, how to start living from it. And, more immediately, whether he should wait until just after he grabbed on to a bureaucrat's position via some pitiable earnestness before he decided to give up on the whole business and just become an everyday Canadian and forestall death by memorizing the many little-known things that Canada was the first nation to do or discover or invent or—

"HOLD ON TIGHT BACK THERE SO YOU DON'T FALL! OKAY LET'S GO I GOT YOU FOR ONE GO AROUND THE KIDDIE CIRCLE AND THEN IT'S BRAIDAN'S TURN!"

His arms lifted a bit and then were pulled forward, the slack on the rope disappearing, and suddenly Bokarie felt the tug more strongly and he broke his crouch at the knees and had to tense his leg muscles to keep from falling over. He heard a little *shush* as the skates cut

through the last little ridge of snow and then they found the ice with
a soft sweet sound like when a needle touches a record, and even
though his entire body was wound up with fear at the strange motion
of it and his ankles felt as if they were about to pop off, he was skating.

The thrill was simple and beautiful and made him forget much and
regret, while he was upright, all the grinning nastiness he'd had towards
this place. He even didn't mind getting pulled around by the rope,
thanks to the helmet. Looking around, Bokarie saw that no one was
taking any notice of him, and that he liked. He did. The adults were
too busy holding kitchen chairs for the littlest ones to push, while the
next sizes up swarmed around him like so many bugs scattered across
the surface of water, some with sticks for balance and others constantly
evolving and devolving from all fours to two legs and all too busy enjoying and concentrating to care what and who was under the red helmet
at the end of the rope switching through them. Farther out on the ice
there were brassy teenagers and glory-hungry men moving around each
other with hot speed, dipping and dive-bombing and dancing and
careening and crashing and howling, and Bokarie had no interest in
joining that lot and bettering them at their game. He'd done enough of
that already. This was enough for him, for now, this anonymous bliss
of glide, the carnival noises around him loud enough to stuff his ears
against any particular encouragements from his immediate fans.
Because he didn't want any of that either. He was content only to be let
alone for a while at this skating, at the joy of doing something for its
own sake and leaving it at that. A happiness.

Enough to be here and enjoy it and stop taking Canada for all it
was worth and instead take Canada for what it was at its looping
best—a wide open cold space whose people stumbled now and then
but always kept trying to do more with their talents than was realistic.
You had to admire this. He didn't feel like laughing at it all anymore.
This could be enough for him, left at that.

Bokarie's fall started with a slow jitter in his exhausted ankles and then a sudden whoop up and slam down against the ice. A cold current shot across the old scar on his back and it started throbbing as he lay there and assured every worried pudgy hot-chocolate-mustachioed face that bent down to him that he was fine, and yes thank goodness he was wearing the helmet.

IV.

Her lips opened.

"How was last week's skating trip with the riding schoolchildren? I'm sure there's pictures enough, so I don't need details just now. Besides, I have some exciting news to share with you."

"Yes?" he asked, wondering if he should tell her this morning of his plan to leave the office at the end of the year. She didn't need him anymore; they'd made their way to the capital city and he was ready to move on. If not as a bureaucrat, perhaps as an ice-skating coach? He'd seen a program on the television recently and found the lead Canadian pair's moves entirely banal. Plus he'd watched enough North American sports to sense that he might find the right audience for his Bible belting there. Jesus Christ seemed to be the personal Lord and saviour of the most successful athletes.

"We're going home."

"But we're not scheduled to return to the riding for another month. Why now?"

"No, not the riding. Home. *Your home.*"

"My?"

"Sorry, your homeland. The news is that I was just added to the Governor General's trip to Africa for next month, and of course, when I told them about you, everyone insisted you accompany me as chief attaché! That means chief attachment. Which you will, there's no argument there. You're absolutely going. I can get my mum to run the office while we're overseas. And get this, the Governor General has even decided to make Think Pink—with your African translation about it being the colour of dawn in your homeland—the motto of the mission! New hope for the continent and all, plus new wristbands, *our* wristbands, to hand out to people. Speaking of your homeland, I can tell from your face you're still a little nervous about going back over there, and I understand. I even mentioned this to Madame GG (as we call her) when she invited us along and she said not to worry. I looked into it and this is a big donors' conference in one of the better countries in terms of plumbing and civil war, and so it shouldn't be too difficult or dangerous for you to go there, especially with a Canadian passport. Do you have one? Me neither. Never been out of the country myself, though I guess you already have, in a manner of speaking. But we can go do the pictures together. Anyway, I didn't have an answer for her about where you're from when she called me earlier today with the invite, and come to think of it, I really don't know which one your homeland is."

Both sets of eyes were cast away at this, one out of embarrassment, the other out of fear.

"It almost feels like you've mentioned so many, which is my fault probably for not listening sensitively enough and I apologize, especially for when I was a little harsh near the end of the campaign. But forget that and just tell me, once and for all, Bokarie, the name of your country."

He swallowed and sucked at his cheeks to get some wet into his mouth before his lips opened. His face was shattered over with shards of the many masks he'd used since starting his cross over the pond and into this place. Shattered with grief and terror and grimace and grin and now desperate pride.

"My country is Canada."

"Right. Of course it is. Sorry about that."

11

HABITAT FOR INHUMANITY

I.

Pulling up from the mess she'd made, Jennifer craned forward and then arced in a semicircle, looking around the cabin. No one else seemed nervous about what to do with their sick bags. If they'd even used them. Jennifer could feel hers, so recently ripped open and now bulging with evidence of her greenness, of this being her first time flying out on a trade and aid mission to Africa. Her first time flying anywhere.

It was steaming beside her ankle and the overhead air nozzle was on high, drying off her scalp and forehead. She was feeling cold-headed and warm-footed. She was looking for something to calm things down but too embarrassed to ding the stewardess to come over. Instead, she decided to remember that this was what it was like in her dad's truck in the months after Christmas and before the spring thaw, when only the bottom heater vents worked. That was a comfort, remembering that time, that place, while squirming, while strapped into this one. As good as any sip of ginger ale.

She would send her parents a card from Africa, and if they had gift shops over there, maybe even bring something back for them. An exotic feathered fishing lure for Dad's tackle box perhaps. Some tribal-coloured thimbles to adorn Mum's sewing room. Jennifer spat into a napkin, a little bilious after-effect. She still didn't like this backward homebody thinking. It was very small-town. Should have been behind her by now. But she needed it. The blipping screen in front of her explained that things were moving forward at hundreds of kilometres an hour, and sure she wanted her rise and hurtle forward to be this way. She just didn't expect it to be so hard to stomach.

After the plane had left Ottawa airspace and settled into its southeast course, Jennifer had been pleased with how little she had shown by way of nerves, especially compared with Bokarie, seated beside her, looking very grim, his lips pursed and his eyes fixed out the window. She wondered if this was his first flight too, but that wouldn't make sense. He couldn't have canoed to Canada from Africa, after all. Perhaps it was the jitters of going back. She could understand that; she had been nervous about her first town hall meeting in the riding after the election. But it had gone well and suggested the town's confidence in her rule. Three concerned citizens had shown up. Fewer, if you didn't count her parents and Bokarie.

Speaking of which, he'd been mighty moody these past few weeks, falling sick whenever a planning session for the Africa trip was announced, asking for a transfer back to the riding because, he said, he missed his old customers. She nearly had to drag him across the icy sidewalks of winter Ottawa to get his passport photo done. He even came to her office one evening, just before they were to leave, to give notice. Said he wanted to go into ice dancing or skate sharpening or something. He sounded almost a little desperate, which was new for him. But Jennifer played it well. Leaning up and over her desk and down into him, she said she regretted that he no longer had interest in serving the public good but she could understand his desire to be an entrepreneur—that was a very immigrant thing. She said she was okay with his wishes and even that she would help him out as much as she could. She reminded him of how far he'd already come with her, the possibilities she'd made possible, indicating what could be done for him now from her latest office.

Afterwards.

Jennifer felt aloud that they had become professionally close enough, after their various struggles together, that she could speak plainly to him. She assumed he thought likewise and she was open to hearing him out. But her first. Bokarie was her ticket onto that plane to Africa. She wasn't going unless he was. And she was going. And when they were over there, he was going to explain to anyone who asked what pink meant in his homeland. Because the whole of Canada was counting on him to show well on this trip; this would, incidentally, guarantee success upon his return and entry into whatever private sector he chose. He'd be greeted and rewarded, she promised, like a medalled Olympian. There was little better than that.

"But if you don't show well," she had continued, "well, maybe, Bokarie, you're not so eloquent as I had thought. Maybe what you'd said at the first Little Caitlin rally was good enough for small-town applause but that's all you've got in you."

His eyes, which had been like broken slate until she said this, suddenly went narrow, hard and harsh. As she was expecting. LBJ attacked the men beneath him on their points of pride. To rip them open enough to make them need to overcome his scepticism. Bokarie nodded defiantly and cut out of the office and was gym-bag-packed and ready to go the next morning. Still, boarding the plane in front of her, he wasn't jangling and bopping around like usual. He was stiff, formal. A walking plank.

While pleased that she'd convinced him, Jennifer had wanted to ask what was wrong with this going back. She decided against it, but doing so was like trudging home with something itching at your ankle when you just want to keep moving instead of reaching down to it and so you decide it will go away on its own. But it didn't. So she accepted the little bites as the cost of forward movement. The extra wondering about why Bokarie's not being fully *himself* had started up after she told him about this trip to Africa. To his homeland.

Jennifer knew to call it his homeland because rather than dowdy old *home*, which everybody had, *homeland* suggested something more rarefied, worthy of cherish, full with the delicate mystery of the distant places that newcomers came from. She liked these phrases, had memorized them from the introduction to an anthology of new Canadian immigrant writing that she'd found in the Parliament Hill library shortly after her triumphant entry into Ottawa.

She'd gone there, as she had to such places in the past, looking for material conducive to her design; this time, it had been to find the right terms to introduce Bokarie to her new colleagues. Not like the people back home, they'd want fancy wrapping for the import she was bringing with her. And so she consulted a glossy book of writings about the immigrant experience in Canada. *New North Strong and Me.*

But none of this thinking about Bokarie was of immediate concern. He was on board and he'd have to be back to his old self by the time they reached Africa. Of more immediate concern was the hot sour lump at her feet.

Jennifer blamed this latest smack of sick on their brief stopover in St. John's to refuel and to participate in a tarmac ceremony involving the Governor General and a handful of starched and permed local potentates. Also present were the requisite award-winning area children's choir and the stooped Legion colour guard. The fifteen-minute event was somewhere between solemn and congratulatory and intended to commemorate a recent commendable achievement that spoke to the long history of commendable achievements in this particular locality. Such sessions were regularly crammed into the Governor General's schedule whenever she touched down somewhere in Canada Minor en route from Ottawa to Toronto or Vancouver or, as in the present case, when off to even more important elsewheres. She and her staff were fine with the disembarking and stiff standing in the strong wind while the bagpipe recording finished, and then the smiling purgatorial wait through a welcome address by a local leader or, worse still, a local youth leader, and then the Governor General's own boilerplate two-paragraph address, and then the nodding graciously through an *only just one more, pleeeease* photograph session, before everyone waved and thanked and went back to their down-loaded playlists and plane novels. On the return flight, the brief stopover was planned for an airport in Nova Scotia so that Madame GG could de-board and quickly officiate, alongside the chatty local member of Parliament, at a ribbon cutting for a centre newly opened to study freshwater parasites in the Maritimes.

For Jennifer, who had gone along uninvited to the St. John's event and been unmovable and smiling from just behind Madame GG's right shoulder the entire time they were on the tarmac, the second takeoff had been too much, too fast. The plane suddenly kicking up and galloping forward and then rearing back and buckling a little from the westerly winds and banking to the left but then righting its course and climbing, climbing, shuddering from a last little bit of rough air, and then a static-clung cockpit apology for the takeoff *but nobody said it was easy visiting Newfoundland let alone leaving it,* which brought off a good laugh in the main cabin save row 11 where Bokarie, who seemed self-lashed to his seat, wondered at this observation before deciding to laugh along. To keep up appearances. Afterwards he sighed and slumped and started readying his faces afresh. Meanwhile, Jennifer was grateful for the cabin full of laughter. It drowned out her catch and hiccup and retch.

At first she had been worried about whether her face was showing it to others. Showing that she didn't belong up here, this far along in her career, this far away from the Ottawa Valley. A strong case could have been made in the spit-strung aftermath of her stomach's knotting and unknotting, during which Bokarie had moved off, smiling and springing over her and into the aisle, where he was immediately snapped up by Madame GG, who beckoned him forward for a little chat.

II.

Wiping the last bits of wet chunk from her cheek and then from her hand, Jennifer peered around once more and noticed that the rest of the flight—the Governor General's staff, the reporters brought along to document historic handshakes and hopefully a few cultural gaffes, the businessmen practising the place names they were looking to invest in, plus Bokarie, now front cabin and seated beside Madame GG herself—none of them, Jennifer sensed, were paying her any attention. Right now, this was fine. She didn't even mind Bokarie getting prime-time face time without her. It couldn't help but reflect back positively, provided he was his usual self. She leaned forward to watch and listen in a bit, just to make sure he was.

He was doing fine, giving a little crook of the neck and an interested grin and half-moony eyes while the Governor General recounted the story of the novel she had been just absolutely consuming! *Prester John*, by John Buchan. Written by one of her predecessors, a former head person of Canada himself. The story was of a Bible-quoting rebel African king who took a simpleton white man prisoner while trying to conquer a nation with his loyal followers, only to get outsmarted by the white man and done in for his efforts.

Bokarie cracked up at this, a short hot HA! HA! HA! that shot through the cabin. Madame GG pulled back quickly, as if the standard poodle she'd been biscuit-feeding turned out to have distemper. The others in the cabin noticed and waited for more of an exchange before deciding on whose behalf to be offended, while Jennifer started fumbling with her buckle so she could intervene and stow Bokarie with the luggage. But then he apologized extravagantly.

"Please, Your Excellency, your forgiveness. I forgot myself. But my noise only meant I don't think this *Prester John* book to be a very realistic story. People in Africa aren't so easily persuaded to follow men who speak from the Bible. I know this to be true, from my own life story."

Madame GG put a hand on his wrist and cocked her head sideways, empathetically cutting him off to assure him she knew this, and further that she wasn't endorsing Buchan's views, only learning from the past so as not to repeat it. Bokarie nodded and then thanked her for sharing and the two were fast friends once more. She noticed that Bokarie wasn't wearing a new pink wristband yet and asked an aide for an extra and fastened it onto him to immediate hums and quick-focus flashes from the seats around them. Bokarie smiled violently for the cameras and was encouraged to tell the story of how pink meant the colour of the dawn where he came from, which he did with the vacant enthusiasm of a tour guide stuck on his last group of the day. Madame GG repeated the lines as instructed, working them into her inventory for coming conversations. Who would remember "Ich bin ein Berliner," she thought, had an aide said it for Kennedy, even if it were a returning native? When she was finished with him, he was excused to another empty seat, where he curved against the window. He smiled out at everyone watching him and nodded his head in meekness and agreement, but behind this was something indeterminate. The others left him alone and went back to studying their host-nation cheat sheets, trying to keep straight their cultural and medicinal do's and don'ts with respect to local food and drink.

Jennifer didn't mind that Bokarie didn't come back to be beside her. Probably because of the smell, she thought. No matter. He could report later on the conversation with Madame GG and also account for his laughing out. Fortunately, it had resolved itself quickly, before she had needed to intervene.

And anyway Jennifer liked this having more time and space to herself. She needed it foremost to do something about the sick bag, which she briskly marched to the bathroom with an in-flight shopping magazine draped over it. She also needed to start reading through her prep materials for the mission; she had the same sheaf the others had been given, which included the latest edition of *Africa for Dummies*, complete with a chummy grave foreword by Bono and Paul Volcker, and also a Coles Notes guide to Joseph Conrad. But more than anything else, she needed to get over her habit of returning homeward when she felt unsure of herself. All this thinking about Mum and Dad and how things were done in town, as if this could help her anywhere else. She'd been doing this since the baggage check, or really since her dad had cupped her cheek and left her at her new Ottawa apartment that day he drove them down.

She had to put all of this behind her, even, she decided, her WWLBJD questions. Johnson never went to Africa. He'd probably barely heard of it, being not just American but Texan. If she was going to get anywhere and anything more than ribbon cuttings and baitfish, she had to be past him, and past her parents, and past the riding and past the embarrassment of the sick bag and past all the rest of it now. She had to be for the here and the forthcoming. Her instincts in first coming to Ottawa had been right: that there was always more waiting to be had in the time to come. She grinned back at that moment in her bedroom when the results had been announced, at what she'd wanted then, how it had been so strange to feel as if that was enough. That with victory, things were wrapped up, over, done with, ended, and she had been happy about it, not wanting more than she already had. She was busting through that small-town politeness and Middle Canadian modesty, too.

Her stomach settling, the warm little heavy bag gone, and munching vacantly on a business-class sugar cookie to freshen up her breath, Jennifer congratulated herself. She was a few months in Ottawa and only nine hours, according to the blipping monitor, from her next get: a trade and aid mission to Africa, with a returning native as her chief attachment no less. So Jennifer had answered What Now. It was directly in front of her, a whole continent waiting for her to swoop in with her dawn-coloured bracelets.

And beyond that, beyond that— She stopped herself from picking out the pie tin before finishing a second piece. Too much sweetness too fast would leave a belly in rot for no good reason other than wanting more than could be swallowed down. Her stomach was empty now and calmly so and would stay that way until they reached Africa, at which point she would get her fill.

III.

From the first moment, the smell and touch of the place was confirmation Jennifer had arrived somewhere she understood. Everything was thick with mushy heat and ripe with the tang of gasoline. While the rest of the Canadian party wilted their way through the welcome proceedings, Jennifer soaked in it, the white-clad schoolgirls' singing both national anthems in all official languages, the elaborate presentation of cola nuts, the equally elaborate sweetgrass ceremony by one of the Governor General's attendants. Then the back-and-forth introductions of the main players while the respective seconds hung back and waited somewhere between nervous and desperate to be recognized and called forward.

Jennifer had planned to ask Bokarie to kiss the ground for the cameras, but then she noticed Madame GG look their way. Look for her, at her, at Jennifer, to come forward. So she pushed past. Dropped him like a slug. She marched over to join the Governor General and the already backslapping business leaders in meeting the always smiling President and his attendants and advisers, who were to a man Wharton-educated and returned home because that's as far as they had to go to find employers still impressed by MBAs. There were reciprocal bows and scrapes and *no, after you's* to the canopied car lane.

The short walk over was quietly humming with repeated requests for pronunciation and reminders of how long the flight was and re-clarifications about the time difference. Nothing much. Jennifer decided she could bust through and better all of this and so leave her mark on this mission from the start. She had devoured the prep materials as if she was night-before studying for an end-of-the-year final. But she had even more than that to work with, and not from Bokarie. She'd finally found her ideal audience.

Her lips opened.

"Mr. President, I believe we have something in common."

He laughed heartily and nodded repeatedly, as did his advisers. A jovial way to avoid anything unnecessary or complicating coming up.

"Yes, we do. We were both recently elected to our offices. Congratulations. Though I must confess, thinking about my election experiences, I envy you."

Even more intense laughter and nodding and a signal to bring the cars around and send the luggage on later because the heat was clearly getting to everyone and best let's continue this wonderful conversation over air conditioning and cool tropical drinks. But Jennifer went on, hard-target in sight.

"Because, you see, the first time I ever ran for president—now of course this was back in a Canadian high school, not a nation rebuilt from the ashes for the fourth consecutive decade, like yours—but I did it just like you. I ran for president against no one. Only I lost."

Absolute belly-busting bedlam and then immediate dispersal. Jennifer was invited to ride privately with Madame GG, who commended her on such a fine opening with the local leadership and then gave her a list of the leaders they were to meet. Many of whom, Madame GG assured her, would find her election confession equally endearing.

As they sped along the empty eight-lane highway from the airport to their hotel, their car's wheels sticky from the freshness of the tar, Madame GG went in for more specific plans for the conference. She'd been thinking.

"Perhaps, Jennifer, when the opening speeches are done and we go into the one-on-one sessions, you can use that line to break some ice now and then, or reserve it for when they ask for something and I need some time to mull. And also, let's plan to end with the presentation of the pink bracelets. By the by, having chatted with him in the plane, I don't think we'll need your Bokarie with us during the private meetings. Together we know enough of his moving backstory to explain why we're thinking the colour we are. Just follow my lead in there. Fill in when I turn and smile at you like this. Understood?" This close to the Governor General, she could see how tight her face was, like dough stretched thin over a baking tin. Jennifer nodded at the bared bonded whites.

"Oh good, I'm glad you're with me. Some members can be so possessive about their bring-alongs, they cry when I tell them they can't have them in high-level meetings. Like babies denied their soothers! Yes, he'll be good for the standard delegation pictures and maybe we'll bring him along to a few minor receptions and perhaps have him share his thoughts for the home crowd when we get back. But you know, he got a little snappish at one point when we were talking on the flight over and frankly that makes him something of an unknown sum. In fact, Jennifer, why don't you just remand him to his hotel room—suggest that it's because you need someone you can trust on call in case there's a situation. Call it the war room or the hardware store or the engine house. Men who work beneath women need packaging like that to keep them proud and happy to be there.

"Because as you can see, Jennifer, out your window, this certainly isn't Ottawa, and that's the last thing we need, an incident, involving one of ours who's also one of theirs no less. Our press would *love* that, especially the reporter from the *Progress*. You know that poor newspaper was just bought by that American, Twin Chambers? You've no doubt heard what that right-wing radical corporate media mogul has already done to the newsroom and editorial. Cultural and intellectual butchery I call it, off the record of course. And you also must know how he's gone on about replacing my position with a battery-operated ribbon-cutter and bilingual applause machine and said he's allowed to say that because he's a fellow Canadian. Calling himself that because he's one-eighth Saskatchewan. A travesty of our funding formulas for underserved minorities. Anyway, he'd just love for something to go wrong on this trip for us, which I think of as an opportunity to show Canada and the world just what a Governor General can do for both. So let's not give him pleasure, understood?"

Jennifer nodded again and liked this *for us*. But she also wondered where Bokarie was. Probably in one of the other cars. She hadn't thought about him much since they dropped down and she was pulled up beside Madame GG for the introductions. Given how things were going so far and her wanting Madame GG to bring her along wherever she went, his getting left out, confined to the hotel, this was fine. All the more for her.

To pass the rest of their drive to the conference site, Jennifer joined Madame GG in marvelling at how efficient the country's highway system was, how wonderful if this was an indication of Africa's progress! Their driver nodded and smiled vigorously in the rear-view to encourage them to say more. As instructed.

The roads were absolutely emptied of traffic save military escorts and diplomat plates. There was none of its daily thickness of over-crowded pickups and horn-bleating taxis and lane-snaking, curse-making, double-backed scooters. Nor were there any chunky transports wheezing to the side, sick from all the downshifting en route from the outer provinces into capital-city traffic and so squatting, useless, on the shoulder while their drivers perfunctorily called out to the gambolling girls trying to sell their fathers' fruit from stands set up around exit signs. Instead of all this, there was only an onslaught of billboards advertising the eternal health and well-being of monogamy and the ruling party. This blocked any views for visitors beyond the fresh-paved road and the gleaming white stalks of new hotels and business centres ahead of them. So Jennifer and Madame GG further missed out on the daily wear and tears of Middle Africa: the crumbling Caucasoid statuary, the erupted sidewalks leading to and from buildings the colour, shape and purpose of crushed cigarette butts, the high clumped mounds of garbage smoking with half-burned tires and a few cooking fires, the successive sets of model new apartment buildings for the people's collective and united future—barely more livable than Baltimore tenements or guest-worker housing in Frankfurt.

In this particular Democratic Republic, residents of the capital city had been lined up for hot-plate handouts in advance of the government's hosting this year's international and All-Africa trade and aid conference. A proclamation was provided along with a gift. There was to be a patriots' vacation week, during which time citizens were expected to not be on the main streets but instead devoting themselves to their family lives and tending to their new hot plates. Those who did venture out would be vacationed elsewhere.

Not that all stripes of African colour weren't on offer for the very important visitors. In fact, they never had to venture outside the parapets of the conference site to get it. In addition to bulging Mandela-faced swag bags, the authentic glories of Africa were on offer nightly. Two shows, at eight and ten o'clock. There were Bushmen cookery demonstrations, native dance and hunting troupes, pantomime re-enactments of creation myths and colonial follies, and, always the favourite, a combination spelling/geography bee by top local students, the topic being capital cities and beloved leaders from around the world.

Of course, a few of the observer-status delegates at the conference and some of the younger aides with the major donor contingents had watched enough documentaries and read enough leaked reports not to buy any of these confections as representative. They snuck out from the conference at night and accepted rides from dangerous-looking unmarked cars waiting across the street, just outside the guard booth's range. When enough money was offered, the drivers agreed to take their fares on hush-hush tours of the *real Africa*, as the request was invariably expressed. The drivers warned their riders in advance that they were going to see things that might shock them and received in response steely-eyed and earnest assurances that *that* was exactly what was wanted.

A nearby and rundown district of the city was chosen for these rough-guide glances, where a pregnant woman was seen standing and smiling ambiguously at a street corner; where a gnarled European aid worker was met who went on in cynical gnomic grandeur about the forces that really ran Africa; where pant-less children were called after in vain as they played at toy guns in vacant lots. After which the cars came upon an unexpected security checkpoint on the way back to the conference. The drivers panicked and swerved and saved themselves and their families, not to mention their riders, from untold sufferings in unmarked prisons. These tours happened nightly, and viral marketing in the buffet lines ensured their continued popularity.

Back at the conference, the enlightened congregated at the twenty-four-hour hotel bar, where they shared with each other how shaken and stirred they'd been by what they'd seen. Confirmations of their worst expectations. They planned to start up defiant blogs full of indignation and little-known statistics. They promised to link to each other's to get the word out about the horrors and resiliencies of the real Africa.

The government had arranged the tours. The drivers were off-duty busmen who knew the right routes to take. Having exiled the documentary makers but failed to suppress the leaked reports, officialdom knew it would have crusading wall-climbers to deal with among the invited guests. It planned and paid out accordingly.

IV.

The speeches that opened the conference itself were a classic duet. Westerners declared that it was time the West finally recognized that it was time to do something about Africa. Africans announced this was not just another hand-wringing session but evidence of a new moment for an entire continent. Both sides agreed that history would no longer be a tragic guide or handouts wasted or promises mouthed, but hands would be joined and agreements would be reached and lives in need would be enriched. The beaming United Nations representative stepped to the podium after the last of these speeches and thanked everyone for their commitment to commitment. Then he announced into the shiny microphone, to great cheer and immediate hustling and bustling, "Let the dialoguing begin!"

The conference organizers adapted the principle of the sixty-second-date service in setting up the individual sessions between donor nations and would-be recipients. Delegations from African nations were assigned hotel suites with bottled water on ice and full audiovisual capabilities at their disposal. The best-prepared had short video presentations on offer, montage images of their nation's past horrors and present struggles and future prospects matched, respectively, to choired ululations and heavy-stringed orchestrals and upbeat synthesizers. So readied, they received Western representatives for short meetings that were a combination of flirtation and coyness and oft-repeated mutual agreements against playing head games. Pastimes and future plans came up, as did needs and offerings, the baggage of former relationships and family histories, health and fitness concerns about the body politic, and, above all else, the type of world they'd like someday for their children. Noncommittal promises were made for longer meetings later on. Phone numbers and awkward affections were exchanged—half handshake, half hug—and then each side, after breath fresheners and index card reminders for their next date, dried their palms and adjusted their lapel pins and moved on, nervous to have someone impressive to show the folks back home but wary of committing too much too fast.

By the time they reached their last matchup for the day, the Canadians were tired, though they'd been pleased with their success so far. In addition to the pink bracelets and accompanying rationale, they presented each of their African counterparts with a sheaf of e-mail addresses that Madame GG had collected from everyday Canadians enthusiastic about making contact with everyday Africans. These were received with gratitude and passed on and made use of. Jennifer and the Governor General's final meeting was with the brain truss of a tiny west central African nation, Atwenty. They had little information on the country even in the confidential prep materials that Madame GG had shared with Jennifer just before going in. A researcher had at least found a picture and brief article about the newly elected president, clipped from a Canadian newspaper from the previous April. He was smiling, en route to the People's Palace.

Atwenty was a postage stamp of a country historically criss-crossed by colonial powers and more recently done in by persisting internal conflicts, including a particularly bloody event that had occurred a year earlier in its northern province. Though never above the fold, reports had been published in a few Western newspapers and there had been dispatches from a BBC team based there. After an American intervention led by a junior senator from Texas with long-standing interests in the nation, a peace-bringing new president with control over the military had emerged, not to mention a slaw of investment in that troubled region and plans for a national reconciliation campaign.

After introductions, the actors took their seats and beamed back and forth and resettled themselves and fluttered their papers until one of them spoke. Jennifer had gone first last time, so it was Madame GG's turn. She went for dinner-party anthropology.

"Monsieur le Président, I'm curious about the name of your country, Atwenty. I know it's terrible to confess, but it's one of the few African nations whose current names evade me. Is it perhaps an ancient tribal designation for your lands and thus an act of cultural retrieval and reunification in the wake of the colonial departure?"

He laughed. A gold-toothed warm gurr.

"No, Madame, it is a joke."

"Oh please, Monsieur, you must take pride in your nation, in its history, in its traditions! The people of Canada do, I can assure you of that, it's something we can teach the world, I believe."

"Good for you, Madame, but the name Atwenty is literally a joke. You see, it was the idea of our first leader after independence. He was educated in England and upon his return, when the government was trying to come up with a name that reflected the nation more truthfully than any of the colonizers' New This's and That's, he proposed Atwenty. He explained that when he was living abroad, the only time he ever saw notice of his native land in a newspaper was a one-line reference on the first page with the direction to see A-20 for further details. So he thought this was the truest reflection of where his nation stood in the world. Atwenty sounded and looked African enough for people back then. It still does."

The Governor General's face was a thin polite blank through all of this. She wasn't sure of how to read this president's tone, whether she should have been outraged or sympathetic or chuckled in solidarity, and so she had nothing to give in response. Except the feeling that she was being quietly laughed at, which was unacceptable personally and nationally. Jennifer was simply confused. With only Canadian high school geography to work with, she was expecting some poetically aboriginal explanation of Atwenty. It should have meant "mighty meeting lodge between two rivers" or something.

The President's first councillor, who was sitting next to him, whisper-reminded him that Canada was high on their wish list of donor nations, that it could offer them more than a couple of easily copied blue passports. The President nodded and changed his tactics with relative ease. He was an ex-army man.

"Madame, you can be assured that we have the very best people looking into how best to deal with this name legacy. I myself am only recently elected. Our beloved President-for-life, as you may know, decided that the recent butchery done to his tribe in our troubled Upriver region made it impossible for him to continue leading. With my support, sympathy and sadness at his departing, he has left the country to join a series of corporate boards. And so now, as the latest leader of this conflicted, impoverished land, I am faced with a series of challenges. They are too numerous to list in our short time together. But you can imagine. I can't do this alone, of course. It's an expensive task."

The air was heavy with hint at these last statements, but the Canadians were ready for this. They'd heard the same lines at every meeting. Jennifer knew what was needed while Madame GG decided whether to open up her purse.

"Mr. President, I believe you and I have something in common—" Only Madame GG didn't want a stay this time. She wanted her hotel bed and decided she didn't care much for this president. He was the one too many of the newly elected reform-minded purse snatchers that she'd met that day.

"With apologies to my colleague, Monsieur le Président, you haven't convinced me that the Canadian people should support your efforts to improve your lands. To be quite honest"—she threw those *t* sounds at him as if they were little spears—"I have little confidence that your nation is capable of moving forward right now. Nothing you've told yet suggests any progress beyond, well, frankly, one big man replacing another."

"I can understand your frustration, Madame, and I can assure you I won't be just another big man, as you say. I certainly don't plan to rule for life, as my predecessors did. I've already set a term limit for my rule and shall respect it, God and the People willing. But you want more immediate evidence of progress, as you call it. I shall give you that, and also show you some evidence of the demons that have plagued us. But first let me share one of my recent decisions. This was part of the agreement for reconciliation and power-sharing that our nation's great friend from Texas, Senator Jellyby, worked up for us last year. We were even on CNN for it. One of my first decisions afterwards was to name a woman to one of our most important positions. The one I chose wasn't my sister or my daughter or even some ex-dictator's widow, like you have when women get positions elsewhere, but her own man, as the saying says. She had previously worked as part of an NGO for women's concerns in our capital city. Before that, she was a sex trade worker in a small village. She managed to escape that life and then devoted herself to making a difference in the lives of others. And as a nation, we have recognized her efforts with this appointment. She's governor of the northern province. In which, as you may or may not know, is located the Upriver region so recently ravaged by a band of butchers. And I tell you, this governor is doing serious work, not ribbon cutting and the like. She has been commissioned to bring healing where it is needed, and also to lead an effort to bring the evildoers to account. And to support her, we have brought with us to this conference rare video footage of one of the nation's Most Wanted giving a speech, the so-called Grin Reaper. This is a smiling killing machine of a man, a leader of poor bendable boys known to have a tongue sweet like honey and sharp like a blade. As you will see. We have brought footage of this madman at his work to raise awareness about the governor's efforts, to give people like you a sense of who, of what type of evil, she's struggling to defeat. Because she's not having an easy time of it and hasn't brought justice to anyone yet. And I'm sure I needn't tell you," he moved in for the kill, "Madame, or you either, young lady, how difficult it is to be a woman in governance, especially one with ideals. So when you make your decision whether to extend us funding, think not of this"—here he ran his fingers down his medal-encrusted bright suit—"but of her."

The Governor General's face was full with vague uplifting identification. She extended her hand with a swoop, dangling three pink wristbands from her fingers.

"Monsieur le Président, I underestimated you and apologize. You have made an eloquent case and I assure you Atwenty will receive the very strongest consideration when Canada sets its Africa aid budget for next year. More immediately, at another point in the conference proceedings I'll be pleased to introduce you to some members of our business community who are with us today. But before all of that, please accept these symbols of our concern and interest, and do pass one along to that brave sister governor you mentioned. In Canada, these are worn to show that we are thinking of Africa these days. And when we do, we Think Pink. Because, as you no doubt know, pink means the colour of the dawn in the homelands of Africa. And with Canada's support, Africans will at last greet rosy pink morning with the hope of a new day for themselves and their nations!"

He stopped grinning and nodding. His face and voice were suddenly very tight. He asked her to repeat what she'd said. Just the last part, about Africans greeting rosy pink morning. Madame GG obliged, unsurprised; it was a very elegant turn.

"Madame, may I ask where you discovered that description?"

"I wish I could claim it as my own, but in fact it came courtesy of my colleague, Miss Thickson."

He snapped to Jennifer, who was ready with the phrases and story and curious to see if it would have the same effect on this listener as it did back home. Though he didn't exactly look curious. Something more intent than that. His nostrils, she noticed, were flaring and his eyes were wide. She thought of how a horse looked just before it kicked out or bolted. But she could bridle this one too.

"And so, my dear, where did you find this phrase? Did you read it on the Internet or see it in one of these so-called documentaries?"

"No, Monsieur President, I know better than to trust anything I haven't experienced directly. Think Pink."

"Good for you. What?"

"I learned about the colour of dawn in Africa from a very courageous young man from there—sorry, from here, who joined our community in Canada recently. He's well spoken and very talented and has worked hard against adversity to become what he is today."

"Which is what?"

"My chief attachment—attaché."

"My goodness! Good for him. And congratulations to you for seeing such potential where others might not have. Oh, if only we could meet such a man, he'd be such an inspirational message for people over here."

"Of course! From what I've heard from Miss Thickson and seen and learned for myself, he's been the same thing for Canadians in his time with us. Would you like to meet him?" Madame GG had decided that was enough prime-time face time for Jennifer and so intervened, sensing possibilities.

"You mean he's here already?"

"Yes. Shall I send Miss Thickson upstairs to fetch him?"

"No, no, just tell us his room number and my associate Charles can go up with my assistants and escort him down." Here the General gestured to the elegant and assured man sitting to his left and to the arm-crossed, lip-pursed wall of men in sunglasses and berets and camouflage that was arrayed behind him. Jennifer hadn't noticed them since sitting down, having grown accustomed to their presence behind every African leader they'd met that day. She hadn't thought of them as anything more than a thick stand of green-clad trees. But they were moving now.

"That sounds fine, Monsieur le Président. I'm so very glad we're making this young man a bridge between our homelands."

"As am I. Yes, everything sounds fine. And now we can watch a short video together before his arrival!" The President's giddiness filled the room. He dimmed the lights.

V.

"He went homeland, back to his people, returned to his old way of life."

Jennifer repeated the phrases she'd earlier practised with Madame GG for the fourth reporter to come back to her seat and ask about Bokarie's absence on the return flight. When, as a follow-up, she was asked how much she felt this loss personally, by grubs hopeful of a little jungle-fever sidebar story to liven up their closing reports on the trade and aid conference, she claimed airsickness and ended the conversation, leaving them a little journalistic licence. But Jennifer wasn't feeling sick, she was just trying to remember one speech and forget another. Trying to remember how LBJ had explained his decision not to stand for a second term. Trying to forget what she'd seen and heard in that video.

He had looked a little thinner and younger and his English was much better than what he'd used when he spoke up for Little Caitlin in Centennial Park, though she recognized some of that in it too. But this was definitely Bokarie at his business—cutting back and forth across the stage, frothing up the audience with his words and moves, smiling out at it all. After the last lines of the speech, *This is why we will at last greet rosy pink morning from the moist earth that your fathers' fathers left to you. Brothers! When they desire mercy, you shall make of them a sacrifice! For our sons, for our General, for our nation!*, Madame GG had shuddered beside her, digging fingernails into her wrist, then gone hard metal and ready to do business.

Jennifer only caught snippets of the President and the Governor General's rapid negotiations, which both sides wanted concluded before anything was brought back to the room. She was wrapped up with what Bokarie had been before, what he was now, what to make of that. Of him. Meanwhile, there had been an efficient and detailed agreement worked out. First, the turn-over of the suspect so as to help along the woman governor of the northern province in her efforts at returning justice to her lands. Second, Canada would relinquish any claim on the suspect, who had forfeited its support by becoming a citizen under wrongful assumptions. Third, the episode would remain confidential. Fourth, the episode would remain confidential. Fifth, an explanation would be prepared that was suitable for Canadian audiences as to why the suspect remained in Africa. Sixth, Atwenty would claim to have caught the suspect in another African nation. Seventh, the episode would remain confidential. This was a question of homeland safety on both sides, it was agreed. The President assured her that it would stay between them, especially since the suspect required a delicate interrogation to determine what had happened to the General mentioned in the speech. They gave each other their word.

Both wanted more.

Soon there were pledges of future visits from freight-heavy C-130 Hercules to Atwenty. These were conditional on the Governor General's possessing political capital back in Canada that only an *entirely* successful trip to Africa would bring, or else she couldn't press for these to be sent. The President understood her situation and said he would do all in his power to make sure no bridge was burned or broken between their glorious nations.

As he was showing them out after the video was done rewinding, the President wanted to break through the young one's numbness. He couldn't resist. Imagine the notes they could compare, trade. He asked Jennifer about what she had said earlier, what she thought they had in common. But when her lips opened, she had nothing to give.

Jennifer and the Governor General didn't speak until they'd been in the elevator for a few floors. There had been a tense moment outside the Atwenty suite when a group of swaggering men came towards it from the right. Each decided she didn't recognize any of them and ducked past. Which was understandable. There were so many such entourages moving around the conference.

"I can't imagine what you must be feeling, my dear. Your Gannibal has turned out to be a cannibal. Living under an assumed identity like that—oh, what an affront! But let me give you some advice. Put all of this out of your head and come back to my suites and we'll work out a good plan for what to do when we go back to *our* homeland, where the people and other things are more reliable. I'm sure you don't need any explanation for why news of this incident would be as devastating to your career as it would be to mine. The PM will never let me go anywhere again. But let's leave aside our professional concerns for a moment and concentrate on you." Madame GG had decided that den mother to wayward cub was a better tack than worried farmer to suspected mad cow. Here she moved in and up to Jennifer, a look of fevered concern on her face.

"You must be feeling so duped by that monster, by how he capitalized on your and my and all Canadians' tolerant natures, on how we go about accepting people from far away and take them at their various words for what they say they are. That such a terror and trickster could do such things to us! Well, it's worthy of a Royal Commission. Not anytime soon, of course—we can't let that rotten apple ruin everything we hope to pick and gather here. You're quiet, and I completely understand you must still be in shock at such betrayal, so just follow my lead about what to do from here on until we're through this. And as far as that Bokarie, that Grin Reaper, is concerned, let such inhumanity be a dangerous lesson learned from and leave it at that."

His inhumanity. That was what Jennifer kept thinking about, as the plane took off and returned to Canada. Because more than that speech, or the things the President had told them about Bokarie, or how uncontrollably things had been mashing and blending and colliding in her head since then, she couldn't get past Madame GG's conclusion. Such inhumanity. But that wasn't what Jennifer had found in the speech.

Because he wasn't just a poor suffering new immigrant, but something more, something else. And yet he wasn't just a videotape of a genocidal African warlord either. Even if it had just been more rewarding, more politic, plain easier for everyone, himself included, to see him either way, to celebrate and punish and make use either way. But these were, because these were, shells. The whole thing. A shell game.

Bokarie had been torn away from her, but she didn't miss him in any real way. She had only known a shard of blackboard and crocodile tears and outsized grins. But behind, there had been something terrifying, calculating, murderous, laughing at her and the rest. No. *Someone.* Jennifer wondered if he might just talk or dance his way out of this new situation he was in, just as he'd danced and talked his way into his old one. She knew that much about him, at least. He'd try. You had to admire this.

She wanted to go home and be done doing politics. She'd lost her appetite in Africa. She would serve out the one term and then see about something else. Maybe even that gym teacher if he was still around. Or perhaps become a civics teacher herself. She would give up her position, even if people would say this was evidence Jennifer Thickson couldn't compete with the big men in Ottawa and beyond. She could, though, she knew that, which had to be enough for her. Because she'd tried for more and got it and then some. Which had led to something she'd never expected. Too much for her. So now the consolation prize of a return to the town, the farm. A habitat safe from the wide loud world and its pulls and pushes. But not that safe, Jennifer realized, thinking back and then forward. Because there would always be more drowned pigtails to dredge up and new Canadians to welcome. That is, if she wanted to get involved. But she wouldn't, she didn't, and was glad of this. Was glad. She was.

VI.

Jennifer's mystical experience over, she left the mushy hot woods where she had seen the slugs wrap around each other and then the bird swoop down and take them still dangling and doing to each other and go back to its tree to swallow down and look for more. She didn't notice the leech until she got home. There had only been a little itchy pull down by her ankle all the way back. Sitting in the mud room, she wrenched off a soaked shoe. She liked the THWUCK! sound that it made. One of her fingers brushed against a rubbery bump when she took the second off. It felt like a Band-Aid, only thicker, humped, rough, wet from the rain and the sludge it had moved through to get to her. She studied it. She'd seen leeches before.

Once, one of the cows, back when they had cows, had somehow made it over the corduroy road and waded into the crick across the way. After her father had dragged it to the barn by the back of its jaws, she held his hubcap ashtray for him while he cut the bloodsuckers off its belly with the lighter-hot blade of his jackknife. Little pink pucker lines were left where the fat black lines had been. Each one slid into the grey ash and curled up around the stubby butts, singed and dying but, she noticed, still trying to grab on to something and keep at its business. You had to admire this.

The cow had only groaned a little and shifted once or twice while her father cut away. So Jennifer wasn't worried by the prospect of a knife soon slicing across her ankle. She could hear her mother on the other side of the swinging door. She was putting down the butter and bread and milk and corn and that bit of leftover roast on the paint-peeled farmer's table they used for meals.

She watched her father through the small square mud-room window as he wiped his hands on the seat of his pants and walked towards his supper, his Ministry of Agriculture journals, and what news his wife and daughter had to tell of their days.

She looked down again at her ankle. She didn't cry or scream or try to pull it off, not right away. She was tempted by the notion of keeping it until school time, to show off to others, to the town kids who just laughed when she asked to jump in on hopscotch. It would be evidence of how much she could do. Evidence of how much she could take. She would show them. Her mouth contorted with fore-thought, with impatience for it to be school days already. Ignoring her parents' calls to the table, Jennifer watched the black band have at her, determined, fixed on her white freckled skin. Immovable, throbbing, growing. She felt a little weak from it, from the hot wet walk to her house in the bright close after-air of a sun shower, and now from breathing in the mud room, close and musky with her father's workboots and the sweet tangs of the spare gas tank and old mosquito repellent. She wondered if she could keep it there long enough to get it working for her somewhere else. She could tell it'd keep going, that it would not stop of its own volition, even if it burst. Her either. But the idea made her feel tired with the time to come, with what she would have to go through if she wanted to catch what she wanted. It'd be easier if she were a bird like that one from the mush. Then she could fly down and scoop up and swallow down and go back up to a new perch each time, always with better sights of the next dangling bit waiting to be had. Her ankle started feeling thin around the bulgy bump. It was pulling at her. Taking more than she knew.

When her father came into the mud room to ask her if she needed a personal invitation to sit down to her roast beef, he found Jennifer in a weak-blooded fever, her lips opened, her ankle fish-belly white. He bent down and saw it and shook his head and had a good idea where she got it from and how. He told her she should have known better than to go and play beyond where she was supposed to. She was grounded the rest of the week for not listening or keeping to what was expected and asked of her. Then he told her to turn away while he got his knife out and did what had to be done. He cut and flung out the door, far from them.

She was drowsy, but she heard a splat against a tree trunk. So that was all. But maybe not. Maybe, she thought, as she was carried into the house, it survived the sudden slash across its body and the hurtling through the air. Maybe it had a taste enough of what it liked and wanted more and would come after it. Wounded, rejected, but insistent, implacable, moving against future banishment, already uncurled and crawling, getting back to the getting place.

THE PRODIGAL LANDS

I.

The tales he told of his old country!

Last week, Bokarie was transferred into a larger cell. He had an audience again. He was coming back to his old self. Before that, he had been confined to an *oubliette*, a pit low beneath the earth, left over from the French days. Successive regimes cited it when decrying the abuses of their predecessors, and also when processing the odd prisoner.

When Bokarie's hosts needed it for another arrival, he was pulled up by his copper-wire arms, buckling and shuddering from the sudden wash of light. The swelling around his eyes had gone down and his face wasn't as barnacled with bruises as when he'd first touched ground. He had his Bible shoved into his shirt, a tumbling brick against his racked body. This was how he'd held on to it before, after taking it from the bedside drawer in the hotel room. When they'd come for him. When his big blond-headed turtle turned out to be the scorpion and also the fish and also the bird.

The General, now President, had greeted him in a cologne-heavy clinch. They were both wearing pink bracelets. A mutual confirmation of their recent involvements. The President marvelled at how thick and healthy Bokarie looked, how fulfilling his time overseas must have been. The People's Palace, Bokarie thought, seemed to have had a similar effect. The President felt the Bible against the small of Bokarie's back when he embraced him and cawed out, harsh and happy, before explaining loudly that it was so hard to find a good security these days. These young men he'd brought with him to this conference, for instance, were too frisky for local girls and pirate DVDs to remember to frisk someone before bringing him to see their President. Bokarie looked at them. He'd dealt with tougher kids trying to buy cigarettes with fake IDs. But there were only water bottles lying around. Plastic. And piles of documents. Paper cuts. If only he had some ice skates.

He had gone to Africa, had let her bring him, had been brought. He could have run, disappeared somewhere else and been some other town's smiling shuffling newcomer. The country was big and empty enough to allow for that again, and then again if necessary, and again after that. But Bokarie had gone tired and empty just thinking of such a future. Going to Africa was the only way to get out of being Africa. Because she'd promised him help upon their return, to be something less than everyone's poor suffering heavy bag. But he also boarded that plane because, more practically, what were the chances, even if the General had become President and went to such a confer-ence, that he would find his old scorpion among all those beetles and ants at their business? Not thinking that the General would find help from other quarters. That *Prester John* story wasn't a bitter funny lesson on his past, but a portent.

Jennifer had said he only had to say some fine words for the very important audience. If he had it in him. As if she knew that he couldn't say no to this. As if she saw through, just enough. Which also meant, he thought, there was more to her than pink and stomp. She had brought him along and then kept him in his hotel room. Perhaps because her General, that Madame, had ordered it that way. That perfumed hummingbird, that shawl-covered laugh-track. But he hadn't minded the confinement, had been glad for it, even if he was again denied the chance to speak. Because this had kept him out of sight. Only now that wasn't it, that wasn't it at all. She had wanted to box him in and wrap him up.

To stop from shaking a little and showing fear in front of this man who had once ordered him killed, who no doubt would have him killed shortly, Bokarie started imagining himself as Jennifer's confection, swaddled in pink ribbon, floating among pink T-shirts, awash in the cream soda she had served town children when he gave them soccer lessons. He worked up a tart smile while watching the President look through his Bible. Probably expecting a bottle neck in the hollowed-out heart of it.

The President grinned back that he'd found God since they'd last spoken, that a man in his position was sometimes in need of even higher powers than American peace brokers! Bokarie didn't join in the laugh, even if he was a little tempted to. Because, he realized, holding oneself above the Americans had become a natural inclination over the past year for him. Like it was in the drinking water.

After enjoying his own joke while the rest in the room barked along obediently, the President found the passage he wanted to share. Something from Isaiah that would explain to Bokarie what his nation and his old mentor needed of him upon his return.

"'Through his suffering, my servant shall justify many, and their guilt he shall bear. Therefore I will give him his portion among the great, and he shall divide the spoils with the mighty, because he surrendered himself to death and was counted among the wicked; And he shall take away the sins of many, and win pardon for their offences.'" He clamped the book shut and kept on.

"That's going to be quite a task, my friend, and I can think of no one better suited or more deserving to do it than you. I am glad you survived your time in the Upriver, and I'm tickled that your talents were appreciated in Canada, and I am overjoyed you are back with us now. You must be planning to tell anyone who will listen that the General you mentioned in those speeches was me, yes? That I am to be counted among the wicked, no doubt. Well, try it and see what happens. You know the people, you know what words can make them do. Just think of what hearing such things about the beloved new father of their nation will make them *want* to do. Now, who do you think they will then count and make to suffer among the wicked? Oh, and please don't bother telling them that you were in Canada these past few months. That's about as believable as walking across water. Or maybe do tell them, and then no one will trust anything you say!"

Bokarie was such a better speaker. The President had missed the roll and cadence of the lines from Isaiah, too concerned with making sure Bokarie understood that *he* was the one being referred to. As subtle as a sledgehammer. He had missed the Old Testament God's greatness, whose sayings Bokarie had heard and memorized as a boy at the orphanage. The gift of angry gab that the grand old man had, always so raging and jealous, and wording his promises of violence with such dash and wit. Bokarie had tried to do likewise in his own career, if not as well or with as much success, but certainly better than the two-bit pulpit bully in front of him. He smiled more now, feeling quietly superior. The President ignored this and gave back the Bible and said he hoped Bokarie would be able to find lines of consolation in it as well. And also that he was off to get freshened up for yet another reception. He understood now why his predecessor had signed his consultancy deals with Nike and Evian—to stay in shape from all the food and drink on the Davos and Doha circuit!

The President left Bokarie in the very capable hands of his assistant Charles—assuming no introductions were needed, that the two must have remembered each other from their beer-bar days. On his way out, the President reminded Charles that Bokarie would have much guilt to bear in the days and weeks to come. Giving him a little portion and spoil now, though, would be fine. Perhaps it could involve a more energetic frisking by the boys? Beginning with his smiling face?

Before the pummels and kicks came at him, Bokarie had to admit that the President had done better by the Bible in that final command, even if it still couldn't compare with what he'd done himself, back in, back in— That was as far as he got before he was concussed into a pulpy lump for his return, finally, to the capital city. For his short flight back to justice.

II.

The tales he told them of his old country.

I have come to you from far off, but please listen to the words of my mouth. I have heard of the tragic loss this community has suffered. Little Caitlin. I have taken courage from her story. I invite you to do the same with me. Listen, then. Because in my country— in my old country, my own mother, my own woman, my own child, were lost to heavy rains, and also to heavy boots. So much suffering between my world and yours. And yet they are no longer apart, but together. And do you wonder why? Because that is the promise of this great land! We are not so different, I tell you. We ask for the same things. That lives may be lived well and easy from sea to shiny sea. This Little Caitlin reminds me of my past, of what I said to my God when I lost everything along a mighty river once. I looked upwards and said, Why? For I desired mercy, and not sacrifice. We have lost Little Caitlin to the high waters, and something must be done so that this can never happen again. In my old country, pink was the colour of the dawn. I am proud to be here with you, to think pink, to make that mean a new beginning, a new hope. Let us together, as a community, raise awareness. My fellow Canadians! For our Caitlin, for our country, for our values!

Bokarie remembered his old speeches while the other prisoners asked him to tell more about Canada. After a couple of days with them—opposition leaders and other accused pederasts, assorted thugs who'd fallen out of favour, unsubtle newspaper cartoonists and their editors and publishers—they were ravenous for his stories. He offered his Little Caitlin speech once, but it did very little. They couldn't understand why all that noise for just one drowning, and not even a boy-child. So he kept his speeches to himself. He never gave them the ice-skating either. But he was free and creative and persuasive with the rest of it, his memories of that promised land of milk and money. Soon a few of the guards were listening as well, taking their smoke breaks nearby and imagining paradise along with the prisoners. They all knew he was the so-called Grin Reaper, the man accused and thus guilty of leading the Upriver Massacres, but they had no interest in hearing boasts or denials of what he had done up there. They were locals, after all; Bokarie was just another fallen warlord waiting to be sprung or punished. It was also known from guard gossip that Bokarie was awaiting a transfer to a court prison outside the capital city, up to the main village of the northern province, where he was to stand trial. There was a holdup because The Hague had recently called with an opening and now the President and the governor were arguing over their options.

When one of his fellow prisoners had asked him where he'd been hiding before he was caught, and he answered, they laughed and called him crazy. So he showed them. He started spinning and weaving around the room, telling fantastic stories. And even if they weren't true, how wonderful still to hear! Of all that wide-open space, of free money from scratch cards and from the government too if you filled out the right forms, of a machine that made ice and syrup into bright thick nectar from the gods. All sounded heavenly to them, crammed into the thick stench and bug fuzz of their cell. "Tell again about the women, how they want it over there!" one of the younger men asked, a one-time government enforcer who had been imprisoned because he couldn't read and had nodded at a sheet of directions and then guessed and roughed up the wrong set of lawyers before some trial.

Bokarie went through it once more, rehashing the storylines of the programs he had watched at night in his old apartment, about the heavy-chested, tight-shirted women with their husbands always at work and their fine gardens that needed pruning. For mutual elevation, he always spoke in the swaggering first-person triumphant.

They loved hearing this from him. It was corroboration. Satellite television was in even the poorest bars in the capital city these days, and so all of them had seen *Desperate Housewives* and wondered if this was what the West was really like. And now, confirmed. Oh, if only they could catch a taste of it for themselves!

But Bokarie wanted to say more this time. He could tell that from his stories they had come to feel as if they knew what Canada was like, what Canadians were like, what their women were like. They had no idea.

"I should tell you," he went on, cutting off their mental fondling, "that the women over there don't just want it from the men. They want more than that. I met two other women while I was there, and you won't believe what they wanted, what they got. And no, not from each other, like that. But power. Real power. Not *Daddy, do this for me and I'll do that on you* power like women who get it over here have it, but people who listened and followed and obeyed and trusted them. But none of you are listening to me. Fine. You cannot understand that place unless you have been there."

They were all too lean for any bellyfuls of giggle, but they still had a good throaty time with his proud declarations about his advanced knowledge of Canada and the extraordinary powers of their women over there. It was then explained to Bokarie that he was the one who didn't understand. His first country, the people who ran it, had changed some since he had gone and come back. He'd find out. Bokarie nodded and thought of the General now being the President. He knew better than they what they meant. Thought he did.

III.

"And you are?"

"Governor of the northern province."

"And you have come here?"

"Yes, to talk to you about the crimes you are to stand trial for."

"And you are?"

"Governor of the northern province."

"And you have come here?"

"Yes, to talk to you about the crimes you are to stand trial for."

"Will these begin with a murder charge? Assault with a deadly beer bottle?"

She turned on the radio she had brought into the room with her. Music. He wondered if she wanted him to dance her again, for the men watching and listening from outside.

"Yes, I remember. I knew I'd be meeting you today—the President told me. And no, to answer your question, there will be no mention of beer bars and bottle fights. That's not the past this nation needs to have healed. This music will drown out our voices while we speak. Because they're listening and watching."

How the men in the cell had laughed at him. At his going on about women and politics. As something that happened over there, in Canada. After a little frisking, he had been taken into this windowless room for a meeting. He had massaged his cheeks and shaken out his arms and legs while waiting, as he used to before a night of dancing at the beer bar. More recently, he'd found this was a good way to get ready for another interrogation session. He was more bendable than breakable then, when the blows started. Only the door opened and it was a woman, and not just a woman but the governor of the northern province, here to discuss his coming trial, and not just a woman in what should have been his position and planning to punish him from it, but more. Marigold. He wanted to believe that it wasn't her, that he wouldn't be able to recognize her since the last time he remembered seeing her, when it wasn't her face but the span of fabric over it, the beer bottle on the small of her back. Her arms shaking like fishtails, caught in her pulled-up dress, her legs blundering around the dance floor trying to get away from Foday. But it was Marigold, and he did remember.

Bokarie's face was cut at a sharp angle, staring at her, and she had expected as much and so told him what had happened to her after they'd all come to the capital city that first time. How she was grateful for having escaped Uncle's beer bar and knew she wanted something more than simply dancing at a better place for richer clients in the capital. And while her girlfriend Elizabeth, Bokarie's old girl, had gone into the palace to become the General's, she had wanted something more than that even. Owed it to the life she'd been taken from, the possibilities given in its place. So she started working for a non-governmental outfit in the capital, trying to help bring young women out of the thumping sex trade. She gained prominence for her efforts and moved up quickly, because she didn't talk, she acted. This was a method she had benefited from herself. She intervened not by compiling case studies but by going into the bars and pulling girls out. Which was how she found Elizabeth again, incidentally. And eventually, when there was a change in presidents and international pressure for something to be done about the terrible events in the Upriver region of the northern province, and also for some evidence of political progress in the nation as a whole, she had been put forward as a possible governor.

Still nothing from him. His mouth so dry he couldn't even spit at what was being said.

"And so I met with the new president. He didn't remember me from our first meeting at his campaign headquarters, back when he was the General. He wasn't hiding his military past, of course, this helped him get elected."

"So did I."

"Yes, that's right, but wait. Anyway, he and I talked about—"

"Possibilities."

"Yes, that's right, but wait. We talked about what had happened in the Upriver region and how part of his promise to the outgoing president and to the citizens and to the internationals was that he would create peace there when he came to rule. And he confirmed that I was from the northern province and that I was indeed of mixed blood, which nowadays makes things like this a lot easier. Then he asked me if I was willing to be governor. I agreed, because I wanted to help—"

"Yes, yes, I know. The People."

"No, wait. That's where you're wrong. I wanted to help *people*. Can you understand the difference?"

That was more than enough for him. He uncoiled from his chair and whipped around the room, his back bending and arching. Like a bird's beak was splitting it. Guards were at the door immediately, truncheons ready to frisk him again, but she sent them away, thanked them for their concern but said everything was fine. There was only music for a few moments. Bokarie mimed an offer to dance, to remind her of what she had been, before her cropped hair and pantsuit, of who he had been for her. She winced a little but expected this much gall and pressed on. She needed to make sure he understood where he was going, what was coming to him. That he understood why. She changed tactics.

"I understand you've been abroad. Tell me, what was Canada like? You must miss it."

He spat. "People are the same everywhere." He spat again. She changed tactics.

"I have come here today to discuss the future, your future and this nation's future. As you know, you are currently charged with crimes against the People for your leading role in the Upriver Massacres. I am not here to discuss the legal side of this case but because I wanted to speak with you, face to face, about what is going to happen. I felt I owed you this much."

He came alive at this, an admission of her dependence, of her not being the person she had become were it not for him.

"And what do you owe him? What did he ask you to do to get this position? And what did you ask of him to call me a liar and a lunatic for saying he's the General I was working for?"

"He doesn't know that I know this. Remember what I said a moment ago. When we met to discuss my becoming governor, he didn't remember me from back when we had all come to his head-quarters. He was all hugs and whispers and dancing with you and your Elizabeth. The rest of us just watched."

Bokarie came back to his chair and slid up the volume button on the radio.

"He doesn't know?"

"No, he told me, when I said I was coming to meet with you, that you'd go on lying and raving that he was the General you mention in the speech on the video and that you had been living in Canada until you were caught. And then he said that the truth was you were caught cowering in a neighbouring country and that of course you would try to blame him as the devil behind it all since he was on top now and that was the way in our country. Then he promised me that he had started a full military commission to learn the identity and whereabouts of the General you mention in that speech, though he predicted the man never existed in the first place, was something you made up in your speech to have someone grander than yourself to inspire the men, someone greater than yourself to blame if things went wrong."

Bokarie gripped the side of the table and breathed hard. Because now wasn't the time for rage against such lies, against being called untalented. The betrayal of it, after what he'd promised him, after what Bokarie had done for him. People were the same everywhere. Just thicker and thinner skins, scales, feathers. But he hoped this was true now, thinly smiling at Marigold. He got up again and started moving around the room, the loud music helping him as he danced up the words.

His lips opened.

"I am glad you have come here to speak with me today. Because the truth about the tragedies of our homeland must be heard! I say, 'Cry out full-throated and unsparingly, lift up your voice like a trumpet blast.'"

"Still dancing with your Bible, aren't you. That was your favourite line back when you were on top of the orphanage wall and we would watch you. But we're not living from that past anymore." He darted past her words, intent upon a chance to save himself and, finally, maybe, a chance to get what was supposed to be his.

"From what you have said, there are possibilities to be had. For you, for us, together. With what we both know of the General— sorry, this President—we can reveal him for the lying filth that he is and then you would be raised up and could become, and then I could be raised up and become, finally become—"

"No. That will not happen. You will stand trial, either in the northern province or abroad—that's still to be determined. But you will, and you can speak as much of the truth as you know it and see what justice that brings. But I won't do it, I won't," she said.

"And why? For your beloved The People?"

"No! For people. Because with this trial comes attention, from the President and others in the capital, but also from the foreign donors and dignitaries. And maybe this means they'll just talk more about how they need to do more for the people in my—in our country, but maybe something more than speeches and wristbands and blue helmets will come. Maybe some interest in us when it's not a natural disaster or a civil war, but for the dailyness of our enduring. But I know there's no getting around it—they need the drama, the terror and the monsters to make it worth their while. So I'm trying to match what they want to give for with what we have to give them. Which means maybe more bucket toilets for the villages you and your men sacked. Or some pedal sewing machines to make up for the arms you and your men hacked. Or another holy order willing to take in some of the boys whose fathers you raged with and raged on. And that's why you have to stand trial, Bokarie. That's why you're needed. So those things happen."

"But haven't you seen enough of this place, haven't you met enough people, whether from here or everywhere else, to know any better? People who always want to get more? Who want us in the package to feel good about doing it? Who never, ever act except for themselves?"

"Like you did, when you saved me?"

His mouth went wide like an open grave, his tongue fell limp, he returned, crumpled, landed back in his chair. He turned the music off. It was over. Because he couldn't do it. He wouldn't answer her why he'd done it. He wouldn't give that up. Because then his saving her, his one secret goodness, would become just more blood and treasure to trade on, to give over to get more. He refused that for himself, to do that to himself. To do that to her. This alone Bokarie wouldn't have taken from him. They could have the rest and keep carving it up and adding to it and inventing it and remaking him into what they wanted, needed, decided he had to be. But not that, because if he gave in and gave it up, then he would only be their heap of broken images. He would be spent. The shell would be empty. There had to be another way.

He looked at Marigold. His lips closed. Bokarie was smiling.